TAMMY
AND RINGO

Creative Texts Publishers products are available at special discounts for bulk purchase for sale promotions, premiums, fund-raising, and educational needs. For details, write Creative Texts Publishers, PO Box 50, Barto, PA 19504, or visit www.creativetexts.com

TAMMY AND RINGO
by N.C. REED
Published by Creative Texts Publishers
PO Box 50
Barto, PA 19504
www.creativetexts.com

Cover photos used by license.
Credit: The National Guard/ Jozef Turoci via Foter.com

Design copyright 2015-2017 Creative Texts Publishers, LLC

The following is a work of fiction. Any resemblance to actual names, persons, businesses, and incidents is strictly coincidental. Locations are used only in the general sense and do not represent the real place in actuality.

ISBN: 9780692504215

TAMMY & RINGO
N·C· REED

CREATIVE TEXTS PUBLISHERS

Barto, PA

As always, For the chef, the clerk, and the ranger.
Love and miss you all, more each day.
For my wife who keeps me inspired when I
want to give up.
For the Wrecking Crew, who remind me
what it was like to be young.
And for you, the readers, who keep me writing.

CHAPTER ONE

-

Tammy Gleason was exhausted. Having twin athletic scholarships was helping her get through college without any debt, but it was always hard this time of year. Basketball and softball overlapped just a little as basketball was winding down and softball was getting started. The games didn't clash, but they were close together.

Having just finished a marathon of practice for both, she was anxious for a hot shower and some sack time. She ignored her phone, and didn't even glance at her dorm room's answering machine, instead grabbing towel and toiletries and heading for the bathroom she shared with three other girls.

Twenty minutes later she was feeling almost human again. Wearing only her towel, she plopped down heavily into her chair and listened to her messages. Coach's announcements, skip. Friend Wendy wanting to get a pizza, skip. Dad warning her to get out of the city while she could, ski...Wait. What? She replayed the message.

"Tammy, for God's sake where are you? I've been calling for over an hour! Listen to me, I don't have much time. Things are about to get really bad. I mean really bad. You need to pack up whatever you can't live without and get back to the base right now! Don't stop for anything but gas and make that quick. Bring everything you can carry but don't hesitate to leave it all behind if you have to. I've got to go, baby girl, we're being deployed right now. Sweetheart, please be careful and trust no one. Understand? Trust no one. The wheels are coming off, Tammy. I love yo--"

Tammy sat back in her chair, releasing a breath she hadn't realized she was holding.

Holy shit. They were deploying her father's Army unit here at home? What the hell? She checked her cell phone and realized that it had been his call that she had ignored. She hastily listened to a similar message, noting the fear in her father's voice. She had never heard him sound like that before.

Her father was stationed at Fort Bragg, North Carolina. Reese Gleason was a Battalion Sergeant Major, one of the highest-ranking NCOs on the base.

For almost as long as she could remember, it had just been her and her father. Tammy's mother had died when Tammy was just four years old. Her parents had been only children and her grandparents had passed before she was even born. Reese had managed to put off deployments until she was of school-age, but it had cost him later with extra deployment in the way of TDY assignments.

The wife of one of his best friends had agreed to take Tammy in when Reese was off-base, leaving her with Mrs. Steele for months at a time. With Sergeant Steele also gone and the Steeles unable to have children of their own it had been a good arrangement for both of them. Lucinda Steele became a surrogate mother for Tammy and Tammy became the same kind of daughter. The two were as close as any mother and daughter might have been, save that Lucinda had not given life to Tammy.

She tried her father's cell phone but got no answer. She left him a voicemail acknowledging his message and informing him she would be on her way within the next hour. It was all she could do. She turned the television on and switched it to a news channel, wondering if there was anything being said. But there was nothing, at least not yet.

She dressed quickly and started throwing her things into a duffle bag. She ignored her stereo, television, uniforms and other less than useful things. She grabbed the small emergency kit that her father had prepared for her and placed it in the top of the duffle. She didn't even know what was in it, since it was sealed, but Reese had always told her to grab it if nothing else and so, she did. She'd open it later if she had time, or had need.

She was almost finished when the television gave an alert sound, indicating breaking news. She stopped and waited.

"Ladies and gentlemen, we interrupt our regular newscast

to bring you breaking news from Atlanta, where the CDC is about to hold a press conference. We go live now to our reporter in the field, Gretchen Danner. Gretchen, what can you tell us?"

"Thanks, Dave. The first thing is that this announcement literally comes out of left field. The CDC rarely makes the time to hold an actual press conference and almost never actually asks for television time when doing so. Their only response so far to our questions has been that this announcement is, quote 'Of vital importance to the entire country' end quote. That's all they've shared with us at this time, but we are trying to get at least some word from. . .Dave, hold on, something. . .Okay, someone's on their way to the podium. . .my colleague is telling me this is Dr. Meredith Baxter, the actual head of the CDC, and that it is Ilesa Bokalu, the press agent for the CDC coming to the microphone. Let's listen in."

"Ladies and gentlemen of the press, I ask you for order, please," the dark-skinned woman rapped lightly on the podium. "We have very little time, so please listen carefully. Dr. Baxter is about to make a statement that is vital to everyone in this entire nation and to people around the world. What she is about to tell you is all the information we have at the moment so please, do not interrupt her with questions. Aides are circulating among you with written information as well, so there's no need to ask her to repeat herself. Dr. Baxter." Bokalu gave way to the graying blonde woman behind her. Baxter looked frazzled. As if she hadn't slept in a while. She wasted no time with pleasantries.

"One week ago, World Health Organization field agents reported a strange sickness in the Montanbu region of Greater Africa. This sickness showed similar symptoms with a certain type of rabies usually found in primates across the continent. It has always been held that this particular strain of rabies was not transferable to humans. This strain of rabies isn't something that can simply be 'caught', to use a phrase we're all familiar with, but rather must be transmitted by bite or exchange of bodily fluids, say the blood or saliva of an infected creature entering an open wound."

"We have since learned, however, that this strain can in fact be transferred to humans, and from human to human. The first cases detected were monitored closely. Those infected began to show signs of dementia, paranoia, and exhibited aggressive hostility toward everyone around them, usually within twenty-four to thirty-six hours..." She paused for a moment, taking a deep breath.

"Approximately six hours after these additional symptoms presented, the hospital's quarantine was broken. Those infected escaped into the city and went on a rampage the likes of which have seldom been seen. Military and police units were called in to stop the resulting riots, but were unsuccessful."

"Worse, many people who were infected and were not yet aware of it managed to board international flights. These flights landed in France, England, Germany, Brazil, Argentina, Mexico, and," she looked up, "the United States."

An immediate uproar went through the press but Baxter held up her hand, and continued to talk.

"Please, I remind you that time is precious here!" she bellowed. The reporters calmed somewhat, but looked rattled.

"We had no idea that any of this had been allowed to escape containment until a few hours ago. By the time we learned of it, it was too late. Those unaware of their infection had reached their destinations and disappeared into the populace. Using the time line for the original subjects, these newly infected are almost certainly past the initial infection and are now themselves capable of infecting others."

"We have no idea how this has happened. Blood samples from the point of origin will be arriving soon and we will start at once working on a way to counteract this virus. Until we can do that however, the risk of infection remains high. We are already hearing of other cases in Europe and South America. It is unlikely we will be spared."

"I am making this announcement without the permission of the White House because it is vital that Emergency Responders as well as civilians be aware of this threat. We will bring you--" The screen went black. Tammy almost jumped.

"Well," 'Dave' came back on the screen, "it appears we've had some kind of technical trouble on Gretchen's end, but we'll try and get her back for you as soon as possible. In the meantime, this announcement from the CDC director is more than a little scary, if you ask me. Joining me now is our in-house medical expert Doctor Jamie--" Again, the screen went black.

"Oh, this is bad," Tammy muttered to herself. She turned off the now useless television, and grabbed her bags. Taking one last look around, she walked to the door, and turned the knob to exit. The door opened against her suddenly, and pushed her back toward her bed.

"What the hel--oh, Gina! You scared me half to. . .Gina?"

Tammy's roommate, Gina Terrio, staggered into the room. Her only response was an eerie moan that made the hair on Tammy's neck stand up straight.

"Gina, what is wrong with you?" Tammy demanded. Gina looked up at the sound, and gave Tammy her first full look at her. Her eyes had a glazed, unfocused look, and her mouth was covered in blood that had leaked down onto her shirt.

"Oh, no," Tammy breathed. And Gina attacked.

Faster than she would have thought possible, Gina crossed the distance between them, reaching for Tammy with bloodstained hands. With that small part of her brain that wasn't in total panic mode, Tammy realized that Gina was missing three fingers on her left hand.

She must have been bitten, that small part of her brain informed her.

Meanwhile, the rest of her brain, the part that was screaming 'oh shit' very loudly, was backpedaling, hands grasping for anything that would help fend off her former roommate. Her right hand fell on her softball bat.

Tammy Gleason was not a waif. She was strong and athletic. And she had been swinging a bat for a long time. Her hands were on autopilot as the bat came up and that tiny, non-panicked part of her brain yelled 'swing'.

So, she did.

The aluminum bat collided with Gina's onrushing head with a sickening crunch and the girl fell to the floor instantly.

"Oh my. . .my God!" Tammy just looked on in shock at what had been her roommate, and friend. She had acted on instinct, defending herself, but the fact remained that Gina was. . . .

"I can't worry about that now, I can't worry about that now," Tammy repeated over and over again. Slinging her bag again, she stepped carefully over Gina's body, pausing to wipe the blood off her bat on Gina's bedding before stepping into the hallway. Looking both ways, she was relieved to see it was empty.

She locked the door and walked away.

-

She walked as calmly as possible to her car, a newer model Honda Accord. Her father had bought it for her when she had announced her intention to attend the University of Memphis. Her decision had been based on the Ranger Training Program the school operated, one of very few such programs in the nation. Such a program would help her gain useful summer work experience which she hoped would give her a leg up when it came time to apply for a position in the Department of Interior.

Throwing her duffle in the back seat she crawled behind the wheel. As she started the car she was immensely grateful she had filled the tank earlier in the week. She rarely used the car during the week so the tank was topped off. It wouldn't get her all the way home but it would take her a long way.

As she put the car into reverse she saw students running through the quad. She could make out a few shouts but not what was being said. She watched a moment longer and saw a male student staggering after those running. His condition was much like that of Gina Terrio, with blood seeping from a wound on his upper left arm and blood around his mouth. She couldn't see his eyes from where she sat but suspected they were glazed over.

Did that plane from Manu. . .Mabo. . .Africa, land in Memphis? She shook her head. She didn't have time for that right now. Once she was home she could think on things like that all she wanted to. Right now, she had to concentrate on getting home.

She put the car in drive and hit the road. Automatically she pulled down University Lane and out onto Poplar Avenue. If she followed this road it would take her all the way out of town and eventually to Pickwick Dam. From there she could go to Savannah and get on Highway 64, which would carry her most of the way across Tennessee toward home.

There was also the interstate. I-40 would carry her well into North Carolina. In her mind's eye, she considered both routes. Which was better? The route down 64 would take her through dozens of small towns, stretches of two-lane highway and any number of possible places for trouble.

The interstate on the other hand would take many more miles, which would mean she would need gas sooner. But the interstate was two-lane all the way and more around places like

Nashville. There were numerous places along the way to get fuel, food, and use the restroom safely as well. Yes, I-40 was the way to go. Decision made, she changed lanes and left Poplar at I-240, heading for the I-40 East and for home.

She had expected traffic to be worse and was pleasantly surprised to find it light and moving without difficulty. She sped down the three-lane highway, careful to keep her speed at the limit. The last thing she needed was to get a ticket. She turned on the radio and tuned in to a local all-news channel to see if there was more information available.

They were talking about how good the Grizzlies were looking in the last few regular season games. Sighing, she turned the volume down but left the radio on in case they had information later. Seeing her exit coming she changed lanes and hit the off ramp smoothly.

And ran smack into a traffic jam.

"Seriously?" she muttered, wondering what the holdup was. She could hear horns blaring, but didn't add her own to the mix. It wouldn't help and it might make things worse. She strained to see around the SUV in front of her, but to no avail.

She placed her car in park and tried to make use of the time by planning her trip. The fuel in the car would take her to Knoxville or thereabouts, but she would be very low by then. She decided to fill the car up at every opportunity during the drive. She glanced at the radio which was displaying the time. Two forty-five in the afternoon. Sunset was usually around seven this time of year. Call it four hours max of sunlight to travel in. No, that wasn't accurate because she'd be driving away from the sun.

Three hours then, just to be sure. She would stop right at sunset and fill the car up again. Hopefully she would be close enough to home that the fuel would see her through.

Her string of thoughts was broken when someone ran past her car. Then two more people. What the hell?

She opened the door just enough to stand outside and look down the road. Her mouth dropped open at the sight before her.

In the middle of the interstate was a young man, maybe a teenager, surrounded by other people. No, wait. Not just people, she realized. They were infected. The teen held a sword, one of those Japanese ones she could never remember the name of, in both hands. Several bodies lay around him already.

Without any real thought, she reached inside cutting off her car and taking the keys, grabbing her bat at the same time. She did not have time for this shit! Running the three car lengths that separated her from the battle she struck without warning, slamming the largest target in front of her on the side of the head with the bat.

The. . .thing, to her right turned at the noise, glaring at her with wild eyes. She hesitated for a second, then recovered, taking that one down with a reverse swing. Without pause this time she swung back to her left and hit a woman. A woman. . .thing, that was turning to attack her. She turned at once looking for more, but. . . .

There were no more. In the time she had taken to kill three, the kid in the middle of the road had killed seven. She looked at him, mouth agape, as he swung his sword to clean the blade off and knelt to wipe the rest off on the clothes of the nearest body.

Seeing her looking at him, he nodded. "Thanks."

"You're welcome," she said without thinking. "What the hell, kid? You always fight in the middle of the interstate?" He shrugged, but made no other reply.

"Where are you headed?" she asked, conscious of the still blaring horns and of the traffic that was trying to get around stalled and abandoned cars.

"Nowhere, really," he shrugged again.

"Want a ride?" Tammy asked.

Now why in the hell did I just do that? she wondered.

"Sure," the teen replied. He walked to the edge of the road and picked up a backpack along with another bag and started toward her.

"You got a name?" she asked. "Mine's Tammy. Tammy Gleason."

"Ringo," the boy replied.

"Just Ringo?" she asked, already walking back to her car. She stopped long enough to mimic his action and wipe her bat clean.

"Yes," Ringo nodded again.

"Well, c'mon Just Ringo, before we get run over." She led him quickly to the car where he deposited his gear in the back and joined her up front.

"I'm not going to regret this, am I?" she asked, starting the car. She steered carefully around the vehicles and bodies to get back on track.

"I hope not," was all Ringo said.

"Me too."

CHAPTER TWO

-

Tammy kept her car just under the speed limit, weaving around slower cars and avoiding cars that were stopped along the way. It took nearly twenty minutes, twice as long as usual, to clear the bulk of localized Memphis traffic. They weren't clear by any means but it was clearer. Tammy would take it.

She looked over at her passenger.

"So, you really aren't going anywhere?"

Ringo just shook his head.

"Then why be out in this?" Tammy asked. "I mean, I'm trying to get home or I'd be hiding in my room."

"I doubt that," Ringo said quietly. "You aren't a hider."

"What's that mean?" Tammy demanded. He looked at her.

"You left your car to see what was going on and then took part in it," he explained. "You aren't someone who hides away."

"Well. . . ." Tammy trailed off. No, she guessed not. Ringo was right. She always had to see what was going on. Damn it.

"So, anyway, that's my excuse. What's yours?" He shrugged.

"Nowhere to go, nowhere to be," he said.

"No family or friends?" Tammy pushed.

"Not anymore," was the quiet answer.

Tammy didn't ask anything else about family and friends.

"Where did you learn to use that sword?" she asked after a few minutes of silence.

"School."

"What kind of school teaches swordplay?" Tammy asked, her tone derisive.

"Private school," Ringo shrugged. Tammy fought the urge to lash out. Ringo's one and two word replies were starting to get to her.

"You don't talk much, do you?" she jabbed. He shrugged again but said nothing. Instead he looked out the passenger window at the passing countryside.

"Got nothin' to say," he said at last. "No point talking, otherwise."

Tammy huffed at that slightly, but the comment did make sense. Ringo was. . .still. She'd never seen someone be so still and quiet. On one hand it intrigued her, but on the other it was a little unnerving.

"Well, you got anywhere you want me to drop you?" Tammy asked.

"Anywhere's fine," Ringo shrugged again.

"Don't be silly, I can't just leave you out here in the middle of nowhere!" she rebuffed him.

"Why not?" he surprised her. "One place is as good as another when there's no place you want or need to go. When you get tired of me traveling with you, just say so. I'll get out." With that he went back to gazing out the window.

What the hell is wrong with this kid? Tammy wondered. He acts like his life is already over and he's just going through the motions. She studied him a little closer, sparing glances away from the road when the way was open.

He's not bad looking, she thought. Tall, lean, kinda athletic really.

His dark hair cut short. He was wearing jeans, boots and a tee. She noted for the first time that there were two straps on his forearm, apparently holding something to his left arm. Similar straps were on his other arm and she suspected around his ankles.

The sword was held between his knees, point down in its scabbard. It had none of the usual affectations that such swords normally had. Of course, those weren't for real use normally, either. This one looked as if it had been made with only one thing in mind. Use.

His hands and arms were traced with scars, some large, others barely visible. Another scar was faintly visible from his left eye, running down his face and to his neck. Still another started behind his hairline, tracing down the back of his neck and disappearing beneath his shirt.

Damn, where did he get all those scars? she thought.

"Well, I'm trying to get to Fort Bragg, North Carolina," she settled for saying. "My dad's in the Army and that's his post. He sent me a message telling me to come home before things got bad."

Ringo merely looked at her, nodding his understanding.

"You're welcome to go with me as long as you want and you don't cause me any trouble."

"Doubt they'd let me on the base, but why not?" he shrugged. "It's as good a place as any to be, I imagine." Tammy fought the urge to roll her eyes.

"You seriously don't have anywhere you want to go?" she pressed. "No one you're worried about?"

"Seriously," he nodded. "I'd as soon take care of you, make sure you get home all right, as do anything else."

"I don't need you to take care of me!" Tammy was angry in an instant. "I'm a grown woman, not some kid with a grandiose idea of himself!"

"Okay," Ringo shrugged. "You want me to get out?" he asked, looking at her again. "Like I said, whenever you want me to go, I will. I feel like I owe you for helping me before. I like to pay my debts, that's all."

Tammy's anger cooled a little at that. Repaying a debt was something she could understand.

"Sorry," she told him quietly. "You just. . .that's a real sore spot for me," she admitted.

"I see that," he nodded. "Won't happen again," he added.

"Look, I'm not. . .I didn't mean to sound mad," Tammy tried to explain. "But I mean how old are you? Seventeen?"

"Nineteen," Ringo replied.

"Oh, well," Tammy's voice was heavy with sarcasm. "If you're nineteen, well that's different then."

"Why?" The simple question caught her off-guard.

"I was being sarcastic," she told him.

"Thought so," Ringo nodded. "Just checking."

Tammy drove in silence for a while, trying to calm down. This kid's seeming lack of any kind of emotion was starting to get to her. She thought about it for a while and finally tried a different track.

"So, are you from Memphis originally?" she asked.

"No."

Tammy waited, but there was nothing else forthcoming.

"Then where are you from?" she pressed. "I mean, where were you born? What brought you to Memphis?"

"I was born in Wisteria, Texas," he replied. "Moved to Memphis to live with my Uncle after my parents died in a plane crash. That was a long time ago."

"Oh." Tammy didn't know what to say to that and stayed quiet for a while.

"I'm sorry about your parents," she apologized a few minutes later. "I didn't mean to drag up bad memories."

"You didn't," he assured her. Tammy's hands gripped the steering wheel hard. No reaction at all. Nothing.

"What about your Uncle?" she asked. "Won't he be worried about you?"

"Not anymore," was the quiet reply.

Uh-oh, she thought to herself. Stepped in it again, Tammy. Not knowing what else to say, she remained silent after that, determined that he would be the next one to attempt conversation.

Only he didn't. He sat quietly and still in the passenger seat, watching the countryside go by the window. If he moved at all she didn't see it.

This is gonna be a long trip.

-

They had managed to get clear of the worst of the traffic for the time being. Tammy looked at the fuel gauge and seeing it was at three-quarters took the next exit. Time to fuel up and get something to eat. Maybe some pogey bait for the road, too.

"I need to fill up the car," she told Ringo. "And we need to make some plans and get some things."

"Like what?" Ringo asked.

"Well, we need to see about getting a couple gas cans, for one thing," Tammy replied. "We need to get some snacks, too, I think. Like jerky and stuff. Water for sure. It's a long way to Fort Bragg."

"Okay," Ringo nodded. "Want me to pump the gas?" he asked.

"Would you mind? That would help. You keep an eye on our things while I see what we can get from inside." Ringo nodded and got out, walking around to the pump. Tammy walked inside and asked the woman behind the counter to start the pump for a fill-up, surrendering her Amoco card for payment.

The store had three five-gallon fuel jugs which she carried

out to the car for Ringo to fill.

"When you're finished, lock up and come inside," she ordered. "It looks like they've got a pretty good sandwich shop and I'm hungry. Might be Beanie Weenies after this so we better eat up. A. And I need to use the bathroom."

"Okay," Ringo nodded as he started to fill the cans.

Once he was inside Tammy ordered their sandwiches and loaded a hand-basket down with jerky. She had Ringo get them a case of bottled water and two sports drinks apiece. She also purchased a cheap Styrofoam cooler and a bag of ice.

"Anything else?" she asked, looking at her travel partner. He picked up a bottle of acetaminophen, another of ibuprofen, and then some foot powder.

"What's the powder for?" Tammy asked.

"We might have to walk," he shrugged. Tammy snorted.

"As long as my car runs, we're driving."

"As long as it runs and we have an open road," he nodded. Tammy got the powder. The woman happily rang up the purchases and ran Tammy's card. She frowned as the machine said 'wait'.

"What's wrong?" Tammy asked. She wanted to get on the road.

"Machine's acting funny," the woman sighed. "All that money for this stupid thing and now it won't work. Hold on." She reached under the counter and brought out an old-fashioned sliding card machine and a card blank. She had the slip prepared quickly and set it out for Tammy to sign.

"I shouldn't be surprised, I guess," the woman sighed again. "Nothin' works this mornin' it seems. Must be all these riots they're havin' in the cities."

"Riots?" Tammy asked, accepting her copy.

"Yeah, couple o' truckers in here a bit ago said it's all over the CB. Got a riot in Memphis and word is there's others in St Louis, Dallas, and Chicago. No tellin' about them city folk," the woman shook her head sadly. "You kids drive safe."

"Thanks," Tammy tried to smile and partially succeeded. "Let's go," she ordered Ringo, who picked up the cooler and followed her to the car.

"I think we better get going," she said. Ringo nodded, placing the cooler in the back seat.

"I want to stay on the interstate as long as we can," she told him, buckling her seat belt. "We'll make better time. I. . .I didn't think this would spread so quickly."

"All it takes is a bite," Ringo told her. "Once you're bitten, that's that."

"How do you know?" Tammy asked.

"I seen it." She remembered the fight she helped him with and nodded.

"Well, we aren't gonna get bit," she said firmly. "We're going somewhere safe and we're gonna stay that way."

Ringo nodded, saying nothing. Tammy shook her head in resignation and headed down the ramp back onto the interstate.

Their first bit of trouble came less than an hour down the interstate. They were about twenty miles outside of Jackson when the traffic began to pick up quite a bit.

"What in the hell is the problem?" Tammy muttered. "Where did all this traffic come from?" Ringo began watching the other vehicles around them.

"What are you looking for?" Tammy asked him.

"Just keeping an eye out," he said softly.

"For what?" she demanded.

"Trouble."

She sighed. One word answers again. Great. Through a short break in traffic she could see blue lights flashing. Now what? A wreck?

"This doesn't look good," Ringo said quietly.

"What? Why? What are you talking about?"

"They're looking for someone, or something," Ringo answered. "Might be us, too," he added.

"Why would they. . . ." she trailed off. "You've got to be kidding."

"Nope," Ringo shook his head. "There were a lot of people back there. For all they know we just randomly killed people on the highway and drove off."

"Well that's just great," Tammy snorted. "What do we do now?"

"Let them look at us," Ringo shrugged as he pushed his sword beneath the back seat along with her bat. "We cleaned up at the truck stop. They don't have a reason to search the car. Unless someone got your tag number, there's no reason for them to stop us."

It was the most he'd said at any one time since she'd met him, but it didn't really soothe her any. Still, he was right. And they were trapped in traffic now, anyway. There was no way off the interstate and no way to turn back the way they came.

Traffic crawled slowly along the highway and angry drivers began to let their frustration be known with their horns. Tammy resisted the urge to join in. No reason to call attention to themselves and the horns weren't working anyway. As they reached the half-dozen troopers, Tammy rolled her window down.

"How you folks doin' this mornin'?" the trooper at her window asked.

"We're fine so far, but the day ain't over yet," Tammy smiled. "Do you need my license, officer?"

"Where y'all headed?" the trooper asked instead of answering her question.

"Home to see my daddy," Tammy answered in her best 'daddy's girl' voice. "He's meetin' my boyfriend for the first time." She jabbed her thumb in Ringo's direction. The boy looked suitably nervous.

"Where's home?" the trooper asked, chuckling slightly.

"Fort Bragg," Tammy smiled. "My daddy's in the Army."

"Is that right?" the trooper smiled. He was looking at both of them closely while his partner was looking at the car through the rear window. "Just the two of you on this trip?"

"Uh, yeah," Tammy looked puzzled. "Why?"

"Oh, we're just doin' vehicle checks," he smiled again. "It's a pain, but the brass expect us to do it every month or so. Personally, I think they just want us to have to be out here in the heat."

"Well, that's not very nice of 'em," Tammy shook her head. "I bet they're all in the air-conditioned office, right now!"

"Wouldn't doubt it," the trooper nodded. "Well, you folks drive safe, hear? And don't let your boyfriend get too anxious. He might pass out on ya."

"Thanks officer," Tammy smiled again and eased away as the trooper motioned her on.

"He's lying," Ringo spoke finally as they sped up, leaving

the impromptu roadblock behind.

"Well, duh," Tammy replied sarcastically. "Ya think?"

"They weren't looking for us," he clarified. "They're looking for infected."

"How do you know that?" Tammy demanded.

"They're all wearing gloves and they have masks around their necks, hidden inside their shirts. The guy on my side, his mask was showing."

"Really?" He had Tammy's full attention now. "I didn't even notice."

"You were too busy playing 'daddy's girl'," Ringo snorted. "Good job, by the way," he added.

"Hey, it worked, didn't it?"

"I just said 'good job', didn't I?"

"Well, yeah," Tammy shot back a little lamely.

"You did good," he nodded. "This might not be our only roadblock, though." He thought about it for a minute.

"I think you're right about staying on the freeway, though. We're less likely to draw any real interest, as long as we aren't looking sick or bloody. If they're looking for infected, that's probably all they'll be focusing on."

"Well, I'm glad you approve," Tammy snorted. Ringo sighed deeply and leaned back.

"This is going to be a long trip," he murmured.

"What's that?" Tammy demanded. "You say something?"

"Not a thing."

CHAPTER THREE

-

Tammy got off the interstate in Jackson to fuel up again. She added another case of water to their stores and four bags of beef jerky, along with a half-dozen cans of Beanie Weenies and some corn chips. She also purchased a soda for each of them and another sandwich.

"Don't drink many sodas," Ringo said once they were back on the road.

"I don't either but this might be the last time we get one for a while, so drink up," Tammy grinned.

Ringo lifted his bottle in salute and took a drink.

"Traffic's picking up," Tammy noted. "Usually not so bad through here, once you're clear of town."

"Word's spreading, I guess," Ringo observed.

Tammy hit the scan button on her radio, looking for news. She stopped it when a station sounded like it was giving a report.

". . .and to repeat, the virus that's supposed to have originated in Africa is now reported to be present in at least forty-three countries. WHO and CDC officials have issued epidemic warnings worldwide and are circulating information on how to recognize the infected, warning people to stay indoors when and wherever possible."

"This morning's CDC briefing was interrupted by Federal Agents, and Doctor Baxter taken into temporary custody, but outrage over that incident, fueled by multiple reports from the attending news agents have forced the White House to backtrack on those actions and reports are that Baxter is now back in charge of the CDC, and that she and a team of epidemiologists are working on a vaccine to slow the spread of the disease."

"In other news, disturbances that were initially reported as riots earlier this morning are now being confirmed as partial outbreaks in Los Angeles, Miami, Chicago, Dallas, and Washington DC. Other nations experiencing these disturbances include

Germany, England, France, China, and isolated cities in Russia and the Ukraine. Additionally, cities in Brazil, Argentina, Mexico, and Venezuela are reported to be experiencing similar issues."

"The stock market has not fared well today with these report of--" Tammy switched the radio off. She didn't give a shit about the stock market at this point.

"Well, it sounds like we got out of Memphis just in time," she sighed. Ringo nodded but said nothing.

"Still have to circle around Nashville and Knoxville, though," she added, thinking out loud. Again, Ringo nodded, but said nothing.

"Lot of rural areas to travel through, too," Tammy said after another minute.

Nothing.

"Have to be on our guard. These small towns probably won't want a lot of strangers coming through."

Nothing.

"Are you listening to me?" Tammy demanded suddenly.

"Have to circle around Nashville and Knoxville, lots of rural areas on our route, expect small towns to be hostile," Ringo repeated it back.

"Getting words out of you is like getting water from a rock," she fumed.

"Already told you that if I ain't got nothing to say, I don't say nothing," Ringo shrugged. "You got things covered, sounds like to me. Anyway, I'm the rider. I go where you say we go."

"I might welcome your opinion," Tammy replied.

"I get one, I'll share it," Ringo nodded.

"I give up," Tammy shrugged. "I just. . .give up." Ringo shook his head slightly, but said nothing else.

The two fell silent as the car kept moving them along the interstate. Traffic was increasing, getting heavier by the minute it seemed. Some of the drivers appeared to be in full blown panic mode too, which surprised her.

"Where do they think they're going?" Tammy wondered aloud.

"Somewhere safe," Ringo replied, startling her. "They think anywhere is safer than where they are. Those in the cities want to be in the country where there's fewer people. Those in the country want to be in the city where there's safety in numbers."

"Which ones do you think are right?" Tammy asked, interested in his sudden philosophical insight.

"Neither," Ringo's answer surprised her. "There is no 'safe'. Not from something like this. No one's immune and no group will risk infection for any one of its members. Herd mentality is to escape and the slow guy get's eaten."

"'Herd mentality', huh?" Tammy mused. "So, where's that leave us?"

"We aren't part of the herd," Ringo shrugged. "You're trying to get home, which in your case just might be a place of safety. Me, I'm just traveling. I don't expect anywhere to be safe, so I'm not looking."

"What will you do when we get to Bragg?" Tammy wanted to know. Ringo shrugged.

"Don't know. Probably take a look at a map and see what looks interesting. I've never been there, so there's bound to be something worth seeing."

"So, you'll be a tourist?"

"Well, I won't be spending any money on 'all I got was this lousy shirt' shirts," he chuckled. "But why not look around? I might never be that way again, especially considering what's happening right now."

"I don't see how you're taking all this so calmly," Tammy admitted. "I'm a nervous wreck."

"No, you're not," Ringo shook his head. "And I'm calm 'cause there's no reason not to be. I can't stop this stuff, can't do anything about it. All I can do is survive and that's not a given. I only worry about the stuff I can have an effect on."

"And if you were a nervous wreck we wouldn't be here," he went on. "You would have panicked somewhere back down the line and still be sitting there waiting for someone to do something. Instead, you're doing something."

She hadn't thought about it like that, Tammy admitted to herself. Hearing him say it made her feel better. Not just about herself but about the decisions she'd made today.

"Well, thanks for that," she finally said, grinning. "I admit, that makes me feel a little better."

"Just the truth," Ringo shrugged. "Hey, I'm glad you're

capable. I could've hooked up with a spazzy drama queen. Or king," he laughed. "Instead, I got lucky. Not everyone will."

"Well, I'm no drama queen, that's for sure," Tammy let loose with a genuine laugh for the first time that day. "I'm more of a tomboy than anything."

"I figured," Ringo nodded.

"What? Why?" Tammy demanded, wondering if she should be hurt or insulted.

"No offense, but you do swing a mean bat," Ringo grinned at her. "No Deb is gonna be able to do that. And you were swinging for the bleachers, too."

"Yeah, I guess I was," Tammy sighed, "Force of habit."

"Serve you pretty well these days."

"Never even thought about it," Tammy admitted. She suddenly had to swerve to avoid an RV that was all over the road.

"Asshole!" she shouted, laying on the horn.

"Ease up a bit," Ringo suggested, watching the RV.

"What's that mean?" she bit out. "He--"

"I meant get some space between us and them," he clarified. "Something's not right, there," he pointed to the swerving RV. Tammy looked back to the careening motor home, and eased off the gas.

"I. . .I wonder if. . . ." Ringo mused.

"Wonder what?" Tammy asked.

"Well, there might be someone infected on that motor home," he told her, his voice thoughtful. "The driver maybe, or someone who's trying to attack the dri-- watch it!" he cut off. Tammy was already hitting the brakes as the motor home swerved off the right side of the road, caught the high shoulder trying to get back onto the highway and suddenly jerked to the left.

The large RV teetered on its right-side tires for a few seconds and then tipped over, seemingly in slow motion. Hitting the road still traveling at a high rate of speed the large vehicle continued to slide down the roadway, sparks flying. An eighteen-wheeler traveling in the left-hand lane was clipped by the RV's front end, causing a jackknife as the wheel was wrenched from the driver's hand, the big truck's front tires cutting left, adding its weight and bulk to the still crashing RV.

"Hit the gas and use the tore-up lane!" Ringo ordered, but

Tammy hesitated.

"The what?"

"The side lane!" Ringo pointed. "Where you pull over when your car breaks down! If you floor it, we can go 'round!"

Finally realizing what Ringo meant, Tammy looked at the maintenance lane. Sure enough, it was empty, at least this very second anyway. She hesitated less than a second before stomping her foot to the floor.

The small but powerful engine in her car wound up in a flash and the car was accelerating into the 'tore-up' lane. Before Tammy had time to second-guess the decision they were past the slowing jumble of RV and semi and accelerating away from the accident.

"Shouldn't we--" Tammy began.

"No," Ringo cut her off. "There's nothing we can do."

"We should at least warn the authorities," Tammy insisted. Ringo took her cell phone from the console between them and looked at it.

"No service," he told her, holding it out for her to see.

"I usually have service through here," she objected.

"Not today apparently," Ringo shrugged, and set the phone back down. "That was good driving, by the way," he added.

"Thanks," Tammy smiled. "It's a good car. My dad got it for me when I graduated high school."

"Nice."

"He's a good man," Tammy said. "He's always felt guilty that I was alone so much. He does everything he can to make it up to me."

"Sounds like a good father," Ringo said softly and Tammy cringed a bit.

"He really is," she nodded. "How many cars followed us around the wreck?" she asked, changing the subject. He turned in his seat, looking.

"Maybe a half-dozen, so far," he reported, settling back into his seat. "Probably most are sitting there waiting for the police."

"Well, like you said, there's nothing we can do."

They continued down the interstate as the world fell apart around them.

The duo encountered their first problem when they reached the Tennessee River bridge. Or rather, when they didn't reach it but were forced to stop two hundred yards short by a massive traffic jam.

"Now what?" Tammy sighed, leaning on the steering wheel.

"If I had to guess, there's a wreck on the bridge," Ringo sighed back, shaking his head at their luck. "Either that or someone on the bridge is infected and that's got traffic stopped."

"I wouldn't stop for infected," Tammy snorted. "I'd floor it and run over 'em."

"Car like this, that won't get you far," Ringo replied.

"Tear your car up pretty quick. Anyway, I'd say whatever it is, it's just happened."

"How you figure?" Tammy demanded.

"Not enough traffic for the bridge to have been closed long," Ringo answered, pointing to the cars in front of them. "And the other lane is still going," he added, nodding to the west bound lane.

"If it weren't for these stupid concrete things, we could at least turn around," Tammy grumped.

"We can anyway if you want to go that route," Ringo shrugged.

"How?"

"We can use the break down lane and go back," he pointed again. "It's not far. From there, we can find a way across the median, and into the other lane. Looks like some are already doing just that."

Tammy looked, and could see he was right. There were cars crossing the median. Some were taking what looked like an old cut through the trees while others were going further back using the side lane.

"What do you think?" she asked.

"I wish we knew what the hold-up on the bridge is," he replied, looking back that way. "If it's something that might be fixed, we need this bridge. If it looks permanent, then our best bet would be to backtrack."

"I've got some binoculars," Tammy offered.

"Get them," he nodded. The two exited the car. Ringo crawled on top while Tammy got her binoculars from the trunk, passing them up to him.

"See anything?" she asked at once.

"Gimme a sec," he managed not to huff back. He focused the glasses on the bridge, looking over the scene. He could see several people milling about and a small bit of smoke drifting toward them from a source he couldn't see.

"I'd say it's a wreck, maybe with a fire judging from the smoke," Ringo relayed what he could see. "If it is, then we're pretty much. . . ." He paused, adjusting the glasses.

"What is it?" Tammy demanded.

"Get in the car," he ordered calmly, sliding down from the roof onto the hood.

"What? Why, what's happening?"

"Get in the car!" he shouted across the hood, moving to do the same. Tammy jumped in beside him, huffing.

"Get us out of here," he told her. "There's a swarm of infected on the bridge. People are already running this way to get away from them. In about thirty seconds this whole stretch of road will go berserk."

Tammy put her car into gear and cut the wheel sharply, angling for the side lane. She just scraped the bumper of the car in front of her, causing no real damage but annoying the already irate driver who exploded out of his car.

"Hey!"

"Get back in your car!" Ringo yelled. "They're coming!"

"You hit my car, you bitch!" the driver ignored Ringo's warning.

"Sorry!" Tammy called, concentrating on her driving. She was finally able to get the car aimed back up the road.

"Where are you going?! Get back here!" the angry driver yelled, chasing after them.

"Get back in your car!" Ringo yelled once more. Tammy sped up, going as fast as she dared.

"Bogeyman's gonna get 'im," Ringo sighed, looking at the man behind them.

"I'm sorry," Tammy said suddenly, her voice soft.

"What?"

"I'm sorry I hit his car," she whispered. "He'd still be inside, safe, if I hadn't." Ringo saw a tear falling.

"Hey, don't go there," he told her. "He knows, or should by now, that things are messed up. You didn't hurt his car. He was already mad and decided to take it out on you. I warned him to get back in his car. Whatever happens to him is on him, not you."

She nodded, unable to take her hands away from the wheel to even wipe her tears. Suddenly Ringo very gently reached across to her and wiped the tears away. She was shocked by his touching her but also surprised at the gentleness.

"Can't have you blinded by tears," he said kindly.

"You may have to drive soon," she tried to laugh.

"Ah. . . ."

"What?"

"Well, the thing is. . . ."

Tammy saw a break in the traffic and shot through it, managing to cross to the median side of the east-bound lane. They were still on the wrong side, but clear of the concrete barriers. She scanned for a place to cross the median.

"What is it?" she demanded, finally able to relax for a second.

"I, ah, can't, um, drive," Ringo mumbled.

"You what?" Tammy asked. There. There was a gap in the tree line. Gravel. Almost a road. She took it.

"I can't drive," Ringo said louder.

"You can't. . .you can't drive?" Tammy demanded in wonder.

"No, Wonder Woman, I can't drive, all right?" Ringo said, a little peeved. "I never had to learn. Never had a car anyway."

"How did you get anywhere?" she demanded. Damn, this was a rough road. Thankfully it was short. Looking carefully, she caught a break in the east-bound traffic and shot up onto the road.

"I walked," Ringo shrugged. "Rode the bus. Rode my bike. Depended on where I was going."

"You can't drive," Tammy shook her head. Suddenly, she laughed. Loud and hard. And kept laughing. Every time she looked at him, saw his look of offended dignity, she would launch into another round of laughter.

"It's not that funny," Ringo finally said sourly, which made her laugh again.

"For God's sake," he sighed, folding his arms over his chest and slumping in the seat.

Which sent Tammy into another gale of laughter. Realizing that she really needed to laugh right now, Ringo loosened up a bit. Listening to her laugh made him smile, and then chuckle just a little.

"Oh, my God!" Tammy gasped for air between laughs.

"Of all the things you could have said, that was the last thing I expected."

"Why?"

"Well, you're so. . .so. . .capable!" she exclaimed. "All this time you're so calm and cool, and, well, I had decided that you could do pretty much anything and you can't even drive!"

"I can do a good bit," Ringo shot back. "Driving just. . .never came up, that's all. It was never a skill I needed to have."

"I've never met anyone who couldn't drive," Tammy shook her head in wonder. "What else can't you do?"

"I can't fly a plane, either," he deadpanned.

He looked for a map while waiting for her to stop laughing again.

-

"Okay. Our options are pretty thin, looks like," Ringo said. Tammy had taken a rural exit off the Interstate near a place called Birdsong. Parking in the shade at a small roadside park, the two had spread a map over the hood of the car, pausing to eat, take care of personal needs, and look at the map.

"Do you think the bridge will get cleared?" Tammy asked.

"I doubt it," Ringo sighed. "It's pretty isolated and most emergency responders will be busy elsewhere unless they've abandoned their posts. Any of them with any sense have already done just that if they're smart, especially if they have families of their own."

"That's pretty harsh," Tammy commented.

"I didn't say I blamed them for it," Ringo reminded her. "A person's first duty is always to their family."

"Anyway," he went on after a moment's silence, "according to the map the next nearest bridge is a good ways south of here, near a place called Parsons. Map shows a bridge across the river on Highway 412. If we can get across, then it's back roads or state highways from there until we cross I-65. If we continue on that way, then there are two, maybe three good ways we can get back to I-40 well past Nashville, which you wanted to avoid anyway."

"I wish we knew if that bridge was clear," Tammy said evenly. "That's a long way out of our way. Cost us some gas."

"Might be able to get more along the way," Ringo suggested. "No way to be sure of that, of course. There'll be a lot of places that let you use cards at the pump, like Wal-Mart and what have you. If they're still working, anyway."

"Other options?" Tammy asked, finishing her jerky.

"Another bridge to the north. Much farther to drive and much more rural. The upside of that one is that it takes us near Fort Campbell. I assume you have ID that will get you on a base?"

"Yes, I do," Tammy nodded, not having thought of that.

"Well, then this might be your best option," Ringo admitted. "You wouldn't be at home, but you'd be safe. Well, safer," he amended. "And they might be able to let your dad know you're okay, too."

"But what about you?" Tammy asked. Ringo smiled.

"I appreciate the thought, but. . .they aren't going to let me on a military base anyway, whether it's Campbell, Bragg, or anywhere else. This is about you, Tammy. Your dad is defending this country. You deserve to be safe."

Tammy didn't know what to say to that.

"Anyway, there are other bridges but all of them take us well away from where we need to be and want to go. We don't know if these two bridges are any safer than the one we just left. All we can do. . . ." He trailed off as a large four-wheel drive that had been passing suddenly stopped, backing up slightly.

"Get on the other side of the car," Ringo said softly, his voice tight. He reached behind him as if to check something.

"What? Why?" Tammy followed his gaze. The truck stopped about fifty feet away and three large, rather scruffy men got out.

"Go on," Ringo pushed her gently. Tammy went, not knowing what else to do.

"Hey, there!" one of the men called, smiling. The smile wasn't pleasant.

"Hi," Ringo nodded.

"Y'all havin' trouble?" another called. All three were advancing toward the car.

"Nope, we're good," Ringo assured them. "Thanks for asking, but you guys can carry on."

"Well, we wouldn't be neighborly if we didn't make sure the little lady there was taken care of," the third said, eyes devouring the athletic blonde.

"She's well taken care of and that's far enough," Ringo replied, his voice taking on a hard edge.

"Look at 'im, boys," the driver laughed. "He's gonna 'protect' his girlfriend."

"I'm asking you, nicely, to go," Ringo's stance changed slightly. "I won't ask again. There's nothing for you here but pain and death."

"Is that right?" the third man smirked and took another step, this time in the direction of Tammy.

Ringo's hand moved so fast that the knife was buried in the man's stomach before the thug realized he was under attack.

"Wha. . .what th. . . ."

The thug's friends froze for a vital second, unable to believe what had happened. It was a second they couldn't spare.

Ringo seized a spike from his left wrist with his right hand and hurled it toward the driver, moving as he did so toward the last man. The spike hit home, taking the driver in his too-large neck, just below his Adam's apple. He probably tried to yell but lacked the necessary equipment to do so anymore.

The last man saw Ringo coming and set himself, preparing for the teenager's rush. Arms curled, fists clenched, he was ready. He was a lot bigger and stronger than the kid coming toward him and, despite the disabling of his friends, was confident.

But Ringo had other ideas. As he approached the last man he leaped into the air, twisting as he did so. His right leg swept around, straightening just as the toe of his boot came into contact with the would-be rapist's temple. Surprise still etched on his face, the man fell in a heap, dead before he hit the ground.

Ringo hit the ground rolling, on his feet in a second. Looking around him, he realized that all three attackers were down and allowed his breathing to return to normal, looking to see if Tammy was okay.

For her part, Tammy was staring open-mouthed at the carnage her passenger had wrought. It had happened so fast she had scarcely been able to follow it.

When she had reached the far side of the car she had instinctively reached into her car for her bat. She still held it tight, her shaking hands making the bat wobble in front of her.

"Are you okay?" Ringo called.

"Wha. . .how. . . ." She stopped, realizing suddenly that her passenger was far more deadly than she had known. Sure, he had a sword and all that, but...

Killing infected was one thing. These three hadn't been infected.

But Ringo had killed them just as quickly, just as easily, as if they had been. From what she could see of his face he wasn't feeling remorseful, either.

"Tammy, are you okay?" Ringo asked again, starting toward her.

"Stay back!" she ordered him, holding the bat in front of her. "Just. . .stay back!"

"All right," Ringo said calmly, stopping where he was.

"I mean it!"

"Yeah, the bat gave it away pretty good," Ringo nodded again. "I'm staying back."

"Why did. . .what were you. . . ."

"Tammy, you do realize what they had planned, don't you?" Ringo called softly. "They didn't stop here to see if we were okay. They stopped because they saw you. You were what they were after."

"You didn't know that!" Tammy shot back, but the inner voice in her head knew that he was right.

"Yes, I did," Ringo told her. "I told them we were fine. Told them we didn't need help, so they could be on their way. And then, when they kept coming, I told them what was going to happen. This is on them, Tammy. Not me."

"You're the one who did it!"

"And you're the reason why," he shrugged. "Quite a pair, aren't we?"

"Don't blame this on me!" Tammy almost yelled.

"I'm not," Ringo said reasonably. "Had I been alone, they

probably wouldn't have stopped. You did hear the man talking about 'taking care of the little lady', didn't you? What did you think he meant, with a look like that on his face?"

"You ki...killed them," Tammy's voice was softer now, and the bat was slowly falling, almost as if it were too heavy to keep up.

"Yeah, I did," Ringo said flatly. "No point denying it I guess, since you seen it."

"Why didn't they just leave?" she asked, her voice much smaller now.

"Because they thought they had two kids trapped here and meant to have some fun," Ringo shrugged. "That's the kind of men they are. Were. We looked like prey and they had a predatory nature. They thought we were easy meat."

Intellectually, Tammy's brain had already told her all this and she knew it to be true. Her subconscious was starting to remind her that early that same day, God was it today? All of this today? That she had killed at least four people herself, infected or not. That the world she knew had turned upside down.

That Ringo had just saved her from something really bad.

The bat fell from her hands and she slumped against the car, suddenly exhausted. Today had been so much. Too much. Her reserves were gone and so was the adrenaline she had been running on. She slid slowly down the car and buried her face in her hands, crying in a way she hadn't since she had been a small girl.

Ringo let her be, turning to the carnage he had inflicted. He went first to the man he'd hit with the knife, finding that he was not, in fact, dead yet. Ringo fixed that and then retrieved his knife, rifling the pockets of the man he had killed with it, producing a switchblade knife, a wallet with what looked to be about two hundred dollars and several rings, all gold, some with jewels. He sighed, realizing now what the three men had been doing.

He performed a similar search of the other two, finding a pair of hand guns, one revolver and one pistol, perhaps three hundred more in cash, and then turned to the truck. He was surprised to find the truck was fairly well kept, which meant it was probably stolen too. There were three cases of bottled water and two cases of canned heat 'n' eat food along with a shotgun and a rifle.

The shotgun was a Remington 870 with a cut down barrel and collapsible stock, a nice weapon for close quarters. The rifle was an AR of some kind with a chrome barrel, very light with a three-point sling. He found several magazines for the rifle, two more for the pistol, and a large amount of ammunition, some for each of the weapons he'd found.

While Tammy cried herself out, Ringo loaded the plunder he'd found into the trunk of the car, hiding the weapons behind the spare and their other supplies. Chances were they were stolen and even with civilization crumbling being caught with them might be. . .bad. And he'd never use weapons he hadn't had time to check out himself.

But they just might come in handy in the days ahead.

By the time Ringo had finished, Tammy had composed herself. She washed her face with bottled water. That, and a few cleansing breaths had left her ready to face Ringo.

"You okay?" he asked. He didn't approach her, giving her space.

"I'm fine," she nodded. "I'm sorry."

"No need," he assured her, hand raised. "Would you rather. . .I mean, if you want me to go, I understand. I'm sorry I scared you."

"You didn't. . .well, yeah, you did scare me," Tammy admitted. "But you were right, too. I. . .I can see that, now. I could see it then, but. . . ."

"But you were a little freaked out," Ringo nodded. "Like I said, if you're uncomfortable with me, we can. . . ."

"No," Tammy's voice was firmer. "You saved me. If you hadn't been with me, I'd still be at the bridge. Or I'd have been here alone. Or. . ., well, you get the idea," she managed to grin.

"I. . .uh, cleaned up a little and there was some stuff in their truck I thought we could use, so. . . ."

"I saw it," she nodded. "What should we do now?"

"Leaving is a fine option," Ringo admitted, waving in the general direction of the truck and its former occupants.

"Leaving it is, then," Tammy nodded once more. She took one last look at the scene around them.

"Let's go."

CHAPTER FOUR

-

They stayed off the interstate. Ringo had noted the time and suggested they try and find a safe place to spend the night. Tammy agreed. If Ringo could drive she would have insisted they carry on. But he couldn't, and she was exhausted.

Three miles down the road they found a place.

Birdsong Bed and Breakfast was a well- kept colonial style house with a large lawn and beautiful flower garden. The two had agreed with a nod that this was a good place to seek shelter for the night.

Tammy parked on the circle drive in front of the house and the two got out, walking up on the large porch. Tammy rang the bell and a moment later an older man answered, opening the door only slightly.

"Help you?" he asked, keeping his right hand behind him.

"We're hoping for a place to spend the night," Tammy admitted. "We've been on the road since early and need to rest."

"We're closed," the man said, though not unkindly. "Sorry."

"Please, sir," Tammy pleaded. "All we want is one night. I'm trying to get home to my father and the bridge is blocked. I have to try and find another way across the river tomorrow, but. . .well, it would be dark before I can reach another bridge a. And I can't drive much further."

The man looked at Ringo.

"I, ah, can't drive, sir," he looked down slightly. "Never learned how."

"Never?" the man's suspicions were overridden by this fact.

"No one to teach me, sir, and no car to drive anyway," Ringo shrugged. "Never came up before now," he admitted.

"Son, everyone should know how to drive," the older man told him seriously.

"I'm learning that today, sir," Ringo sighed. "Too late to do me any good, though."

"Hiram, who is it?" An older woman joined him at the door.

"Two kids, looking for a place to stay," Hiram replied.

"Let them in," the woman said, eyeing the two.

"Helen, we agreed. . . ."

"They need help," Helen shook her head. "Look at her," she whispered, too soft for the 'kids' to hear. Hiram looked back and realized for the first time that the girl was shaking like a leaf.

"Come in," he said, opening the door wider.

"Thank you," Tammy almost sobbed but caught herself.

"I'll get your bag," Ringo offered. Tammy nodded and allowed the older woman to guide her inside.

"She's had a...it's been a hard day for her," Ringo told Hiram. "Thanks."

"Looks like you ain't had it so well yourself," the man replied. His right hand deposited a Colt .45 into his rear waist band. "You need a hand?"

"No, but. . .I do have something to tell you," Ringo hesitated. Would Hiram turn them in? He didn't know. "If you can listen while I get our things, it would keep her from having to hear it. Again."

"All right," Hiram surprised him. "Sorry I was a little short, by the way," he continued as the two stepped down to the car. "Been a rash of trouble around here today. Several people killed, robbed, things like that. Can't be too careful." Ringo stopped short.

"You know who did it?" he asked.

"Just two, maybe three men, in a big truck," Hiram replied.

"Hiram, you can probably forget about that," Ringo said softly. "Three men in a truck like that tried to attack us a little while ago, not far from here."

"Tried?" Hiram's eyebrow rose a bit.

"Yes, sir," Ringo said respectfully. "They were after Tammy."

"Lot of past tense in your sentences, son," Hiram said gently.

"I. . .took care of it," Ringo told him evenly. "I have something that. . .well, they had these," he admitted, reaching into his pockets and removing the jewelry, handing it over. "Two had blood on them. Well, other than their own," he added. Hiram took the rings and other jewelry from the teenager.

"Son, I don't mean to be suspicious, but. . .how did you manage to take on all three of them and win?"

"They underestimated me," Ringo shrugged. "And I'm a little tougher than I look," he admitted.

"I'd say that's a given," Hiram snorted. "I'll have to call the sheriff," he warned.

"I understand," Ringo replied, taking Tammy's duffle and his own backpack from the car. "Do what you have to. I did what I did to protect her. If there's consequences, I'll accept them. But only after she's safe," he added.

"Sheriff Ball might not agree to that," Hiram warned again.

"It would be in his best interest," Ringo shrugged. "I intend to see that girl home, or as close as I can get her. And I'll walk through or over anyone or anything I have to in order to make that happen."

Hiram looked at the boy in front of him, reappraising his early assessment.

"You two together?" he asked.

"Just met today," Ringo shook his head.

"She must have made a good first impression."

"Saved my life," Ringo agreed.

"Well, I reckon there's no need to call until. . .tomorrow, anyway," Hiram grinned slightly.

"Thank you, sir," Ringo nodded.

"No, thank you, son," Hiram sighed. "Might sleep better tonight, now."

"I wouldn't," Ringo shrugged. "World's gone crazy."

"Ain't it though," Hiram agreed. "C'mon, let's get you two some hot food and maybe a bath. You might need a new shirt, too," he nodded. Ringo noticed for the first time he had blood on him.

"I've got a spare," he nodded.

-

"You poor dear," Helen consoled Tammy, who had just told essentially the same story to her hostess. "I'm glad your young man is so capable. Good men are hard to find these days."

"He's not mine," Tammy smiled. "I just met him this morning."

"Well, I'm glad you did," Helen insisted. "Some things are meant to be, honey, and God always leads us to the people we need most. I met my Hiram at a USO dance at Fort Campbell."

"That sounds very romantic," Tammy smiled.

"He was on his way to Korea," Helen smiled softly. "A perfect gentleman."

"Hard to find nowadays," Tammy nodded.

"They weren't any easier to find back then, either," Helen frowned. "But once in a great while you get lucky. I got very lucky indeed." Helen stood.

"And it appears you did, too," she smiled. "Now, you sit here and rest. Bathroom is down the hall, on the left. I'll fix the two of you something hot. Trail food isn't enough in times like this."

"Please, don't go to any trouble," Tammy asked.

"It's no trouble, child," Helen replied. "I'm blessed to do it." With that she disappeared into the kitchen.

Tammy was asleep before Hiram and Ringo made it back inside.

-

"Tammy," Ringo called gently, shaking her shoulder. "Tammy, Miss Helen has supper ready," he told her. Her eyes suddenly flared wide open, panic running wild as she looked at Ringo, then at her surroundings.

"Hey, it's okay," he said softly. "Remember, we're safe. We're at the Bed & Breakfast. Miss Helen said you should eat something." He watched as recognition dawned in her tired eyes and the panic subsided. She smiled up at him wanly, accepting the hand up he offered her.

"I'm sorry," she murmured.

"Don't be," Ringo shook his head. "You've had a rough day. C'mon, Miss Helen sets a mean table from the look of it." His voice was a little hoarse, she noticed.

"What's wrong with your voice?" she asked, concerned.

"Talked more today than I have in a month," he shrugged. "Throat's a little sore."

"You really don't talk much, do you?" she said kindly.

"Not usually," he shrugged again. "Have to make exceptions once in a while." The two entered the dining room, where Helen had indeed set a mean table.

"You two sit," she ordered kindly. "You need a good meal and then a good night's sleep."

"Yes, ma'am," both answered in unison, then laughed.

Once the blessing was said the food started making the rounds.

"Mister Hiram, is there anything you need help with around here?" Ringo asked between bites of ham and mashed potatoes. "Long as I'm here, I'd like to help if I can." Hiram looked at the boy, young man, with something akin to affection.

"Son, that's right kind of you, but as far as I know we're in good shape."

"You think of anything, you let me know, okay?" Ringo insisted. "You folks have done us a great kindness today. I'd like to help you some way, if I can."

"You helped me plenty a little while ago," Hiram said cryptically. "But if we think of anything, I'll tell you." He hesitated, then looked to Helen, who nodded.

"If you two are of a mind to stay, you're welcome," he said suddenly. "We're in a good place, and if things get more pear-shaped than they already are, this is as good a spot to be in as any."

Tammy looked at Ringo, who simply nodded to her. This was her trip and she was trying to get home or to something like it. He'd do whatever she wanted.

"That's very kind of you," she said softly. "You don't even know us."

"I know enough to know you two are good folks," Hiram replied and Helen nodded her agreement.

"Don't think we need help," she said, her voice kind. "It's just. . .well, the two of you alone, out in all this mess, I don't like it. If you need a place to ride out this storm, we have one."

"Let me sleep on it," Tammy temporized. "I'm too tired to make a good decision, to be honest."

"Smart girl," Helen nodded again, pleased. "Never make a decision when you aren't at your sharpest if you can help it."

"Where did you two come from? Memphis, was it?" Hiram asked. The talk then turned to what the two had encountered during their adventure so far, a bit more detailed than their earlier accounting. The older couple was forthcoming with information they had and what their day had been like as well.

"I'll call a friend of mine with the State Troopers later on," Hiram promised. "To see if he knows about the other bridges and traffic in general. Maybe he'll know."

"The bridge here is probably not going to re-open at least for a few days," Ringo told him. "There. . .there were infected on the bridge. No way of knowing how many. Or what damage they've done."

"I remember," Hiram nodded. "Well, there's the HAM and the CB. I can try and reach out to folks I know and see what information they have. Can't hurt," he shrugged.

"We're grateful to you," Tammy said softly. "I can't begin to tell you."

"All I ask is that you help someone else if you have the chance and the means," Helen smiled. "I've lived my whole life like that, sweetie. It's never failed me."

"I promise," Tammy replied, meaning every word. She sighed, looking down at her cleaned plate.

"I think I'd like to clean up and get some sleep," she said. "I know it's still light out, but today. . . ."

"Don't you worry, honey," Helen nodded, rising. "Come and let me show you where you'll be staying." The two women left the room, still talking. Hiram looked at Ringo.

"You'll do whatever she decides, won't you?" he asked after a minute.

"Yes, sir."

"Yeah, I recognized that look," Hiram chuckled. "Give it to my missus all the time."

"We're really not a couple," Ringo shrugged. "I. . .I just don't have anywhere to go, anywhere I need to be. She helped me when she didn't have to. I didn't really need it, but she did it anyway. So, I made it my business to see to it she can get home if I can manage it."

"You've no family, then?" Hiram asked.

"None," Ringo shook his head. "Not anymore."

"I'm sorry, son," Hiram said gently.

"It's okay," Ringo shrugged. "You can't miss what you can't remember. My parents were always traveling. Died that way, in a plane crash when I was a boy. My uncle took me in, taught me. . .well, he taught me to be a man. This sickness got him, late yesterday. Seems like a lifetime ago, now," he admitted. "So there's no one to miss me, now."

"I'd say that girl would miss you if something happened to you," Hiram noted.

"She'll have to miss me if I can get her home," Ringo replied. "No way they're letting me on an Army base. But if I can get her to one, then. . .well, then I'll go my way and see what I see."

"This virus," Hiram changed the subject, "you know it's spreading fast. Too fast."

"Yes, sir."

"The news people have started calling them 'zombies' late this afternoon, you know that?" Hiram was watching him closely.

"Just panic, I'd say," Ringo eased back in his chair, finally full. He paused to drain his tea glass. When he set it down Hiram refilled it.

"They have to call it something," Ringo went on. "But they aren't really zombies. They're not 'undead', or anything else supernatural. They're just sick. Rabid."

"And there's no cure or vaccine," Hiram nodded. "One bite is all it takes, according to the news, and you're infected. Takes a few minutes to a few hours according to what information they're giving out. Any rabies I ever saw took days to show itself. Sometimes longer'n that."

"This is something new," Ringo nodded. "I don't think it's entirely natural, either," he added.

"What makes you say that?" Hiram asked, eyes bright.

"It spreads too fast, like you said," Ringo shrugged. "If this strain of rabies was entirely natural, there's no way it hasn't been seen before, either. I know it sounds like conspiracy crap, but. . .I think this form of rabies escaped from some lab somewhere in Africa. And now, it's too late to put the genie back in the bottle."

Hiram leaned back at that, as if thinking about what Ringo had said. In reality, however, he was making a decision. Once it was made, he leaned forward again.

"You're right," he said suddenly. "It is man-made, at least that's what my sources tell me. You're right about it being too late, as well. This thing has spread too far, too fast and response has been far too slow. In all likelihood, there's no stopping it now. It may burn itself out, but billions will probably die before it does."

"Do your sources know of any way to protect yourself from it?" Ringo asked.

"Don't get bit and don't let any of their bodily fluids enter your bloodstream," Hiram replied at once. "There is point zero four percent of the population that will in all probability be naturally immune. From the virus, mind you. No one is immune to the damage one of these poor deranged individuals can cause them physically."

"Leather would be a good protection," Ringo mused. "But it's awfully hot for that this time of year."

"Man would have to make sure and stay hydrated," Hiram nodded. "Take salt tablets, drink electrolytes if he can get them. Have to be careful where he gets his water, too. Even a good filter might not be enough to filter out the virus."

"Will boiling work?" Ringo asked.

"Should," Hiram nodded, his eyes showing approval. "And some Clorox bleach."

"Really?"

"Best thing for making water drinkable, especially in the field or from an unknown source." Hiram stood up suddenly.

"I need to try and make those calls," he said. "Helen should still be upstairs. She can show you around. If you need anything, holler."

"Thank you, sir," Ringo stood as well.

"Don't mention it, son."

CHAPTER FIVE

-

Ringo was awake before sun-up, and slipped outside with no one the wiser. He made a quick check of the area around the house then went through his workout. He didn't want anyone to see if he could help it. He wasn't really hiding anything, he just. . .well, it was his time, that's all.

As he went through motions that had long since become automatic, his mind drifted across the previous day and his conversation with Hiram after the women had gone upstairs.

That was one cagey old man, he decided. Played his cards close to the vest. He knew more than he was willing to let on, that was for sure. Ringo felt flattered that the man had shared as much as he had. Hiram didn't know Ringo from dirt so he had made that decision on simple faith. Ringo appreciated that almost as much as he did a good night's sleep in a comfortable bed and a good meal.

Tammy was another dilemma. If not for her, Ringo would stay here with Hiram and Helen. They could use him here and it would be almost like a home for him. He felt at home here. Comfortable. Probably too much so, he decided. If he got too comfortable he'd probably get careless.

Yesterday getting to Fort Bragg hadn't seemed insurmountable. Troublesome, sure, with things going the way they were. But now, with the bridge closed and no idea if any of the other ones were, the trip seemed much longer.

How many bridges were there between here and there? How many were over streams or rivers that there would be no other way to cross unless by boat and then go on foot? Ringo didn't know.

He had learned yesterday however that every bridge was now a potential obstacle to getting Tammy home to Fort Bragg. If they walked. . . .

Walking made a one or two day trip by car an odyssey. Even if they covered twenty miles a day by foot, that was still. . .well, at least two months. And that was if everything went perfectly, which it would not.

How many gaggles of infected were between them and where they needed to be? How many towns would they have to skirt around because the locals wouldn't let them go through? How many gangs like the three thugs he had killed yesterday would be waiting to see two people alone, especially a woman who looked like she did?

He paused, wiping sweat from his forehead. He had been at it for over an hour now without realizing it. He flipped his sword once more, sliding it into its sheath, then turned to go inside and get a shower only to see Hiram sitting on the front porch, watching him intently.

"I haven't seen anything like that in a long time," Hiram said quietly. "Nicely done."

"Thank you," Ringo bowed slightly.

"Have a seat, son,' Hiram pointed to another rocking chair. "Your options are a lot thinner than you thought." Ringo walked onto the porch and sat down. Hiram offered him a glass of water from a pitcher on a small table.

"When I was in Korea, I used to get over to Japan once in a while on leave," Hiram said casually. "I made friends with a Japanese liaison officer and he took me out one night to see a show where a man 'bout as old as I am now put on quite a show with a sword. Cut a candle without movin' it, kinda like on Zorro, never thought to see such in my own front yard."

"My uncle taught me," Ringo said softly. "It was how he drew me out of my shell, I guess. When I realized how much I enjoyed it, how good I was at it, it became all I cared about pretty much."

"Well, I'd say you're pretty good at it sure enough," Hiram smiled. "Sure takes me back, though." His grin faded and he grew serious.

"I spent a long time on the radio last night," he said gently. "There's pretty much no way across the river by vehicle at this point. All the bridges are blocked either by wrecks that can't be cleared due to traffic or by gaggles of infected folk that can't, or won't, move away from the cars they've abandoned."

"I suspected as much," Ringo nodded, drinking more water.

"Society has pretty much broken down since we went to bed

last night," Hiram admitted. "Was already on its way by supper mind you, but a few hours really makes a difference, seems like. President declared Martial Law, which is about as useful as an empty toilet paper roll in an outhouse." Ringo snorted water through his nose at that one.

"Military is out, working to and I quote, 'restore order', but anyone with an ounce of intelligence knows that's not going to happen. Not without an all-l out slaughter, anyway. There's no bringin' order to a bunch of folks that's gone plumb mad."

"No, sir," Ringo agreed.

"Lotta action, or at least talk and threats of action by so called 'militia' groups here and yon. Most of 'em sound like they know the script to Apocalypse Now and Red Dawn by heart. Probably where they got their 'training' too." Again, Ringo had to be careful not to shoot water from his nose. Hiram had a biting sense of humor this morning.

"Anyway, damn near ever little town between here and Bragg is tryin' to close itself off to outsiders. You and your Miss will have to go through places like that, most like on foot, to get her home again. I hate to say so, son, but. . .I don't think it's doable. Not without a lot of blood, sweat, and tears." He looked at Ringo.

"And some of it'll probably be your blood. Or hers."

Ringo nodded silently. He'd already worked most of this out during his workout this morning.

"Not really telling you anything new, am I son?" Hiram asked.

"No, sir," Ringo admitted. "I'm not used to being responsible for anyone other than me. It's. . .difficult to get used to."

"So, it is," Hiram nodded. "Well, the offer to stay here stands. If you're determined to go, I've got a friend who can take you across the river, but from there it's on foot, or bike, maybe. No way to get the girl's car across. Sorry."

"It is what it is, sir," Ringo shrugged. "It brought us a long way, no matter what. I'll talk to her when she wakes. We'll see what she says."

"Well, I'm going to sit here and watch the sun come on up," Hiram said, shifting in his chair slightly. "Helen is still sleeping, so I'd take it kindly if you were quiet."

"Yes, sir."

-

Tammy awoke with a start, sitting up in her bed. She didn't recognize the room she was in and looked around her. Slowly, as she saw her things on the night stand, her bag in a corner and realized she was wearing her favorite sleep shirt, she relaxed.

"It was just a bad dream," she thought to herself. "That's all." Standing and stretching, she grabbed her bag and started for the shower. She opened the door to see. . . .

"R. . .Ringo?" Tammy almost stammered.

Ringo, shirtless as he was leaving the shower, hurriedly threw his towel over his back and shoulder, but not before. . . .

"My God, Ringo, what happened to you?" Tammy asked softly, her hand moving to his back without thinking. Ringo deftly avoided her touch, pulling his toothbrush from his mouth.

"I'm good. You look better after a good night's sleep," he added, changing the subject.

"I. . .until I saw you, I had convinced myself it was a bad dream," Tammy admitted.

"Sorry," he offered, not knowing what else to say.

"Not you, me," Tammy shook her head. "I'm not dealing very well, I guess."

"I'd say you're dealing fine," Ringo replied. "Ain't every day the world goes straight to hell, ya know."

"No, I suppose not. I'm going to get a shower and then see about making some breakfast."

"Need any help, call me," Ringo nodded. "I'm gonna check a few things, see what's what."

Tammy walked into the still steamy bathroom and couldn't help but inhale the inherit maleness Ringo had left behind. There was something about him, she admitted.

After taking her shower, Tammy headed back to her own room where she dug into her duffle looking for clothes. As she did so she came across the emergency kit her father had made for her.

"I wonder what's in here," she murmured. Taking her pocket knife she worked at the small zip tie that held the handle secured. Once it was gone she opened the kit, exhaling sharply when she saw its contents.

Laid out in perfectly cut sections of the egg shell foam used in gun cases, each component of the case had its own little place.

First, there was a small handgun with an extra magazine and a box of shells. She picked it up, realizing it was her own XD Springfield. Replacing it, she looked at the small plastic tubes and picked one up. It was full of silver coins, ten to be exact. Each one contained a full troy ounce of silver. The other tube was smaller and contained one-tenth ounce gold coins, ten in number.

Tammy sat down abruptly. She'd never imagined why this case was always so important. Now she knew.

There was a knife inside, a small fixed blade RTK, one of the best blades available. It wasn't Rambo sized, but she would never need something like that anyway.

The last item was odd. It looked like a radio but when she picked it up she realized it was a satellite phone. On the back was one number with the name Dad on it. She looked at the phone stupidly for a moment before it hit her.

"I can call my dad!" she almost shouted. She was halfway out the door before she realized she wasn't exactly dressed. Slamming the door closed, she quickly dressed then grabbed the phone and sprinted downstairs.

"Ringo! Ringo, where are you?!"

"Here I am," he called from the front porch. "What's wrong?" She ran out to see Ringo talking with Hiram.

"Mister Hiram," she nodded. "Ringo, my father, he. . .he made me this emergency kit. I've never opened it but I found it in my bag this morning and so I opened it just 'cause, you know, I never had, and I found. . .well, I found a lot of things, but most. . .well, not most importantly maybe, but. . . ."

"Hey, now," Ringo raised a hand. "Slow down, girl."

"Look!" She thrust the phone at him. Ringo took it and looked at Hiram, who held his hand out.

"Sat phone," Hiram said at once. "Good one, too. Well, what are you waiting for young'un? Give your old man a call and let 'im know you're okay," he smiled.

With trembling fingers Tammy dialed the number on the back of the satellite unit. She waited, hearing a series of clicks then a growling noise she finally realized was the phone ringing through. It rang twice. Then a third time, and then a fourth. Just as she was starting to think there would be no answer she heard her father's gruff voice.

"Tammy? Tammy is that you? Dear God, let it be you!"

"It's me, daddy!" Tammy almost shouted. "Daddy! It's me, I'm all right!"

"Thank the Good Lord," Reese Gleason sighed in relief. "Where are you?"

"Well, I'm near a place called. . ." she looked at Hiram.

"Birdsong," he provided.

"Birdsong, Tennessee. I. . .I can't get across the river, at least not here. The bridge is blocked. Where are you?"

"I'm in. . .I'm in Atlanta, baby," her father's voice cracked slightly. "Listen, Tammy," his said haltingly. "I don't. . .I'm not sure we're going to get out of here, honey," he admitted. Tammy felt the air rush out of her.

"Daddy?" she almost whispered.

"Honey, this is pretty bad," Reese told her. "Worse than anyone is saying out loud, so far. We. . .we were supposed to try and restore order but that's not really working out. A lot of our people are. . .we've lost a lotta men."

"Daddy, what are you saying?" Tammy's voice was trembling. She knew deep down what he was saying but couldn't, wouldn't, admit it to herself.

"We're pretty well cut off, baby," he finally said straight out. "There's no way out of here that we can find so far. We. . .we may not make it."

"No, Daddy, don't say that!"

"Tammy, listen to me, I don't have much time." Gunfire could be heard in the background now, along with a high-pitched scream she didn't recognize.

"You're going to have to look after yourself, honey," Reese told her. "You'll be on your own from now on. We've lost contact with Bragg. I don't know what the situation there is, so even if you can make it, you may not find any help."

"You're going to have to make your own way now. And I don't know what kind of world you're going to find. All I can tell you is to stay safe, baby, and be careful. Remember that I love you."

"I love you too, Daddy," Tammy cried. She waited, but there was no more coming. Her father was gone. Slowly she lowered the phone, not bothering to shut it off. Ringo took it gently from her fingers, handing it to Hiram who shut it down.

Tammy stood silently for a time taking in all that she had just learned. Suddenly she turned and buried her face in Ringo's shoulder, sobbing uncontrollably. Hiram got silently to his feet, nodding to Ringo over her head and eased into the house.

Ringo held her a little awkwardly perhaps, but he tried to comfort Tammy as she sobbed. Yesterday they had been headed for her home where it was assumed she would be safe. Now, just twenty-four hours later, things had changed so much.

Her father was in the middle of a hot zone and sounded like he wasn't going to get out. He didn't have any contact with Fort Bragg, either. For all anyone knew the base had fallen. All of this on top of what they had learned yesterday. For Ringo, on top of what he'd learned from Hiram this morning.

After a few minutes Tammy seemed to cry herself out. She raised her head from Ringo's chest, looking up at him sheepishly.

"I'm sorry," she said softly. "I've got your shirt all wet."

"It'll wash," Ringo assured her, smiling very slightly. "Feel any better?"

"Oddly, yes," Tammy admitted. "Don't know why, though. Nothing's changed."

"You let out a lot of stress," Ringo pointed out. "That's not nothing. And it's good for you, too." He guided her into one of the chairs around the table where he and Hiram had been sitting and poured her a glass of water. She took it, nodding gratefully, and drank. Ringo let her finish before speaking.

"What do you want to do, Tammy?" he asked. She looked at him.

"What can we do?" she asked.

"We can do whatever you want to do," he promised.

"My father said Bragg was off the grid, maybe lost," Tammy sighed, forgetting that Ringo had been able to hear that for himself. "There's nowhere to go, Ringo," she said sadly.

"The offer to stay here is still good," Hiram said, walking out onto the porch. "We're in a good place here. I'm not saying we're safe because we might not be, not completely. I honestly have no way of knowing. But, we'll eat and we have safe drinking water. There's a roof over our heads. We're off the beaten path."

"We may never see a single infected person around here."

"That's possible, I suppose," Ringo nodded. "On the other hand, we're not that far from the bridge as the crow flies. I don't know anything about how these things behave. For all we know they'll attack each other when there's no one else to attack."

"Well, breakfast is ready," Hiram interposed. "Let's all get fed and then we can talk. Or you two can and we'll join in if you like. Always think better on a full stomach," he grinned.

-

"Thank you, Miss Helen," Ringo leaned back in his chair, rubbing his stomach. "That was pretty awesome."

"You're welcome, Ringo," Helen smiled. "That's an unusual name," she added after a minute.

"Yes, ma'am," he nodded. When he offered nothing else Helen let the matter drop. Instead she looked at Tammy.

"Dear, I'm sorry for your bad news. Is there anything I can do to help?"

"Ma'am, you've already helped us more than anyone would have a right to expect," Tammy smiled. "And I appreciate it more than I can say."

"You're quite welcome," Helen smiled. She rose and started gathering the dishes. Tammy got up to help.

"I've got it, dear," Helen told her but Tammy shook her head.

"I want to help," the younger woman said. "I need something to keep me occupied." Helen nodded and off the two went.

"Let's take a walk," Hiram said suddenly and Ringo got to his feet. The two went outside and began to make a circuit of the property. Ringo had pulled his sword over his shoulder without thought. Hiram settled for a shotgun held in the crook of his arm.

"I've been retired for a while," Hiram said. "I made a career out of the military. Didn't plan it that way, just sorta happened. I been a lot of places, but this. . .this has always been home," he waved to the area around them. "I'm not from here, mind you, but Helen is, and, well. . .Helen is my life. Has been since I met her."

"I ended up working in Intel," he continued after a minute. "That's Military Intelligence. Sort of an oxymoron, I always thought," he chuckled, and Ringo snorted.

"Anyway, I made a lot of contacts in a lot of places back in the day. Kept in touch with most of them. Still in touch with them, in fact," he added, looking at Ringo. The younger man nodded, indicating that he understood.

"It seems like this has all happened overnight, but in reality, it took at least a week. I'd say closer to a month, but I'm guessing. The powers that be, for whatever reasons, sat on it until that woman with the CDC, Baxter, let the cat out of the bag."

"We heard something about that on the radio," Ringo nodded. "About how she was arrested, but there was such a uproar over it she was let go and was back in charge."

"That's right," Hiram nodded. "Well anyway, the CDC is locked down now. That place is nothing short of a fortress when it's shut down, at least normally. They're working on the virus, of course, and looking for a vaccine, maybe even an antidote."

"I don't think an antidote's gonna work," Ringo said gently. "I'm not saying it won't, but. . .from what I've seen. . . ."

"Lot of people agree with you," Hiram nodded. "Me included. See, I think that this rabies is causing a fever, and that fever is burning the infected up. Could be wrong of course, but that's my thinking."

"The question is, what happens now?" Hiram stopped near the river's edge and the two looked out over the water. It was strangely calming.

"Once a fever reaches a certain point it literally starts to cook the brain," Hiram continued. "That kind of damage is pretty well irreversible. In a normal setting, there are anti-inflammatory drugs that might help fight the fever, but. . .last few days have been anything but normal."

"I don't think we're gonna see normal again anytime soon, sir," Ringo agreed.

"No, son, I don't think we will," Hiram sighed. "Anyway, so far we don't know squat about what happens to the infected over even a few day's time. What changes does the virus make inside them? If it is rabies, then the infected will soon die of dehydration because of their fear of water."

"That same fear will make someone infected very cautious about being around the river. Or a lake. Probably even a small pond. If, that is, they really have rabies and this strain of rabies affects them like it normally would." Hiram stopped, looking at Ringo again.

"You see the problem?"

Ringo nodded, mind working. Hiram might look like an old innkeeper, but he wasn't. The younger man had to wonder just how many others Hiram had shared his background with. Probably none, he decided.

"Yeah," he replied, looking again toward the water. "We need information. Or rather, the people working on the vaccine need information."

"Got it in one," Hiram nodded in satisfaction. "Not second-hand, he said she said stuff. Or the usual fear and panic reports, either. They need real, honest to goodness, usable information. And there's only one way to get that kind of information."

"Go out and find it," said Ringo.

"I'm afraid so."

"I assume you've been in contact with people who can use this information?" Ringo asked.

"I'm in regular contact with them," Hiram's voice was soft. Calm. Expectant.

Ringo took a deep, cleansing breath, forcing it out in one long exhale.

"What do you need me to do?"

CHAPTER SIX

-

"You realize that I am in no way qualified for something like this, right?" Ringo mentioned, looking at Hiram. The old man nodded, his face a study of sadness.

"I do," he agreed. "I also know that no one else really is, either. I've got that covered. Well, sort of," he amended.

"Sort of?" Ringo asked, eyebrow raised.

"My communications are pretty secure," Hiram revealed. "If you're willing to be one of their scouts, for lack of a better word, then the people at CDC are prepared to teach you everything you need to know in order to get the job done."

"I assume they're gonna want blood samples and the like," Ringo sighed.

"Probably," Hiram admitted. "I don't really know. This is way beyond me, kid. I'm not a scientist. Never was. I'm an operator."

"For the phone company, right?" Ringo snorted and Hiram grinned, albeit a bit bashfully.

"Something like that."

"Well, I guess I ought to be able to find some infected somewhere," Ringo thought aloud. "Trick'll be catching one alone and getting him or her, it, down and out to get the sample."

"Think about it," Hiram encouraged. "You don't have to do this, Ringo. No one can make you and someone else, somewhere, can get it done, I'm sure."

"How will we get the samples out?" Ringo asked, thinking ahead.

"Helicopter," Hiram told him.

"That'll need to be picked up somewhere far from here," Ringo pointed out. "You don't want that kind of attention. From anyone," he added darkly.

"We'll work it out," Hiram promised. "Like I said, think it over. I figure you'll wanna talk to the girl about it anyway. Let me know what you decide."

"Do you really think this'll help?" Ringo asked, looking the older man in the eye.

"No idea," Hiram answered honestly. "Like I said, not my area. The squints at CDC think so, though. And some of them are pretty smart."

"Squints?"

"Nickname. Squints, geeks, nerds. You know, smart people. They squint at stuff and then tell you all about it."

"Ah. Nice."

"Wasn't meant to be," Hiram snorted. "All too often their bullshit gets you into a mess in the field. But like I said, these at least seem to know what they're talking about."

"You're a very jaded old man, Hiram," Ringo grinned in spite of himself.

"You have no idea, kid," Hiram replied. "I better get up to the house, see what's doing."

"I think I'll just hang out here a while," Ringo said, seeing a bench near the waterfront. He wandered over to it as Hiram departed and sat down. He rubbed his hands down his face in a scrubbing motion, looking out over the water.

Of all the things he was thinking about when he woke up this morning, crazy as some of them were, this had not been on the list. Leaning back on the bench, he took stock.

Ringo knew he was able and fit. His training, the only thing that had mattered to him for a long time after his parent's death, had seen to that. He could do this.

Probably, he qualified. A lot of that depended on exactly what Hiram's 'squints' would want from him. Kill an infected, take a blood sample and slip away, that sounded pretty uncomplicated. Not easy, but straightforward.

Hiram had also mentioned observation, though. Watching, taking notes, trying to determine what was happening to the infected as they roamed the countryside. How would he know what was important and what wasn't? How would he figure that out?

"Hey," Tammy's voice broke him away from his thoughts. He turned to see her walking toward him.

"Hey, yourself," he smiled. "Have a seat," he waved to the bench he was sitting on, offering to share. She sat down, placing her hands between her knees, looking out at the water.

"How you makin' it?" he asked.

"One foot in front of the other," she admitted. "You?"

"Just peachy," he shrugged. "Made any kind of decision?" He needed to know that before he could answer Hiram.

"I don't see that I have one," Tammy shrugged. "This is a good place, off the beaten path and they're nice people. It's safe here, at least for now. We can earn our keep and help them out. I don't see many other options."

"True," Ringo nodded, a ball of dread settling into his stomach. Until she had said that, the idea of going out looking for 'answers' had been just that. An idea. Now, it was a plan waiting to be put into place. But there was no way he was going to tell her that.

"Well, it works for me," he settled for saying. "I like it here and they are good people."

"So, what were you and Hiram talking about?" she asked. He froze for just a second but relaxed before she caught it.

"Stuff," he shrugged.

"Man talk?" she laughed gently, and he grinned in spite of himself.

"Right. Super-secret man-type things. I could tell you, but. . . ."

"Yeah, yeah, I've heard how that one ends," she held up a hand, laughing outright now. "He passed me on the way down. Seemed pretty preoccupied."

"He's got ears everywhere," Ringo told her. "He's hearing news from all over the place. Probably going to check on some of them right now." Almost certainly, in fact, he didn't add.

Tammy turned her gaze back to the lake, watching the waves.

"It's so peaceful here," she said after a minute. "Seems crazy, doesn't it? How quiet, peaceful it is here, considering that the whole world's gone crazy."

"Can't be crazy everywhere, I guess," Ringo shrugged. "We got lucky coming by here," he said seriously. "Very, very lucky."

"I know," Tammy's voice was soft. "I was able to tell my dad. . .tell. . . ." Her tears started despite her best efforts and Ringo slid over to her side.

"Hey, I know," he told her softly, placing an arm around her shoulders. "You may as well let it out. There's not enough room for it inside."

"I've got to stop," she shook her head, wiping her eyes as she did so. "It doesn't help and it won't change things. And all things considered, we're blessed to be here."

"I'd say that's accurate," Ringo agreed. "So, you're going to stay here, then?" he asked.

"Yeah," Tammy sighed. "At least as long as I can. As long as it's safe and we're welcome." Ringo nodded absently, looking back out over the water.

"What?" she asked, looking at him.

"Well, I said I wanted to get you home or some place safe," he said, leaning forward, bracing his elbows on his knees.

"I told you I can take care of myself."

"So, you did," he nodded. "And you have. If this is where you're going to stay, then. . .well, I have something I have to do."

"What's that mean?" Tammy asked, her face showing puzzlement.

"It's just a job," he shrugged. "I'll be leaving soon," he told her.

"What?" For all that she didn't raise her voice he could hear the desire to in her tone.

"The CDC needs people in the field to observe the infected and gather samples. Blood and tissue samples, I guess," he added when her face showed confusion. "I'm going to be one of those people." Well, so much for not telling her about it, he thought.

"What can you possibly know about that kind of stuff?" she demanded, harsher than she had intended.

"Nothing whatsoever," he admitted. "But Hiram says the CDC people can teach me what to do over the next day or two. What information they need and how to get it. Once I'm finished with that, I'll be leaving."

Tammy just looked at him for a long moment. Suddenly she shot to her feet, her body rigid. Rather than speak she simply turned away from him and walked back toward the house, her posture stiff. Ringo watched her go, sighing to himself.

"Well, that went well."

-

Tammy stalked toward the house furious with her travel partner. What was he thinking? Going out there was suicide! And it could only get worse.

"I take it you talked to Ringo, then," Hiram's voice broke her out of her fuming. It also gave her a target for her ire.

"How could you ask him to do something like that?" she demanded, hands balled into angry fists.

"I just mentioned it had to be done," Hiram replied evenly. "And he's far more capable than anyone else I know of."

"He's nineteen years old!" Tammy wanted to scream but settled for a yell instead.

"He's a grown man," Hiram replied calmly. "When I was his age, I was lying in a rice paddy looking across the DMZ into North Korea. And he's a hell of a lot more capable than I was at his age," he added almost reluctantly.

"How do you know?" she hissed. "We just got here yesterday! You don't know us at all!"

"I know a warrior when I see one," Hiram smiled sadly. "I've known more than one in my lifetime. And Ringo is a warrior, pure and simple."

"Warrior?" Tammy goggled. "Is this some kind of game? Wizards and warriors, dragons and demons, whatever the hell it's called?"

"Well, there's demons I'd say, based on what I'm hearing and seeing, anyway," Hiram shrugged. "And don't scoff at the word warrior either, missy. Have you forgotten where you came from already? You're the daughter of a warrior, as I recall."

That brought Tammy up short, the words hitting home in more ways than one. Even the thought of her father hurt, but. . .Reese Gleason was definitely a warrior. He had admitted once talking to her before a deployment that being a soldier was what he was meant to be. He couldn't imagine being anything else.

Then she remembered where he was the last time she'd spoken to him, and the likelihood that she would never see him again. That was what being a warrior was good for.

"It's his decision, Tammy," Hiram said softly. "He doesn't have to go and I made that clear. He may still not. Completely up to him and if he decides not to go I wouldn't blame him one bit. I told him and I'll tell you, there are others, probably, that can do the same thing, somewhere."

"But you still put him up to it." Her teeth were clenched so tight they hurt.

"No, I mentioned it needed to be done," Hiram shook his head. "He was the one who noted that he could get it done. And he can. Of that, I'm sure."

"Why?" Tammy demanded.

"I've been a soldier of one kind or another all my adult life," Hiram said simply. "I don't know how well you know Ringo, but he's a very dangerous young man, and one more than capable of making his way in a world like the one we seem to be living in now."

Tammy opened her mouth to object but reconsidered. She thought back to the day before, first at the traffic jam in Memphis and then to the three men who would have attacked her had Ringo not been there. Even though she watched the entire thing he had killed the three would-be rapists with a speed that had been hard to follow.

"I don't want him to do it," she said softly. "He's done enough."

"Then tell him that," Hiram urged. "Might be what changes his mind."

"You wouldn't be angry?" she asked.

"Hell, no," Hiram scoffed. "I like the boy. The thought of him out there alone makes my skin crawl."

"Then why even mention all this to him?" Tammy demanded.

"It needs doin' and he can do it," Hiram shrugged. "It's more for you and others like you than for anyone like me. Helen and I, we've lived a good life. Your lives, yours and his, are just getting started. I don't want you two to have to try and live in a world where most of the population has been reduced to animals."

"That's why it's important," he continued. "If there's a way to stop it, or even just slow it down, maybe a vaccine to protect the rest of us, anything that would help, then it's worth the effort to find it. That's all."

Tammy deflated at that, sitting heavily onto the porch steps. She didn't want to live in a world like this either. Even if there was a 'fix', the damage already done would mean that her plans for the future were already shot. Survival had become everyone's primary job, now. Just surviving.

She got slowly to her feet, walking back the way she had come, almost against her will. If Ringo was willing to risk his life to do what had to be done then she could at least be supportive.

If she couldn't talk him out of it.

-

Ringo was walking slowly toward the house, still deep in thought. His talk with Tammy had gone about like he'd thought it would. He liked her and hated to see her upset. She'd lost her home and her father, her entire future, in one day. She'd been through enough grief and misery in the last day-and-a-half to last anyone a lifetime.

Here, she was safe. If anyone could keep her that way, Hiram could. Ringo didn't really have any doubt about that. And Tammy could take care of herself, too. With the old soldier's teaching, she would become even more capable and self-reliant than she was now. Her father had taught her pretty well already.

"I'm sorry, Ringo," her voice broke through his thoughts. He looked up, surprised to see her standing right in front of him.

"What?"

"I'm sorry about earlier," she said. "I. . .well, to be honest, I didn't know what to say, so I ran away. I'm sorry."

"Nothing to be sorry for," Ringo shrugged. "Believe it or not, I understand. You've been through a lot since yesterday."

"So have you," Tammy pointed out, joining him in walking back toward the house.

"Not like you," Ringo shook his head. "I already lost most of the things that you lost. Only I lost them along the way. One here, another there. You lost them all at once. No matter how tough you are that's a hard blow. If anyone's got some leeway coming, it's you I'd say."

"And you did great yesterday," he added. "Most people would have panicked at one time or another going through what we did yesterday. You didn't."

"I might have if not for you," Tammy admitted.

"And I might still be in Memphis fighting for my life or dead without you," Ringo shrugged. "It evens out."

"You're determined to do this, aren't you?" she asked as the two stepped up onto the porch and sat down.

"I don't know yet," he admitted. "Until I talk with these people Hiram wants me to speak to, I don't know what they want or if I can do it. He thinks I can, but. . .I won't know until I know. If that makes sense," he added, snorting.

"It does," Tammy assured him. "I wish you wouldn't go," she added.

"I plan on coming back," he told her honestly. "This is supposed to be a one- time thing the way I understand it. Once I've done what they want, I'm planning on coming right back here. And stay as long as Hiram and Helen will have me."

"You're welcome to stay as long as you want, dear," Helen said, walking out onto the porch. "Not to intrude, but I couldn't help hearing that. Both of you are welcome to stay here with us." She sat down.

"I've had a word with Hiram about this scouting trip, too," she continued, her voice almost frigid. "He had no right to lay that on you."

"Why not?" Ringo asked calmly. "It needs doing. Maybe I can do it. He's trying to help, that's all. Do whatever he can to make things safer."

"That doesn't change the facts," Helen said tartly. "You're not trained for this kind of thing. I think he forgets sometimes that not everyone has his background. Or his sense of adventure."

"I've never had much of a sense of adventure," Ringo nodded. "But I'm not untrained. I can take care of myself just fine. I'm more worried about actually being of any use to these scientists."

"We'll talk to them later tonight," Hiram promised, following Helen onto the porch and taking his own seat. "I don't know what all they'll want but you can be sure they'll want samples, pictures, maybe a video of their behavior. Behavioral patterns, how they respond to what stimuli. . . ."

"I think we can talk about something else right now, dear," Helen said firmly, and Hiram nodded, contrite.

"Right. You and me'll talk later about it, Ringo. And to the CDC, too."

"I still wish you wouldn't," Tammy said softly.

"And I still may not," Ringo reminded her again. "We'll

see."

-

The first thing Ringo noticed about Doctor Meredith Baxter was that she probably hadn't slept much lately. There were dark circles under her eyes and her face had a drawn, haggard look to it.

The second thing was that she did indeed squint at everything, including the web cam she was using to talk to Hiram.

"This is the young man I was telling you about, Doctor," Hiram said, once the connection was established.

"Thank you, Colonel," Baxter smiled tiredly and Ringo looked at Hiram, eyebrow raised. Hiram just shrugged.

"What is your name, young man?" she asked kindly.

"Ringo, ma'am," he replied. She waited a few heartbeats.

"Just Ringo?" she asked finally.

"'Fraid so, ma'am," he nodded.

"Well Ringo, you're very brave to do this," Baxter told him. "I'm sure the Colonel has explained how dangerous this will be."

"I pretty well figured that out for myself, ma'am," Ringo assured her.

"I imagine you have if you've been out there," Baxter nodded. "Believe it or not, the virus hasn't spread everywhere as of yet. There are still a few areas that aren't affected at all, but not many. And I don't expect that to last."

"I wouldn't either," Ringo nodded.

"What I need are specimens to work with," Baxter got to the point. "I need tissue samples, blood samples and some video of their behavior. The Colonel can provide you with the containers for the samples but I cannot stress enough how careful you must be. Use gloves and glasses at all times to avoid any type of fluid contact."

"All right," Ringo nodded.

"Otherwise, just be observant. Write down anything you see that seems important."

"How will I know what that might be?" Ringo asked, frowning.

"Well, do they act in a group or pack, or do they act individually? How do they respond to stimuli? Does sound attract them? Movement? Do they all respond at once, like a herd mentality, or do they seem to follow the leader? Things like that."

"Okay," Ringo nodded. He could probably do that.

"We also need at least one intact head," Baxter added, her face sorrowful. "That will require you to dismember the. . . ."

"I've already been there and done that, Doctor," Ringo raised a hand. "Won't be a problem."

"Well," Baxter almost frowned. "It's a problem for some people. There's a lot of people in the government insisting that the infected are simply sick and must be treated humanely. At least that's what they're saying in public," she added.

"Ma'am, I've seen the infected close up and personal," Ringo said flatly. "There's no humanity left there. And I mean none."

"I know," Baxter nodded slowly. "Unfortunately, many, many people are buying into the theory, and that's just adding to the problem. You'll have to be careful that you don't run afoul of any of them. Even some peace officers are coming down on that side of the argument."

"I'll mind it," Ringo promised. "Anything else?"

"Yes," Baxter nodded. "If you can see any of them around water, I'd like video of their behavior there. This is supposed to be a rare strain of African rabies. Rabies is the common name for hydrophobia, which is--"

"Fear of water," Ringo nodded. "Already thought about that."

"You are a very intelligent young man, Just Ringo," Baxter smiled after a minute. "And I really appreciate this. We don't have many people willing to do this kind of work, and without samples to work with we're helpless."

"How many are there?" Ringo asked. "Besides me, I mean?"

"Five," Baxter replied evenly. "That's all we could get that we can reach by helicopter. You make six. Hopefully it will be enough."

"I'll get what I can for you, ma'am," Ringo promised.

"Thank you. Again," she added. "Colonel Wilkins will finish your briefing. Please be careful." With that the screen went blank.

"Colonel Wilkins," Ringo tried out the name. "You know, I don't think I'd heard your last name until just now."

"It's not my last name," Hiram assured him. "There's no way I'm telling her or anyone else who I am. Or where I am, either," he added.

"Then why let me tell her who I am?" Ringo demanded.

"I've never heard you use anything but Ringo," Hiram shrugged. "How hard will it be to find someone named Ringo? Just Ringo," he added with a snort.

"Guess that's true enough," the teen shrugged. "You got what I need to get this done?"

"Yeah," Hiram sighed. "Gonna have to show you something, kid. Don't really want to, but. . .reckon I gotta trust somebody, sooner or later. You're elected, looks like."

"I can wait here," Ringo offered.

"No, you can't," Hiram sighed. "There's a lot to do and a lot to show you and it's better we do it somewhere. . .outta the way."

CHAPTER SEVEN

-

Hiram led Ringo outside to the garage behind the house. Ringo was a bit puzzled but held his questions, following quietly. The garage was two-story with what was probably an apartment over the vehicle bay.

Once inside Ringo looked around, but . . . it was just a garage. A nice one he admitted, with room for three vehicles. Two sat inside, a late model SUV and an older pick-up. The third bay held a side-by-side ATV. Hiram ignored all of these and headed to the back of the garage.

In back of the ground floor Hiram opened a door that exposed a small storage area, full of tools and auto care products and supplies. Walking to the back of the storage closet, Hiram motioned for Ringo to close the door. Frowning, he did so.

Hiram looked at Ringo, eyes flinty hard.

"I'm about to trust you with my life and the life of my wife, kid," he said flatly. "Don't make me regret it." Before Ringo could reply Hiram reached in between some of the stored oil cans and pulled. Ringo heard what sounded like a lock mechanism throwing and suddenly the rear wall of the closet swung open, revealing a set of stairs.

"Watch your step," Hiram warned over his shoulder. He flipped a switch inside the newly opened door and started down the now illuminated steps. Ringo followed, cautious. As they descended the steps Ringo found it difficult to contain his surprise.

"This is my hole card," Hiram told him. "Everything the loving couple needs to survive. . .well, anything."

Ringo nodded slowly, taking in the view. Shelves filled with cans of freeze-dried foods and other supplies lined the walls. The room was somewhat Spartan but still. . .comfortable was the word that came to Ringo's mind. There was carpet over the concrete floor, simple yet inviting furniture including two recliners and a sofa, and all the touches of a small but comfortable living room in what could be any house in America. Books lined shelves in every available wall space.

Several doors opened off of this main room. Hiram started pointing them out.

"Bedrooms," he indicated two doors at opposite ends of the larger room they were standing in. "Baths," he pointed to a room toward the center. "Kitchen," was a doorway to their left. "And. . .the armory," he pointed right. It was this door he headed toward.

"C'mon."

Ringo followed, still taking in what he'd been shown.

"No one other than Helen and I and two other people who helped me have ever been down here," he told Ringo over his shoulder. "Not until now."

"Wow," Ringo finally managed. "I've never seen anything like this."

"Everyone needs a bolt hole," Hiram shrugged. They reached the 'armory' and Hiram keyed in a number on an illuminated key pad. Once again Ringo could hear a locking mechanism disengage. Hiram gave the oversize door handle a twist and opened the door.

Ringo hadn't known what to expect when Hiram had said 'armory' and followed the older man inside wondering what he would see.

The first thing he noticed was that the well-lit room was big. At least as large as the room they had first entered.

The second thing, hard to miss, was that one wall was basically a weapons rack. Rifles, shotguns, handguns, and some other items Ringo was unfamiliar with lined the wall on padded rests. He could see the reflection of a light sheen of oil on all of them.

There were cabinets along the far wall, all locked. Several looked almost like safes and two were refrigerators he noticed with some surprise.

"Powder," Hiram shrugged, seeing where Ringo was looking. "I re-load, plus make custom rounds." Ringo nodded as if he understood, which he did in part. Ringo noted there was no wasted space anywhere, shelves and cabinets filling the walls all the way around the room.

From the doorway down the front wall was a long work

bench. Odd machines here and there sat with plastic covers over them, while tools unfamiliar to Ringo hung along a pegboard over the bench itself.

"My reloading presses and gunsmith tools," Hiram offered, waving at the bench.

"Wow," Ringo repeated, shaking his head.

"I'm showing a lot of trust in you, Ringo," Hiram said matter-of-factly.

"It's occurred to me," Ringo snorted in amusement. "And you just met me yesterday. Not under the best circumstances, either."

"True," Hiram nodded. He pointed to a stool, taking another for himself. Ringo sat down.

"I'm a pretty good judge of character," Hiram explained. "And I've watched you like a hawk, too," he admitted. "Once I figured out that you and the girl really weren't together except as traveling partners I decided you were okay. Not many men, especially your age, would help a pretty girl like her and not expect something in return, if you know what I mean."

"I know," Ringo said softly.

"I also watched you practice this morning," Hiram continued. "It's obvious you have discipline and training." He paused then, looking Ringo dead in the eyes.

"It's also obvious you're hiding something," he said flatly. "Concealing might be a better word since you aren't harming anyone with it. But. . .I want to know what happened to you, son. And I want the truth."

Ringo's face flushed for a second and in that second Hiram saw the dragon lurking beneath the lamb's exterior. Ringo hadn't moved an inch, but his eyes were almost glowing with barely-held rage. Hiram held up a hand, forestalling Ringo's response, if there was to be one.

"That's good enough, right there," he said. "Your parents didn't just die in a plane crash, did they, son?"

"No," Ringo replied flatly.

"You saw it happen, didn't you?" Hiram's voice was gentle, kind.

"Yes," Ringo's single word answer was strained.

"Did you see who did it?" Hiram asked. This time Ringo

just nodded.

"How old were you?" Hiram asked.

"Five."

"Five years old," Hiram shook his head slowly. "How long did you stay hidden, afterward?"

"I don't remember," Ringo admitted. He had never spoken of this to anyone other than his uncle and the authorities. Ever.

"I'm sorry, kid," Hiram's voice rang with sincerity.

"Long time ago," Ringo managed to shrug.

"I'm guessing you don't feel much anymore," Hiram speculated.

"No," Ringo admitted. "I don't. I never saw a point, afterward."

"And that explains the sword, the martial arts, the edge on you." It wasn't a question.

"I suppose it does," Ringo replied, almost against his will.

"Thanks, kid, for trusting me as much as I do you," Hiram said softly. "Let's get you outfitted, and start looking at what you need to get the job done."

There was no more talk of Ringo's past.

-

Ringo let out a long exhale looking at all the equipment gathered on the table before him. He had thought he'd known what he was agreeing to, but now he wasn't so sure.

"This is a lot of stuff," he said, still looking over the gear.

"You'll need it," Hiram promised. "More than you expected I take it?" he almost smiled.

"I travel pretty light," Ringo admitted. "I didn't think about having to haul all this shi. . .stuff, around while I was doing this."

"I've heard the word before," Hiram chuckled. "And had the same thoughts myself, I assure you. Thing is, you're going to be out in the field, alone. You might be able to find what you need and you might not. That means you carry the things you absolutely have to have with you. Understand?" Ringo nodded.

"Good. Now," Hiram picked up the small camera. "This thing is supposed to hold a shitload of video. I don't know exactly how much, but a lot. More than the squints should need, especially if you use it right. There's a small roll-up solar charger that will help you keep it charged," he set the camera next to what looked like a roll of rubber matting. "Takes a while, but it's light, easy to carry and simple to use."

"These are MREs," he continued, picking up a foil wrapped package. "I would tell you they're good eating, but I like you. They taste like cardboard, especially if you have to eat 'em cold. But they've got all the fuel the body needs to keep going, even in combat. There's enough here for five days at two a day." He set the package down and picked up a plastic bottle.

"Food tabs," he explained. "Actually taste better than some of the MREs. Two of these have about fifteen hundred calories between them. Good to keep your body up and running when you're on short rations. These," he pointed to a collection of what looked like candy bars, "are called survival bars. There are thirty-six hundred calories in each bar. Coasties use them in lifeboats. Also good for keeping you going on short rations and a lot easier to carry. And not bad eating compared to some stuff."

The lecture continued with a filtering water bottle, water purification tablets, GPS, satellite phone, waterproof map, a very small camp stove with fuel tabs. That one brought a question.

"Little warm for a stove, isn't it?" Ringo asked.

"Until you're soaking wet and night falls," Hiram nodded. "Then, there's no fire large enough until you're dry again." Ringo nodded. That made sense. Finally, Hiram's hand touched on a pistol with an attached suppressor.

"You know how to use a gun?" he asked. Ringo nodded.

"I do. Not as well as my sword, but. . .I do," he settled for saying.

"Got one of your own, do you?" Hiram asked, smiling slightly. Ringo just looked at him but nodded.

"Use it if you want, then," Hiram shrugged. "This one's quiet, though. Line of work you're about to go into, you need to be invisible. Noise is death in Indian Country." Ringo looked at him and Hiram shook his head.

"Never mind, just an old saying. Anyway, take this with you, you'll find it handy. I've got plenty of knives and machetes so if you want take your pick. I know you favor edged weapons." Ringo looked the selection over and did select one good knife that he liked the heft of.

"Good choice," Hiram approved. "Randall Knives.

Excellent all-around blade."

"It feels good in my hand," Ringo nodded. He placed it with the rest of his supplies.

"All right," Hiram sighed. "We've got sample containers and a bio-hazard container. I cannot stress enough, do not let any of their blood get inside your eyes, mouth, open cut, anything. If it does, you may find yourself infected. Use the gloves and the goggles, got it?"

"I got it," Ringo promised.

"This one," Hiram took the second bio-hazard container, "is for the head. Once you put it inside, seal it like this," he demonstrated, "and then open this tab," he pointed, "and push the green button...in that order. Got it?"

"Seal, green button," Ringo repeated dutifully.

"This container will flood with a tiny capsule of liquid nitrogen when you seal it and then activate it with the button," Hiram explained. "It will keep for up to forty-eight hours. As soon as you've got this and can get to a secure location, use the sat phone to call the number on the back. Give them the GPS coordinates and they can send a chopper to recover them."

"How do you have all this stuff?" Ringo's curiosity got the better of him.

"Leftovers from a by-gone era," Hiram shrugged. Ringo waited but Hiram offered no more, instead returning to his instructions.

"Wherever you decide to leave your collection, attach this to it," he gave Ringo a small cylinder. "Hit this button and it activates a light that only a thermal image will see and a small tone that the chopper can home in on." He looked at Ringo, his face serious.

"Do not be around when that chopper lands, Ringo," he warned. "Do not trust these people, even for a second. She may mean really well, but if Baxter is on the level, and that's not a sure thing, she doesn't have a clue the kind of men who will be collecting this stuff for her or I'll eat my hat. They're just as likely to take you with them as not. Or kill you."

"Why?" Ringo was puzzled.

"I'm not saying they will," Hiram told him. "I'm just saying it's possible. We've already agreed that this virus is probably man-made. Just because someone wants an antidote or a vaccine doesn't mean they want anyone to know where it came from. I know how these kind of people work and think, kid. Trust me on this. Let them come to get the samples and you be long gone when they get there."

Ringo absorbed all this without comment, but inside he was wondering what kind of person Hiram had once been. Had this no-nonsense old man once been like the people he'd just described?

"A long time ago and a long way from here, yes, I was like that," Hiram said softly, seeing the look on Ringo's features. "All I can say is that it made sense at the time. They were enemies, Ringo. People that would have killed me, Helen, anyone of us they could have. I tell myself the world is a better place without them. Almost helps me sleep better."

"But this is different," he went on, voice firmer. "We're Americans, and we don't do that to our own people. At least, we aren't supposed to. But. . .times change, Ringo, and I don't know all the players anymore. So you do like I said, okay?"

"I will," Ringo promised. "I'll call them after I've set things up and set off the beacon."

"Smart boy," Hiram grinned, slapping the teen on the arm. "All right, let's get you packed up. Once we're done you can go when you're ready. Did you leave the keys in that truck you said those three thugs were driving?"

"No, I took them," Ringo replied. "Why?"

"I was just thinking that truck would be a good way for you to get around and get away," Hiram shrugged. "I'll take you to get it. Using it, you can take that case a good ways from here, leave it, and then get back. I'd prefer it be dropped at least fifty miles away," he added.

"I really don't know how to drive," Ringo reminded the older man.

"Just a preference," Hiram shrugged. "If you can't, we'll deal with it."

"Is this putting you at risk, Hiram?" Ringo asked, suddenly concerned.

"No, and I volunteered to help," Hiram sighed. "Damn my patriotic heart. But there's no reason for them to have any better idea where we are than necessary. I don't want them thinking they can come here later on, if you catch my drift."

Ringo did. He nodded his understanding and returned to packing his gear. Finally, the pack bulging, he lifted it. At least fifty pounds. He shook his head, chuckling.

"This is going to be an experience," he sighed, heading for the stairs.

"That's why it's always the young that get these jobs," Hiram chuckled. "Gotta be strong enough to carry all this crap."

The two were still laughing when they emerged from the storeroom, the bunker once more sealed and concealed.

-

That evening following supper, Ringo sat on the porch for a while watching the very last light of dusk fade into night. He looked up as the door opened and Tammy walked out onto the porch. She sat down in the chair next to him, saying nothing at first. The two sat in companionable silence, watching as the stars came into view. Finally, she spoke, her voice soft.

"Are you still planning on going?" she asked.

"Yeah," he replied equally softly. "Already got the stuff ready and everything. Shouldn't take long. A few days at most, I figure."

"I still wish you wouldn't," Tammy sighed softly. "It's too dangerous.

"It won't be that bad," Ringo shook his head, wondering all the time if he was wrong about that. "I'm just going to sneak around some, that's all. Take a few videos, get their samples, then I'm done. This is a one-time thing for me."

She said nothing else for a time and the two returned to the silence. Ringo had rarely been comfortable around others but Tammy he was okay with. He wondered why that was. Sure, she was attractive, but. . .it wasn't that. Her looks were nice but it wouldn't make him comfortable around her like this. It was something about her. Her attitude maybe, or her strength. Maybe it was a combination of the two. Either way, he genuinely enjoyed her company.

His defensiveness raised its head at that point, warning him not to be too comfortable. It was weakness, being comfortable, to desire the company of others. He tried to ignore the innate feelings and was partially successful. Meaning he didn't get up and leave her sitting alone.

For her part Tammy was thinking about many things. Her father was on her mind, of course. She had tried his phone three times since talking to him this morning, without success. She wanted to believe that he was still alive but the odds were certainly against it.

She thought about the friends and near family at Fort Bragg, wondering if the base was still safe and them along with it. She had tried calling Lucinda Steele but the landlines were completely jammed as were cell phone circuits. All Tammy could do was pray that the woman who had been like a mother to her was safe at home.

Despite the tragedy of the last two days Tammy had to admit that she was extraordinarily fortunate, first in finding Ringo and then finding Hiram and Helen Tompkins. She had gotten their last name from Helen while the two were cleaning up after breakfast that very morning. It hadn't seemed important to know their last names really. The older couple had opened their home to two strangers and taken them in when there was no real reason to do so. Tammy was thankful to them and never ceased to tell Helen so.

Helen had made it clear that more thanks were unnecessary. She was happy to have them there; the older woman had told her. She and Hiram had never had children, Helen had confided in her that afternoon. Both were only children, so the family they had was distant at best. Instead they had a few very good friends as a substitute family.

It was unlikely they'd see them any time in the near future.

Tammy understood Helen was essentially making Tammy and Ringo part of her family. That realization brought with it a warmness that Tammy was unable to explain but that pleased her very much.

That warmness evaporated again as she thought about Ringo leaving, being out there with all those infected and being all alone this time, with conditions much worse and growing more so with each passing hour. She sighed suddenly, a long, sad sound that drew Ringo from his own thoughts to look at her, a hint of concern showing on his face and in his eyes.

"You okay?" he asked carefully. She shrugged, not really knowing the answer herself.

"Just thinking," she told him, still looking out at the night. "Lot of things have happened since yesterday."

"So, they have," he admitted with a nod. "We've come a long way in less than forty-eight hours, Tammy Gleason."

"So, we have, Just Ringo," Tammy looked at him, smiling softly. Just then, Hiram and Helen came out onto the porch, each carrying two small plates.

"Pie for dessert, dears," Helen smiled as she and Hiram sat down with them. Hiram ate his with gusto while Helen picked at hers. Ringo decided the woman was still a little angry with her husband.

The four sat talking quietly about anything other than the present crisis or Ringo's pending departure. Eventually Helen excused herself and headed to bed, Tammy following perhaps ten minutes later. Ringo and Hiram sat quietly in the darkness for a few minutes.

"I'll be gone when they wake up," Ringo broke the silence. Hiram nodded, having expected something of the sort.

"Want a lift out somewhere?" Hiram asked, but Ringo shook his head.

"No. I studied the map this afternoon. I can cut across country pretty well it looks like. I think it's probably better to stay off the roads. Crossing them might be okay, or following along parallel, but I'll be better off staying off of them, I think."

"Good idea," Hiram nodded. "You already know that not everyone who isn't infected will necessarily be friendly. Keep that firmly in mind."

"Count on it," Ringo agreed. "I'll try and stay in contact."

"Don't keep the phone on," Hiram warned. "I don't know that the girl won't try to call you. You don't want that phone ringing at an inopportune moment."

"Hadn't thought of that," Ringo admitted. "I'll do it." Hiram stood suddenly.

"Be careful, Ringo," he said sternly. "Don't try too hard. If you can't do this without endangering yourself then pull back and come home. Don't try to be a hero."

"I won't," Ringo promised. "You're second-guessing this, aren't you?" he asked.

"Maybe a little," Hiram admitted, thrusting his hands into his pockets. "Not that you can do this," he added. "That I'm sure of. I'm just wondering if it will really help; if we aren't already too far gone for it to make a difference."

"If we do all we can, then at least we have that," Ringo offered. "There's not much else to cling to."

"I suppose," Hiram sighed heavily. "Just make sure you come back. I don't like to think of the impact on Tammy if you leave and don't return."

"She'll be fine," Ringo assured him. "She's strong. And I know you and Helen will take care of her."

"Me and Helen won't be here forever," Hiram said flatly. That startled Ringo a bit, but he merely nodded his agreement.

"I'll be back."

Hiram looked at him for a minute longer, then turned abruptly and went inside. Ringo sat in the darkness a little while longer before going inside himself. He needed to sleep, if he could.

Morning would come early, he knew.

CHAPTER EIGHT

-

Ringo studied his map, eyeing the road lying just below the hill he was on. If he was where he thought he was, the road below would take him in the general direction of the river bridge. He didn't know how far he'd need to travel because he wasn't sure exactly where he was.

He pulled the GPS receiver from the case on his belt and hit the refresh button. The small screen popped up with a digital map that roughly corresponded with the paper one in his hand. A few taps on the scroll button revealed the river, and the bridge, lying six miles, plus or minus, to his east. He returned the receiver to its case and started making his way through the woods, keeping the road in sight.

He'd made pretty good headway this morning, he decided. He had left in the dim light of dawn, making his way down the road from the house until the road turned away from the woods. The dawn had broken by then and there was enough light for him to proceed safely into the woods.

Ringo had to admit he was pretty pleased with how things had gone so far. He was far from a wilderness scout but careful planning and good equipment were paying off. He was close to his objective and had remained unseen. At least, that he knew of.

He didn't like the uncertainty of 'that he knew of', but there wasn't much he could do about that. The going was slower than he liked but there was simply no help for that. There could be infected anywhere, including here in these woods. Blundering into one, or a dozen for that matter, would be bad. His mission was to stay quiet, stay unseen, and observe. He would take the best of those opportunities to take his 'samples'.

For now, he concentrated on making his way quietly toward the bridge. The GPS would guide him home if necessary.

-

Tammy Gleason was unhappy to say the least. She had

awakened early, intending to help Helen prepare breakfast and see Ringo off only to discover that he was already long gone. Hiram was sitting on the porch with a cup of coffee when the young woman stormed out onto the porch.

"You knew!" she accused. Hiram looked up at her calmly.

"That Ringo was already gone? Yeah, I noticed it as soon as I got up."

"You knew last night he was leaving early!" Tammy expanded her statement, hands on her hips. "Didn't you?"

"He might have mentioned that he was leaving early," Hiram sighed. He wasn't going to lie.

"Why didn't you tell me?" Tammy looked betrayed.

"You were already asleep," the older man shrugged helplessly. "And honestly, if he'd wanted you to know, he'd have told you," he added.

"Why would he not tell me?" she snapped.

"Oh, I don't know," Hiram pretended to muse. "Maybe to avoid the same kind of scene we're having right now?" The calm words brought Tammy up short. She closed her mouth, open to make a snappy comeback, and stood there looking at him.

"Sit down," Hiram offered. "Coffee?" he asked, picking up the small pot and another cup. Tammy nodded glumly, plopping into the chair. She took the proffered cup of coffee, adding sugar to it before trying it.

"Not bad," she complimented, almost grudgingly.

"What they call Navy coffee," Hiram told her. "Add a little salt to it, believe it or not. I always have liked it ever since I tried it."

"They should sell it at Starbucks," Tammy snorted, then remembered there might not be any more Starbucks soon.

"I know your mad right now," Hiram told her gently. "But try to give the kid a break, okay? He's not used to having anyone depending on him and he's not entirely comfortable with it, yet. I'd bet he's also not used to anyone making a fuss over him or caring whether he lives or not."

"What do you mean?" Tammy asked, frowning.

"He's an orphan and was raised by an uncle, right?"

"Yeah."

"Well, that same uncle, assuming he was the man who

taught Ringo his marital arts and sword skills, was probably not the most nurturing man ever to live. I haven't heard Ringo mention an aunt. Have you?"

"No," Tammy admitted. "I haven't."

"So there probably wasn't one," Hiram nodded. "Which means that he grew up with a man who was probably just as emotionally closed off as Ringo is himself. Not the best environment for a kid to grow up in, for starters. Throw in the traumatic loss of his parents, factor in the absence of any kind of nurturing environment or maternal influence and you end up with a young man who is completely uncomfortable with any kind of emotional reaction to his well-being. Not because he doesn't appreciate it," Hiram added firmly. "But because he isn't accustomed to it. He simply doesn't understand how to react to it." He leaned back into his chair again.

"So, try to cut him some slack, okay? He needs time to adjust to the fact that people care about him."

Tammy considered that. Did she care about Ringo? Of course, she did. She'd only known him two days, that was true, but they had been through a lot together in those two days, and she felt. . .well, she owed him, she told herself. That was all.

"I just feel like I owe him," she said aloud to Hiram. "He not only helped me get this far, he saved me from something pretty bad. Something I might not have reacted to in time to protect myself. Something I didn't see coming," she admitted finally.

"I know," Hiram said kindly. "But I think he'd be the first one to tell you that you don't owe him anything. If I haven't badly misjudged him, anyway."

"I don't think you have," Tammy replied. "I really don't." And she didn't. She couldn't understand why she was so certain of that, but she was. Just as certain as she knew her own name.

"I don't either," Hiram didn't bother to hide his smirk. "And anyway, we've got plenty to do right here, waiting for him to get back."

"We do?" Tammy asked, straightening.

"We do indeed," Hiram nodded. "It's about time to start putting in the garden. If we want fresh vegetables this year I'd say we'll have to grow them ourselves. What do you think?"

"Now that you mention it, yeah," Tammy snorted. "I guess

that answers the question of what I do with all this spare time."

Helen wondered what had Hiram in such a good mood this morning. She could hear him laughing clear upstairs.

-

Ringo smothered a curse as he looked at the scene below him. According to the map, the road he'd been following was Highway 641. He was still a good way from the bridge, he realized, looking at the map along with the GPS. He hadn't paid attention to the fact that the highway below him was actually leading him slightly away from the bridge even as it led him back to the interstate. But that wasn't the problem.

The problem was that he had run out of woods to hide in along his chosen path. To stay hidden, he'd have to strike out across country. He was fairly confident that he could do that using the map, compass, and GPS.

But as he sat on a small rise surrounded by sage brush and scrub oaks he wondered if that would be necessary. There were five infected below him right now, stumbling around as if confused by their surroundings. True, there was no water around, but. . .he figured if he could get everything else then Doctor Baxter could get her information about how the infected reacted to water from somewhere else.

Using the small, but powerful, binoculars he'd received from Hiram, Ringo watched the scene below him for a few minutes then turned to his pack. He removed the video camera and set it up on the small tripod, careful to move the brush aside so that the camera would get a clear view of what happened below. No sense wasting this opportunity to get her the video she wanted.

Now all he had to do was figure out some way to provoke a reaction from them. Preferably one that didn't see him ripped to shreds by angry, infected, homicidal maniacs. After a few minutes, he realized there was only one way to go about things.

Leaving the camera set up, Ringo took his pack and retreated into the heavier cover afforded by the trees behind him. There he hid his pack, taking only his sword, the suppressed pistol Hiram had given him and the sawed-off Remington that he'd taken from Tammy's trunk. The same one he'd removed from the would-be attackers the day they had met Hiram and Helen.

If he wanted a reaction from the infected, he'd have to do

something to get it. The only thing he could figure out to do was go down there and get their attention, hoping all the time that doing so wouldn't prove to be fatal.

-

"This is your garden?" Tammy's eyes widened, looking at the huge plot.

"Yep," Hiram grinned. "We used to do a brisk business, believe it or not. Plus, we'd truck patch the excess. This year though I imagine we'll be eating or storing most of it. If things don't get better we'll be glad to have it all."

"True," Tammy nodded. "Well, let's get started," she smiled. Hiram nodded and started the small lawn and garden tractor. Soon he was breaking the almost one-acre plot with the plow while Tammy was sorting through the seed containers. Helen joined her before she'd finished and the two of them began to set containers at the end of the rows for later planting.

Once Hiram was finished he replaced the tractor and then took his shotgun to make a round about the property. The tractor was noisy. He wanted to make sure they hadn't attracted any undue attention.

With Helen showing the way, Tammy was soon planting the garden alongside the older woman. While not physically demanding, especially for an athlete, it was time consuming and monotonous. It also served to take her mind from her father, the events of the last few days, where Ringo was at the moment and how he was doing.

Hiram returned soon and began to assist the two of them. Before Tammy realized it, the sun was high in the sky and Helen was preparing lunch.

"That's enough for today," Hiram told her as Helen called them in for lunch. "We'll get the rest in a day or two."

"Why wait?" Tammy asked, curious.

"Couple of reasons," Hiram shrugged. "We don't want everything coming in at once, for one thing. We'll wind up with stuff rotting on the vine if we can't get it all at once."

"What's the other reason?" Tammy asked, cleaning up before going inside.

"I'm tired," Hiram told her flatly. "I'm an old man and I've done more'n enough work already today," he winked. "Course, the real reason is to give Helen a break. She can't keep up like she used to," he added, much louder.

"I heard that!" Helen called from inside and Tammy couldn't help but giggle. The older couple clearly loved one another dearly. She hoped someday she'd have someone that she could. . .
.

The thought trailed away as she remembered why she was here and why they needed the garden. No, she admitted to herself. She'd probably never have what Helen and Hiram had shared. That made her sad.

It was something she would have looked forward to.

-

Ringo checked the camera once more making sure he would know which area was covered by the little recorder. No sense in making the infected react if it wasn't on film. Satisfied, he eased down the hill on his belly, coming to a stop about eight feet from the highway and perhaps twenty feet from the nearest infected.

Taking one of several rocks he'd collected, Ringo chucked it out onto the asphalt hitting a car hubcap with it. The sound rang along the highway like a church bell. The reaction was instantaneous.

All five of the infected whirled toward the sound, their lethargy gone in a flash. All of them hurried that way, searching for the source of the noise. Ringo watched, impressed by their speed. This really was nothing like the old horror movies. The infected weren't dead and they weren't slow, either. No shuffling and moaning for this bunch.

Instead, they screeched in what could only be described as an animal-like rage, doing a running stumble toward the sound. Ringo noted that some motor control seemed to be deteriorating along with balance. He also reminded himself that five infected didn't make a study. He couldn't depend on all infected to react as these had.

With the five of them distracted he tossed another rock, this one farther down the road away from his own position. Again, all five infected turned at once and shuffle/ran toward the sound of the rock skittering along the asphalt. Ringo watched them carefully, trying to determine if there was any deductive reasoning to their movements or if they we simply following the sound.

It was almost as if they were blind, Ringo thought. Using sound to hunt. He caught all five looking away from him and tossed another rock toward the same place as the second, almost right on them. This time one of the infected seemed to notice the rock bouncing and held his ground. The other four went chasing after the sound.

So they could see. Ringo sat back for a minute, wondering what else he could try. Before he could think of anything, he saw movement across the road in the field beyond. As he watched a dog burst from the grass, barking and growling at the infected. As one the three men and two women turned to the noise.

Emitting a screech that made the hair on Ringo's neck rise, all of them started for the dog. A medium-sized shepherd mix, Ringo thought. The dog stood his ground for a second longer then turned and loped away, the infected pursuing.

Ringo stayed put for another five minutes watching the infected trail the dog out of sight, then he crawled back to the camera. Speaking softly, he described what had just happened and the shut the camera off.

So much for getting his work done here on the first day, he thought sourly. He gathered his gear and set off through the woods toward the bridge. He was more careful now, however. He knew that the least noise would bring the infected down on him and that was something to be avoided at all costs.

He decided that he wasn't going to offer to do anything like this again.

-

Tammy settled onto the front porch after lunch. She had assisted with the clean-up and both Hiram and Helen had announced they were going to lie down a while. Tammy tried her satellite phone again, calling her father and Lucinda Steele. Neither answered her. She kept the phone with her anyway. There was always the chance that she'd hear from her father, at least.

Looking out over the yard she leaned back, slowly drinking cold water from the glass she'd brought with her. Helen and Hiram had a beautiful place. In spite of the events of the last few days, she could honestly say she felt as comfortable here as anywhere she'd ever been. The place seemed to embrace her, hugging her close, keeping her warm and making her feel safe.

She was careful with the last part, however. With things the way they were now nowhere was really safe. Not anymore. Despite the safety brought by isolation here, there were no guarantees that things would stay that way. Maybe they would and she hoped for that, but her father had taught her to always be prepared for the worst even while hoping for the best. The idea was to not be surprised when things turned bad.

She had forgotten that on the first day, she admitted. She'd done well at first, but the three thugs that meant to attack her and Ringo after the debacle at the river bridge had caught her unawares. She hadn't been thinking about threats from people who weren't infected and that had been a mistake. Ringo had, though, and that was all that saved her from a terrible fate.

Thinking about that afternoon brought to mind once again how quickly and efficiently Ringo had dismantled the three would-be rapists. Even though she was watching, the event was a blur to her, both when it was happening and in her memory of it now. She had never seen anyone move that fast.

Ringo reminded her of a cobra. Fast to strike and deadly when it did. She wondered again at the notion that had made her invite him along. She would never understand it. Normally she wouldn't have even considered it. Whatever the reason, it had been a good decision. One that had ultimately saved her life and brought her a good friend.

The thought of Ringo as a friend made Tammy re-evaluate her relationship with him. She snorted mentally at the word 'relationship' even as it flitted through her mind. They didn't have a relationship, other than a friendship forged in the heat of battle, for lack of a better term. She hardly knew him, knew next to nothing about him. She knew more about Helen and Hiram in point of fact.

Still, she had to admit that Ringo was special. He reminded her of her own father in many ways. Strong, quiet, but with a determination to get things done and an attitude that should serve as a warning to anyone who would dare attack him or anyone he cared about. She remembered the scars she had seen on him and wondered again where they had come from.

He was a mystery in so many ways. Tammy couldn't help but be intrigued by that, even when she knew she shouldn't be. The worst thing she could do was allow her imagination to run away from her. There were any number of reasons for those scars, for his attitude or for his solitude and silence.

On top of it all he was good looking, she admitted, if only to herself. Dammit, Tammy, she chided herself. Here you are in the middle of. . .well, maybe the end of the world, and you're thinking about how good looking the man who saved you is. You're treating all this like some romance novel!

Shaking her head at her own foolishness, Tammy got to her feet. While there was no work to be done at the moment she decided she wanted to walk around and stretch her legs. She wouldn't leave the grounds of course, but she could roam around the house and down to the river.

It would distract her from things she didn't want to think about.

-

Ringo mentally cursed the sinking sun as he made his way through the woods. The sun was going to be setting soon and he was still in the middle of nowhere. He wasn't lost, thanks to the map and the GPS, but he still wasn't where he needed to be. Worse, he hadn't found anywhere that could serve as shelter for the night. He had a tiny tent strapped to his pack, but. . .he really didn't want to trust that tent in the woods at night. A random infected could stumble across him and have him bitten before he knew what had happened.

He had hoped to find a shed or a barn, something that he could secure at least nominally. He needed anything that might afford him some protection, or at least some warning of impending attack. So far, that hadn't happened. There was nothing out here but trees and more nothing.

He estimated he had another hour, hour-and-a-half at most, before it would be too dark to see well inside the trees. He had until then to find some place of safety and get undercover.

As he continued to make his way through the trees and brush a new thought occurred to him. Did the infected move after dark? Would they be active without the light of day? Probably another 'observation' that Doctor Baxter would interested in. Hiram had shown him how to work the night vision on the small video recorder so he could document whatever he could see after dark but that was not for today.

Today he was more interested in simply finding protection and making sure he was at least marginally safe before dark. Tomorrow or the next day, if he could find a safe place to observe from, he'd use the camera to see how the infected handled the dark. For today he was more worried about how he would handle the dark.

He saw a lighter area ahead of him and was soon at the edge of a small clearing. The area of grass, maybe an acre, was almost surrounded by trees save for a gap in the tree line that opened into a much larger pasture. In the distance, he could see what he thought was a farmhouse. Between his position and the farmhouse sat an aging barn. It was one with a hayloft, if the small doors high on the eaves of the building were any indicator.

It wasn't exactly isolated but it was better than nothing and the light was fading fast. Moving through the clearing, Ringo used the woods on the other side to screen his movements from anyone inside the house, placing the barn completely between him and the distant dwelling. Satisfied that he had done all he could to avoid detection, Ringo began to slip toward the barn. He had to travel about one hundred fifty yards to get there and every step was laced with the anticipation of a gunshot from an angry farmer, or worse, that hair-raising screech from an infected farmer. Neither threat materialized, however, and sooner than he'd thought he was standing at the entrance to the barn.

There were no actual doors, he was sorry to see. He could have secured the doors to give himself an added bit of security. At least there was only one ladder into the hayloft. He could probably jury rig something at the top of the ladder to help cover himself and provide at least some warning of an intruder, infected or not.

He climbed cautiously, slow but steady, making as little noise and disturbing the dust and dirt as little as possible. At the top of the ladder Ringo poked his head carefully above the entrance, looking around the loft.

A screech coupled with movement almost gave him a heart attack and nearly caused him to lose his grip on the ladder. He managed, barely, to keep from falling while grabbing for the pistol Hiram had given him. He stopped short of drawing it, however, when he realized that he was face to face with an enraged cat, hissing in anger and back raised like the proverbial Halloween feline.

Swearing under his breath, Ringo climbed into the loft, keeping clear of the angry cat. For her part, the cat watched him intently, following his every move. Shaking his head, Ringo made a quick inspection of the loft. Finding that it was just him and the cat, he shrugged out of his pack and removed the shotgun from its harness.

Taking four bales of hay, Ringo made a short, but effective, barrier around the hole in the floor, then placed another two bales across the top of the first four, closing off the opening completely. While someone could still get in, they would have to work at it and that would make noise, noise that should wake him in time to defend himself.

That being done, Ringo took his binoculars and moved to the open loft door at the front of the barn. Inspecting the farmhouse through the powerful glasses, he could detect no sign of movement within or around the homestead. After ten minutes of careful watching he decided either no one was home or they were very wisely staying out of sight.

He didn't blame them one bit for that. If he had better sense he'd still be at Hiram's enjoying Helen's cooking and sleeping on a comfortable bed. Using a flush toilet and taking a hot shower.

Instead, he was spending the night in a barn in the middle of No and Where. Sighing in regret, he moved back to his pack and dug inside for one of the MREs. Opening the self- heating meal pack, Ringo looked at the roast beef substance inside and shrugged. It didn't smell all that bad. He added a bit of water, activated the heating tab as Hiram had shown him and set the bag aside to wait for it to heat.

As he waited, he fished through the remainder of the contents; spork, toilet paper, some kind of peanut butter treat, salt and pepper, crackers, and what looked like a small container of jelly or jam. All the comforts of home, he snorted to himself. Movement drew his eye and he looked up to see the cat edging forward, drawn in by the smell of the roast beef, no doubt.

"Oh, you want to be friends, now, huh?" Ringo said softly. The cat hissed silently, but didn't arch its back. Ringo decided that was an improvement. He took the now warm meal pack and fished a small amount out with the spork, tasting the roast beef.

It wasn't Arby's, but it wasn't bad, either. Or else he was just hungry. Using the spork, he lifted part of the contents out and placed it on the outer package the meal had come in, pushing it slowly toward the cat.

Suspicious, but drawn in by the smell, the cat took several steps back but didn't run away. She watched Ringo for signs of treachery for a minute, then moved slowly toward the offered meal. Ringo continued to eat slowly, his movements slow and steady so as not to startle the cat again. He was going to have to share the barn with the cat tonight and figured it was in his best interest to be on at least neutral terms, if not friendly.

The cat sniffed, always keeping one eye on Ringo, then leaned forward and licked at the substance. Realizing what it was, the cat suddenly attacked the meal with gusto, gobbling it down as if it hadn't eaten in days. Ringo had to smile at the cat's actions. Maybe she hadn't eaten in a while.

Once finished, the cat backed away a few steps then proceeded to clean herself of the gravy that had wound up on her fur. Ringo chuckled at the haughty attitude, finished his own meal and leaned back. His movement drew a look of suspicion from the cat, but didn't result in any outrage.

For his part Ringo ignored his temporary feline roommate and considered his situation. He had managed to gather some information today and had covered a good bit of ground. He wondered idly how the dog had made out. Had the infected on the highway followed the dog far? Had they lost interest when they didn't catch him right away? Were they even now still chasing after him?

These were all good questions for which he had no answers. He took out his notebook and noted what he had seen, using the last of the dying light to make his entry. Once that was done he laid his sleeping bag out and placed his flashlight next to him. He didn't plan to use it, but figured if he needed it he would need it bad and need it in a hurry.

He hadn't realized how tired he was until he stretched out. He wanted to remove his boots but decided against it. He wasn't secure enough here to ensure that he would have time to put them back on if he had to run for it. Better to leave them on and be a little uncomfortable than have to go running who knew where in his sock feet.

He wondered idly what Tammy was doing right about then and if she had ever managed to contact her father. As much as he hoped she had, he doubted it. At least she was safe with Hiram and Helen. As safe as possible, anyway, considering that the whole world was going stark raving mad.

He drifted off to sleep thinking about what he would have to do come morning. He was so tired that he didn't even notice when the cat curled up on his stomach and went to sleep as well, its belly warm and full for the first time in two days or more.

The night passed peacefully for both.

CHAPTER NINE

-

Tammy Gleason rose early the next morning. Standing by her bed she stretched and instantly stopped. She was sore in places she hadn't even known were there. She was finding out the hard way that athletic, active and 'in good shape' did not necessarily translate straight to 'able to do hard labor'.

She snorted at that thought. Gardening didn't especially qualify as hard labor, but it had required her to use muscles she obviously didn't use often. She was paying for that now. Knowing there was only one way to fix the problem, she dressed and headed downstairs to stretch and exercise the soreness away.

Much like Ringo with his martial arts and sword work, Tammy's stretching and calisthenics were pretty much locked into her muscle memory. As a result, she didn't really have to concentrate much on what she was doing, leaving her free to consider all kinds of new things.

The world had definitely gone to hell in a hand bag, as her dad would have said. Thinking of that made her think of her father and that made her a little sad. She tried to avoid thinking that he was gone, but she was honest enough to admit that his chances of survival hadn't sounded good. It was obvious from his last few words that Reese Gleason hadn't expected to survive the situation he'd found himself in. But then her father had never been anything but a realist. He looked life in the face and rarely flinched. When he did, it was normally over his daughter. She smiled, remembering the first time she'd had a boy pick her up for a date while Reese was at home. He had been at his very intimidating best and had gone next door as soon as Tammy had disappeared down the road to ask Lucinda Steele to have 'The Talk' with his daughter. When he discovered that it was far too late for that, Reese Gleason had actually not known what to do. So, he went home and got very drunk.

Returning to the present, Tammy considered her situation.

She'd already decided to remain with Helen and Hiram. Not only could she probably not reach home, it might not be there when she did, at least not like she remembered it anyway. Tammy hoped that Lucinda was all right. She missed the older woman's steady influence. At least she had Helen now.

Tammy found it difficult to admit to needing anything. She supposed it was partly because she'd been on her own so much. Part of it was that she was her father's daughter and Reese Gleason avoided anything that might make him appear weak or 'needy'. It was not that he didn't often need the help of others, because he did. He just didn't want it to show. Tammy had inherited that innate stubbornness from him.

She sat back on her left leg and extended her right, stretching out the muscles there. As the soreness radiated away, she wondered where Ringo was at the moment. She found herself thinking about him more and more with each passing day. She frowned at herself, not really in annoyance but in puzzlement. What was Ringo to her? A friend? Even though they'd known each other only days, she had to say that there was friendship there, if nothing else. Her father had always said that combat forged tighter relationships between people than anything else he knew of. Looking back on the wild trip that had brought her to where she sat at the moment, she could almost see how the ties of friendship, of companionship, had been built between them. They'd had little choice but to trust one another. Thankfully, each had come through when the other needed them too.

Tammy honestly didn't think that Ringo was interested in her in any way other than friendship, but he was extremely hard to read. Hiram had hinted more than once that Ringo thought more of her than he let on and she had begun to realize that Hiram was a pretty sharp old dude. But was she interested in Ringo that way? It wasn't an easy question to consider, let alone answer.

They just hadn't known each other long enough for her to know. She didn't think he knew, either. One of the things that made her trust him, then and now, was how he treated her. Even when he told her he would 'see her home', he wasn't condescending about it, just. . .matter of fact. I'll just do this and then move on to something else. To him, it was probably just that simple.

Ringo seemed to think very straightforward and he

probably did at times, but all it took was one look in his eyes and you realized that Ringo's mind was always working, always running. She switched legs, extending her left leg out before her, and began again.

She hoped that Ringo was safe. She also hoped he managed to get whatever it was that this Doctor Baxter needed and that she, in turn, could give them some hope for the future. As things stood right now, she wasn't sure there was much hope for the future without it.

-

Ringo had awakened before sunrise, surprised to find the cat curled up on his belly, purring loudly. He smiled slightly but didn't move just yet, preferring to lay still and listen to his surroundings. He couldn't hear anything out of sorts and the cat was still sleeping peacefully so things were probably all right.

As light began to dawn Ringo stirred finally, the cat stretching slowly before abandoning its warm bed on his stomach. While the cat had deigned to use his body heat for a comfortable bed, the morning found little improvement in their relationship.

"Don't worry," he told the aggravated feline. "I'll be gone soon enough." He quickly packed away his gear and then made a quick meal of one of the ration bars. The cat sniffed at a piece that Ringo had broken off and placed on the floor, but the smell wasn't enticing enough and was ignored. Ringo shrugged. If the cat got hungry he was sure the small piece of food bar would be welcome.

In less than twenty minutes Ringo was on the ground just inside the barn door, using his binoculars to scour the area around him. He could see no movement and couldn't hear anything other than nature; birds, crickets and other insects, and once in a while a dog barking. Normal stuff you'd hear every day in a place like this.

He thought back to his encounter on the highway the day before and wished he'd paid more attention to whether or not those same sounds had been present when he was looking at the infected. If the birds and insects grew quiet when infected were around then that might make a decent early warning system. Any advantage he could gain he would take and be glad for it.

Satisfied that there was no threat around him at the moment, Ringo eased out of the barn and began his trek anew. He'd checked his map and GPS before exiting so he knew exactly where he was and which way to go. As he entered the woods, the cat sat in the hayloft, tail flicking, watching him out of sight.

When it could no longer see Ringo, the cat turned to gobble down the bit of ration bar left for it. No sense letting it go to waste, the cat decided.

Ringo was much more cautious than he had been the day before. He had learned a good deal from his brief experiment with the infected and was putting that information to good use. Stealth was definitely the best way to move, but he also needed to stay hidden. The infected, unlike the movie zombies they'd been named after, could see just fine, apparently. He didn't want to know if they would respond to seeing him moving through the trees. He especially didn't want to see how well they moved in the trees when chasing someone, namely him.

According to the GPS, Ringo was a little more than three miles from the bridge. Following the highway had been a good idea in the sense that he had something to follow, and the presence of the road made reading the map easier using intersections as landmarks.

But, it had also carried him a good bit out of his way. While it had added steps to his journey Ringo was still satisfied with his decision. Had he not followed the road as he had, the opportunity to record the infected he had the day before might not have presented itself. Their behavior was puzzling to him, but maybe Baxter could use it. He'd reviewed the recording and was pleased to see it had been in focus and most of the activity had been captured on the screen.

Ringo halted abruptly, his thoughts of movies and the CDC left on the floor. Cocking his head to one side as a dog might, Ringo strained to hear. He was almost certain. . . .

There it was again. Ringo felt his pulse quicken just a bit as his blood pumped a bit harder. Somewhere ahead of him were infected and from the sound of it there were a lot more than what he'd seen the day before, a lot more.

Ringo checked his watch, eyebrows rising in surprise. He'd already been moving over two hours? It seemed like just minutes.

He would have to watch that, he chided himself. Being aware of his surroundings was important these days. He obviously hadn't been as alert as he'd thought if his wandering thoughts had allowed him to move for over two hours without him even realizing it. That was dangerous and a habit he could ill afford.

He stepped into a small, dense grouping of trees that afforded him better concealment, then consulted the GPS. He was less than a mile from the bridge. Which meant he was right on top of an entire gaggle of infected. He swore silently at his own stupidity. He took a deep breath to clear his mind and then focused on the job at hand.

In a way, he wished he had left his bedding and other gear in the barn. That way he could move quieter, without the risk of abandoning his pack and its contents. Of course, if he needed to leave the area in a direction other than the barn he'd still have lost them. Either way it was a moot point now. He examined the small copse of trees he was using.

It was a small area and provided a good hiding place. He was still hesitant to use it for storing his gear. If he couldn't get back here, then it was gone. After a few minutes of mental debate, he decided to keep his pack with him and plan his moves accordingly. He checked to make sure he wasn't making any noise, and that everything was tied or strapped down tight. Next, he made sure that anything he might need in a hurry was within reach and easy to hand. Finally, he couldn't put it off any longer. Taking a deep breath, he eased away from his hiding place and started moving again toward the bridge and the horrors he knew awaited.

Oh, I really don't want to do this.

-

Hiram walked around the place after breakfast, looking over everything. His fence was in good shape and he'd closed the gate across the driveway. It wouldn't stop a determined thief or attacker, but it might confound some poor sot whose brain was burning up with fever. Hiram wouldn't hesitate to shoot one of the infected, if needed, but he'd prefer not to have to. Most would be innocents, infected without even knowing it. He didn't want to think about it and he wouldn't, he knew from experience. If the need arose, he'd kill as many as necessary to keep Helen, and now Tammy, safe. It wasn't as if he had never killed a man before, or a woman, if it comes to that, he remembered grimly.

Hiram tried very hard to be the kindly old innkeeper most people saw him as. He really did. But too many years doing his nation's dirty work had left its mark on him and he knew it. Without constant discipline, he wasn't fit to be around good people. The part of him that still cared regretted that. As he'd grown older he realized what he'd missed through the years, always being gone, always moving from one dirty job to the next. True, if he'd stayed in the Army's regular forces he would have still been deployed, but he'd have been home more, too. And maybe he'd be better for it. He just didn't know anymore.

He didn't know Reese Gleason but felt a kindred spirit to the man that had raised Tammy the way he had. Tammy had called him the 'Battalion Sergeant Major' which Hiram knew made him a Command Sergeant Major for an Airborne Battalion in the 82nd Airborne Division. He hadn't bothered to correct her, but he doubted Tammy realized just how important or influential her father was. He was, for all practical purposes, the third highest ranking man in his battalion. No Captain who assumed command of a battalion would dare ignore a man that almost certainly would have more experience than he did. A good CSM could easily make or break a battalion commander with about as much effort as most people put into making breakfast.

All of which meant that Reese Gleason was a capable man. If there was a way out of the pickle the man was in, Hiram was willing to bet he'd find it. And now he knew where his daughter was, too. That would let him free his mind to work on his own problems instead of worrying about her constantly. Hiram silently wished him well and knew that Helen was constantly praying for the man. Hiram would pray for him, but didn't figure the Creator wanted to hear anything from him these days. Probably hadn't for a long time. He shook his head, trying to get rid of thoughts like that. They were unprofitable and useless, especially now.

His thoughts turned instead to Ringo. They hadn't heard from him as yet, but that in itself didn't concern Hiram too much. It was easy to forget to check in even when things were normal. And things were anything but normal these days.

He hoped to hear from him tonight, at least. He wanted to know the kid was okay. In the short time he'd known Ringo, Hiram had come to like the teenager. He liked to think that if he and Helen could have had a son, he would have turned out to be like Ringo. Not many men his age would have done what he'd done for Tammy

Gleason. And that kind of thing stood out to a man like Hiram.

Hiram finished his inspection and headed for the house. They would need to get to work on the garden soon or it would get hot on them.

-

"Hiram is coming in," Tammy said from where she stood washing the breakfast dishes.

"Finished his inspection, I suppose," Helen chuckled lightly. "He did that most every morning before all this blew up. Now he's almost fanatical about it. He misses the military."

"I know how that can be," Tammy nodded absently, placing the last glass in the drainer.

"I know, dear," Helen said easily. "Hiram lied about his age and joined the Army at sixteen, I think. He was almost twenty when I met him and already too old for his years. I'm afraid he's been to a lot of bad places. He never speaks of it, though, and I don't either. I pretend I don't know anything about the nightmares he has or the distant look he gets once in a while and he can believe he's 'protecting' me from his past. He needs that," she finished from where she was looking at a hand-written list for the garden.

Tammy marveled at Helen and her casual acceptance of the trouble Hiram had. Would her mother have been like that for her dad? Probably, she decided. Lucinda had known her mother and had always praised her.

Tammy looked out the window once more and sighed. No word had come from Ringo last night. She found herself fighting not to worry that he was hurt or worse. There was no profit in it, nothing to be gained.

"Stop thinking about it, dear," Helen said absently. "He'll call when he can and thinks of it."

"Thinks of it?" Tammy blurted, too surprised by that statement to claim she hadn't been thinking about it.

"Sometimes you forget simple things, dear," Helen nodded, finally looking up from her list. "He's in danger, Tammy, and has no one to depend on but himself. I'm fairly certain he's also not accustomed to having to answer to anyone or account to anyone else for his whereabouts or his actions. That takes getting used to. Give him time."

"It's not like he answers to me," Tammy objected slightly.

"Or that he owes me a phone call."

"I'm glad you can still say that," Helen smiled faintly, once more perusing her list. "You can fight it all you want child, but you're worried over him, though I daresay you haven't figured out why just yet."

Tammy had to work to hide her shock. It was like the older woman could read her mind!

"You aren't the first young woman to fall for a man who seems to seek out danger, Tammy," Helen smiled warmly, looking up again. "And probably not the last. I was young once, you know," she added impishly. "There was something dark and dangerous about Hiram the first time I saw him. I didn't know what it was, but I could see it even then. And I'll admit, here in private, that it drew me like a flame draws a moth." She got a faraway look in her eyes then, like she was seeing something else. Something that was somewhere Tammy couldn't see.

"I've never regretted it, either," she said at last, turning her refocused gaze upon the younger woman. "So, it's okay for you to be worried. Just don't let it rule you. What will be, will be."

With that Helen fell silent, rising to go and get her straw hat and gloves. Tammy followed her. It was time to work in the garden. That would distract her...for a while anyway.

-

It was worse than Ringo had imagined and that was saying something.

He was lying in thick woods about one hundred yards north of the bridge and the interstate. The line of cars in the east-bound lane extended up the hill and out of sight to the west, while the west-bound lane was practically empty, of cars.

Hundreds of infected roamed the highway. There were groups and gaggles of infected in some places while others roamed alone. He noted that a few of them fought between themselves and wondered what about. Realizing he should be taping, he quickly removed the small recorder from its protective case, set it on its stand and turned it on. He whispered briefly into the camera recording the date, time and location, then set the camera up where it would capture as much of what was happening as possible.

That done, he took his binoculars and began looking over the scene once more. He was farther away than he wanted to be, but couldn't see much of a way to get closer without risking detection. He still wasn't sure how sharp their hearing or their eyesight was. Yesterday's experiments were far from conclusive. He spent about thirty minutes lying in watch, panning and zooming the camera to capture anything that seemed like different behavior from the bulk of the infected.

Why don't they leave here? he couldn't help but wonder. Why bother staying around here? Is something attracting them to this place?

He kept the camera moving. He passed by one infected then pulled the camera back to her. There on the highway was a woman, obviously infected, the bite wound in her shoulder still bleeding just a little. That wasn't what caught Ringo's attention, though. While most of the others were just ambling around aimlessly, this one was trying to open a car door. Ringo recorded her actions for a two full minutes, then spent the next fifteen examining the roadway looking for others who were doing the same thing or anything that remotely resembled a coherent action.

Two others were also trying to gain entry to a vehicle, including one with keys in hand. Ringo made sure to record that one for a full five minutes though he watched the battery meter carefully. After a few more minutes of looking he discovered an infected man trying to open what looked like a bag of some kind of chips and got three minutes of his behavior. Another was trying to open a trunk and at least one was trying to have sex.

Oh, I did not need that image in my head, Ringo thought to himself, closing his eyes and trying to erase the scene. He wasn't sure the selected partner was a willing participant and preferred not to think about it too much. Still, it was behavior, so he recorded it even though it made him feel dirty.

Finally, he shut the camera off, saving the rest of the battery in case he saw anything else interesting. Returning the camera to its bag, Ringo prepared for the next phase of his job. He needed to take blood and tissue samples…and a head.

Slipping behind a tree Ringo got to his feet and began to make his way closer to the road. He had seen a bit of movement further up the road. He knew that there was a fence along the interstate that kept traffic access controlled to the exit and entrance ramps and hoped that it was keeping the woods clear. He planned to use that same fence to break contact once his grisly job here was done.

He moved west through the woods following the interstate, watching the roadway. When he'd moved perhaps a half mile from his original position he found what he was hoping to see. Three infected, pretty much alone, along a partially open area of the road. There were cars he could use for cover and he was fairly sure he could take three without raising an alarm.

He found a good hiding place and shrugged out of his pack. It was too bulky and heavy to try and take over the fence so he would leave it here. He also left the shotgun. He kept the suppressed pistol that Hiram had given him, his sword and his knives. He donned the protective gear he'd been given and then gathered the sample containers. Once he was sure he had everything he headed for the fence line. He would leave the containers at the fence until the job was done, then retrieve them as quickly as he could, get what he'd came for and make himself scarce.

The fence was sturdy along this section of road, he was glad to see. That should slow down any infected who might give chase should he be discovered. He'd take any advantage he could get today. He made his way over the fence without noise and placed the containers on the ground, careful not to let them rattle against one another.

There were two women and a man wandering along the roadway in front of him, maybe fifty yards away. He watched them for five minutes, looking for any sign of a pattern or that he'd been noticed. Satisfied that they were unaware of his presence, he rose to a crouch and made his way to an abandoned SUV sitting on the side of the road.

As he reached the truck he had a horrifying thought. One it was too late to act on. What if there were infected inside some of the cars? If the ones outside couldn't get in, then maybe they couldn't get out. But they would probably make noise and noise was death. Why hadn't he thought about that before?

Because you've never had to think about it before, he answered himself mentally. This waking nightmare was one that no one had ever dealt with before. It wasn't like there was a training manual for how to move in zombie country. He grimaced at the thought of the word 'zombie'. Some of the behavior he'd seen today had disturbed him. These poor people weren't 'undead' or any other kind of crap. They were sick and that sickness made them violent and dangerous, but it was obvious that at least some of them still recognized or remembered certain actions and behaviors from before their infection.

He thought back to what Baxter had said and decided that maybe those clamoring for 'fair treatment' of the infected were not completely wrong in their assumptions. That didn't change the facts, however. Right now, regardless of their attempts to carry out basic functions, the people on this stretch of interstate were violent, dangerous and beyond reasoning with. There was no 'talking' to them. Every time he'd seen infected react, it was violent. There had been no other response. Maybe if he did his job right then Baxter and her colleagues could find a way to fix them.

He put those thoughts aside. It was unprofitable, especially since he was about to kill three more of them. He eased his sword from its sheath and rose slightly to peer through the glass of the SUV. His targets were directly in front of him, one just on the other side of the Suburban. Nice.

Ringo moved to the rear of the vehicle, forcing himself to breathe slowly and deeply several times. His mind cleared, he exhaled the last breath and walked around the vehicle to where the infected stood milling about the other vehicles. The first female never saw him coming and died when his sword decapitated her. Unfortunately, that made noise.

The male turned to look for the source of the sound he'd heard and saw Ringo immediately. He crossed the twenty feet between them faster than Ringo had expected and the teen was forced to roll away from the larger infected man, regaining his feet with a smoothness that would have made any street-dancer proud.

Even so, it almost wasn't enough. The enraged male recovered much faster than Ringo had anticipated but Ringo's own movements were faster. As the man reached for him Ringo's sword sliced through both arms. The creature roared in rage and Ringo realized that the infected could feel pain. He hadn't thought about that before. Another thing he'd overlooked. Ringo spun away from the man who was still reaching for him despite the loss of his hands. Continuing his spin, Ringo transferred his weight to his front foot as he turned back to the larger man. Using his weight and momentum for added power to his next swing, he once again decapitated an infected.

Ringo was hit hard from behind before he could recover and lost his grip on his sword hilt as the weight of the final infected, the other female, bore him to the ground. Though caught by surprise, Ringo managed to twist himself around enough to take the fall on his right shoulder and at least partially face his attacker.

The image he saw was one that would haunt him for a very long time. Until now he'd never been that close with one of them. It was clean and clinical to strike with the sword and keep moving. Now he was truly up close and personal with an infected.

The gaping maw of blood and teeth didn't look human. It looked like the mouth of a shark at feeding time. And right now, it was planning to feed on him. He managed to get his left arm from between himself and his attacker, forcing his forearm beneath her jaw and then pushing her face, and that mouth, away from him. The infected woman continued to shriek in what Ringo could only recognize as rage; pure, unadulterated, primal rage.

Trying to keep the pressure on with his left arm, Ringo managed to remove a steel spike from his web gear. It wasn't the ideal weapon but it was all he could reach with the weight still on him. The woman was strong with her insanity and it was all he could do to move. In the back of his mind was the fact that her constant screeching had to be alerting others of his presence. Before he could worry about that though, he had to survive here.

Still holding his attacker at bay with his left arm, Ringo reversed his grip on the spike in his right hand so that the point extended below his hand rather than above it. Turning as much as he could while still in her grip, Ringo raised his shoulder as much as possible and then slammed the point of the spike into her left eye.

Ringo hadn't known what to expect but the sudden silence hadn't really been it. One second the infected woman is screaming at the top of her lungs, the next she's dead quiet. Because she was dead, period.

Her weight fell on him partially as her body collapsed. Ringo managed to shove the falling body with his left arm so that he wasn't directly beneath her, but blood from the eye socket shot over him.

Ringo shoved her the rest of the way off him and scrambled to his feet, noticing as he did that his right arm didn't want to obey him fully. Leaving the spike where it was, Ringo retrieved his sword before he bothered to look down the road.

Nothing. He hurriedly scanned the area around him expecting to see infected any and everywhere he looked. Despite his fear, he could neither see nor hear any sign that other infected were close by or even cared to investigate the noise. Maybe they hadn't heard it at all. Ringo didn't know and had other problems to concentrate on anyway.

Realizing that his shirt was covered in infected blood as was his webbing, Ringo was close to panic.

Don't let their blood or other bodily fluids get on you. Was that what he'd been told? Or was he okay so long as it didn't get into his blood? He was wearing the goggles so his eyes were protected. What about his arms? Had any of the blood gotten into his mouth? He didn't taste anything, but would he? There was too much he didn't know.

Why didn't you ask more questions?! In his assurance that he could do the job, he hadn't asked enough questions. He hadn't taken enough precautions. Now he was probably infected.

How the hell am I supposed to tell if I'm infected? he asked himself, mind racing. He didn't know and what he didn't know could cost him.

I can't think about that now, he told himself. I came here to do a job. If I'm infected and don't finish what I came to do, then I'm infected for nothing. I might as well have stayed where I was. If I'm done for, it won't be for nothing. He took a deep, calming, cleansing breath and steadied himself. Cleaning his sword on the pant leg of one of the infected, he sheathed it and went to retrieve the containers he needed.

Donning another pair of rubber gloves over his leather ones, Ringo quickly performed the work he'd come to do. It was grisly, but he'd known that from the start. Since he'd already decapitated two infected he chose the head that was in the best shape, the man's, and inserted into the cryo container. Securing it the way Hiram has showed him, he hit the button that released the nitrogen into the container, effectively freezing the head.

Taking the other containers, he took skin and blood from all three of the bodies labeling each one male or female, about all he could do in that regard. The work took less than ten minutes, but it was a very long ten minutes for a young man who thought he might now be infected with the virus. Added to that was the need to constantly be on guard against the arrival of other infected. By the time he was finished, Ringo was nearly a nervous wreck. He wasn't often scared, but he would have admitted to anyone who asked that he was as scared now as he'd been when his parents had been killed.

Dropping everything into a bag with Biohazard markings, Ringo took one last look around him. Seeing nothing he moved back to the fence and then over it. He hurried to where his pack still sat and then paused. Clean himself up now? Get the hell away from here and then do it? The debate lasted less than five seconds before he snatched up the pack, crammed the shotgun into it and took off through the woods back the way he'd come.

He needed to clean up, but he needed to be away from here first. He was in trouble maybe, and if he was he didn't know how much time he had. For now, he needed to find a place to leave the samples, then get cleaned up and then make a terrible phone call.

One he really didn't want make, since he'd be asking questions he wasn't sure he wanted the answer to.

CHAPTER TEN

-

Hiram jolted in surprise when the satellite phone by his side rang. He'd been waiting to hear it all day but when it finally rang it was a shock nonetheless. Despite his eagerness to hear from Ringo he was hesitant to pick it up, a feeling of dread settling in his stomach. He activated the phone.

"Ringo?"

"It's me, Hiram," the boy's voice rang out. "I got it. Got it all."

"Everything okay?" Hiram asked. The silence on the other end was answer enough. "Ringo?" Hiram spoke hesitantly.

"I need you to do something for me," Ringo said rather than reply. "I might have a problem." Hiram felt the dread in his belly congeal into a hard ball.

"What happened, son?" he asked gently.

"I need you to call that Baxter woman for me," Ringo said calmly. "I need to know how long it takes for infection to show up in someone."

"Are you bitten, Ringo?" Hiram hated to ask. His eyes were closed against the answer.

"No," Ringo's reply seemed to take hours. "But I. . .I got some blood on me. I'm not sure, but I maybe got some in my mouth, too. One of the infected got on me and I killed her, but. . .well, blood went everywhere. I just don't know Hiram. And I really need to know."

"I understand, kid," Hiram managed to keep his voice even. "I'll call her right now. Have you activated the beacon yet?"

"No. I'm about to as soon as I'm done here. I want to be somewhere else when they get here, like you said. Especially now. I'm trying to get cleaned up in a creek and get rid of anything that's got blood on it. Then I'll be on the move. I spent last night in a barn so I'm going to try and get back there. If it's still safe I'll hang out there for a day or two and see if. . .wait and see. . .well, you know."

Ringo sounded defeated for all that he was calm about it.

"Yeah, I know," Hiram answered. "I'll get on the horn with her right now, son. I'll get your answer for you. Now, you get gone from there once you activate that beacon. Where are you?" Ringo rattled off the GPS coordinates for his position.

"Room there for the chopper to land?" Hiram asked, writing quickly.

"Yeah. No wires and plenty of room," Ringo affirmed.

"All right, then," Hiram tried to sound upbeat. "You get clear and I mean right now. I'll give you twenty minutes to get moving and then place the call. Call me back in two hours or whenever you get holed up. I should have some answers for you by then. Sound good?"

"Sounds good," Ringo replied. "Thanks, Hiram. I'm sorry," he added.

"Hell, son, don't be sorry. I'm the one who should be sorry for mentioning this shit to you in the first place. And I am," the older man admitted.

"I didn't have to do it, Hiram. You made that clear."

"Yeah, well," Hiram replied lamely. "Get moving."

"See ya," Ringo said, and then he was gone.

-

"Son-of-a-bitch!"

The curse was accompanied by the sound of porch furniture being thrown about. Helen looked up from where she was peeling potatoes, frowning in concern. Tammy was at the stove preparing to place bread in the oven. She started toward the porch but Helen stopped her.

"No," the older woman said firmly. "That. . .he's not in a good frame of mind at the moment, dear," she settled for saying. "Let him work it out first, then we'll talk to him."

"Do you think it's Ringo?" Tammy asked, worry in her voice.

"I don't know," Helen admitted, but her voice said something else. "We'll have to wait and see. But now isn't the time to ask him about it. You'll just have to trust me on this dear."

"But what if--?"

"I said not now!" Helen snapped suddenly, her voice taking on an edge. She instantly schooled her features and in seconds was the kind older woman Tammy had come to know.

"Not now," she repeated more calmly. "Hiram is working through a problem and he needs space and peace. When he's calmed down, he'll tell us what the problem is, if it concerns us. I know you want to know about Ringo," Helen held up a hand to stave off the coming objections. "But now is not the time. Now let's get back to work." For all that her voice was calmer now, gentler, the steel in her voice was plain. Tammy nodded, cowed for once, and returned to what she'd been doing.

Her mind was still running away from her, though, in fear.

-

"I'm sorry to hear that, Colonel," Baxter said evenly. "I did warn him."

"I don't want to hear that shit," Hiram snarled. Unlike his wife he made no attempt to rein in his anger. "I'm well aware you warned him. Now I'm asking for information. Are you going to give it to me, or will I have to make you regret withholding it from me?" Baxter blinked at that. What did the man think he could accomplish from so far away was beyond her. . . .

"I can see the wheels turning, lady," Hiram growled softly. "Don't think even for a second that you're beyond my reach. Understand? All I'm asking for is some simple information. Information I know you have and that I need. Now tell me what I need to know so we can still be friends."

Baxter was not accustomed to being threatened, but she dealt with enough people like this Colonel that she knew the difference between someone who was serious and someone just talking out of their ass.

This man was serious.

"If he's contracted the virus, there's simply nothing we can do for him, Colonel," she explained gently. "So far nothing we have tried has been successful in even slowing the virus down, let alone stopping it. If he's infected he should begin showing signs within twenty-four hours, give or take six hours. That depends on how he was infected and how deeply."

"He may not be infected at all," Hiram's tone was more congenial now. "He had to kill an infected woman who was on top of him and her blood went all over him. He was wearing the protective gear but he can't be sure his mouth wasn't open. He isn't bitten, scratched, or cut and he's already cleaned up, disposed of the clothes and gear that were bloody and set your samples where they can be picked up."

"Have him wait for the helicopter and they can bring him here," Baxter told him and Hiram didn't miss the slight excitement that crept into her voice. "We can treat him--"

"I'm going to pretend you didn't say that, Doctor Baxter," Hiram replied, his voice as cold as the liquid nitrogen used to freeze the severed head of the infected man. "Because if you did say it, I'd have to kill you," he continued, his voice conversational despite the frigid tone.

"I only meant that we could care for him here," Baxter stumbled over the words. "It's the least we can do after all he's done for us."

"I know exactly what you meant," Hiram told her flatly. "Do us both a favor and don't say it again. Now, if he's still clear after seventy-two hours, would you say he's safe? In the clear?"

"Most likely," Baxter nodded. The Colonel had seemed much easier to deal with before. "Every report we have has indicated that infection sets in within twenty-four to thirty-six hours, usually the low side of that. In some cases, it's been much lower but in all of those there was a direct fluid transfer of some kind, it seems. How direct I haven't been able to determine. If he hasn't shown symptoms in three days, he's probably going to be okay." She went on to briefly describe the onset symptoms for him to relay to Ringo.

"Now that wasn't so hard, was it?" Hiram smiled over the video link and the smile made Baxter shiver despite the safety afforded her by distance and the bunker she was currently housed in. She'd misjudged this man badly.

"I appreciate your help, Doctor," Hiram finished. "I doubt we'll speak again. For the record, I had thought that you weren't like the majority of the people I'd run across in your line of work during my service. I can see now I was wrong. If I'd known you were like that I wouldn't have offered my assistance. Mark me well, Doctor Baxter," Hiram leaned in closer to the webcam "If your men try to find that boy, I will hunt you down and make you beg for death. Understand? If you have any doubt about it, then let me ask you a question. Is there a man working for you by the name of Williams, perhaps? Large man, white hair, bad eye with a scar running through it?"

"Yes," Baxter answered without thinking. "There is."

"Then tell him the Goblin sends his love and let him tell you if I'm serious or not, Doctor. I'm sure he'll enlighten you. Oh," Hiram added almost as an afterthought, "tell him not to bother looking for me. I'd take it personally. He'll know what I mean. Good luck to you Doctor." Hiram literally stabbed the button that killed the connection and stood still for a full two minutes, breathing, trying to bring his temper under control.

That two-faced, lying, back-stabbing bitch! For a few seconds, his anger threatened to override his common sense and send him on an errand to erase her and all her kind from the planet. But common sense came knocking back, reminding him that the two-face lying bitch was needed to try and get some kind of control over this virus if that were possible.

"I shouldn't have said all that," he spoke aloud. "I was hidden and I should have stayed that way. Lord, forgive me for bein' stupid, please." With that Hiram headed outside to call Ringo and give him the news.

After that he was sure Helen would want to know what his fit earlier had been about. Some days it didn't pay to get out of bed.

-

"Hiram?" Ringo's voice answered.

"Yeah, it's me kid," Hiram affirmed. "Chopper's inbound. Are you clear?"

"A mile gone and moving," Ringo replied. "Beacon is lit off."

"Good, that's good," Hiram answered. "Baxter tried to get me to have you wait for the chopper to bring you to her, Ringo," he decided the boy deserved the truth. "I convinced her that wasn't a good idea. She didn't really want to talk to me about this, but I guess she felt like she owed you for the work you've done. Basically, if you're still good in seventy-two hours then you're golden."

"If you start running a high fever then you may be infected, son," Hiram broke the news gently. "The fever is the first sign, followed by capillary bleeding around the eyes, nose and sometimes the ears. You may start to cough up a bloody phlegm, but not everyone they know about has. Those are the signs you need to be concerned with. If they show up, then. . .well if you start having them show, you're. . . ." Hiram couldn't bring himself to say it.

"Then I'm screwed and the rest won't matter," Ringo said it for him. "Well, that's what I needed to know. I've got food for several days and I'll filter some water before I hole up. I've got that collapsible water-bag I can fill. Should last me long enough to know if I'm gonna need more or not," he tried to chuckle.

"Ringo, son, I'm sorry," Hiram blurted, eyes closed as he imagined the fear the teen must be feeling.

"It don't mean nothin', Hiram," Ringo replied calmly. "If it wasn't this, it'd just be something else. At least I got the job done. So maybe it's not for nothing, yeah?"

"Yeah," Hiram replied, thinking how many times he'd said those same words. They had always tasted like ashes in his mouth then, and they were no better now. "Get back to your barn and lay low, Ringo. Call if you need anything, or if you just want to talk."

"I won't," Ringo told him, though not unkindly. "But if I turn up with the symptoms I'll call and let you know. You deserve to know, just in case. Otherwise I'll call you when I start back." He paused a minute, then added; "I'm glad you and Helen are there to look after Tammy. I wanted to get her somewhere safe, and I did."

"You sure did, kid," Hiram smiled in spite of himself and the dire situation. "Now I'm gonna have to go and explain to her and my Helen why you aren't coming straight on back."

"Lie to 'em," Ringo said. "Ain't no reason to tell 'em the truth."

"Son, you ain't married, but just in case you get the chance, let me give you some advice," Hiram chuckled this time. "Don't never try to lie to the woman you sleep next to at night. It ain't healthy." Ringo's laughter rang through the phone and Hiram was glad to hear it.

"All right then" Ringo said finally. "I'll let you deal with your problem and I'll go deal with mine. Take care, Hiram."

"You too, son," Hiram returned, but Ringo was already gone. Hiram secured the phone, setting it down beside him. With a deep sigh, he stood and headed inside.

He had a problem to deal with, as Ringo had said.

-

Ringo had put the landing zone he'd marked out far behind him by the time he heard the helicopter in the distance. He kept to the trees so long as he could hear the aircraft, only moving to lighter cover once the *whoppa whoppa* of the chopper's flight fell away. Evidently the beacon had led them straight to the sample containers with no problem. To his ears, the chopper had been on the ground less than five minutes, closer to three by his count.

As he plodded through the woods on his way to the barn, Ringo pondered his dilemma. There really wasn't much to ponder on, he admitted. Either he was or he wasn't. There was no middle ground. In a few days, he would know if he was sick or not. If he wasn't, then he could finally move back to Hiram and Helen's place and enjoy some well-deserved rest and peace. If he was. . .well, if he was he'd be haunting that barn for a while, he figured.

He allowed himself to play over the mistakes he'd made on this little venture and there were plenty of them. The biggest in the bunch, of course, was his failure to keep the woman who might have infected him in sight. If he'd done that, she could never have gotten the jump on him. If he lived then he could file that away as knowledge gained by hard won experience. If he didn't then it wouldn't matter how well he'd learned the lesson, since he'd never have a chance to employ it.

He'd made other mistakes as well. He decided that once he was set in the barn he would devote the waiting time to the small journal he had, making an assessment of his movements and mistakes on this little jaunt. Even if he didn't need it, someone might find it later on and be able to use it.

And it would give him something to do. That would be important over the next three days, he decided.

-

Helen and Tammy looked up expectantly as Hiram entered the kitchen. He got himself a glass of water and then moved to the small table indicating that Tammy should join him, Helen already being seated.

"Heard from Ringo," he said simply. "He got his job done and got clear. Samples he collected ought to be on their way to Atlanta by now." He stopped there, weighing his next words very carefully.

"He was attacked while he was gathering what he needed,"

Hiram went on after a pause. "He defended himself and wasn't bitten, but he did get a good deal of infected blood on him. He's going to wait out the incubation period and a little more in a barn he came across on his way up to the bridge. He knows the signs and what to look for. He can safeguard himself from being out and able to hurt anyone if. . .that is in case he. . . ." Hiram finally trailed off, completely out of steam. He was suddenly very tired.

"I see," Helen spared him any more need to talk. She kept herself calm but did cast a look at Tammy. The younger woman was as stoic as Helen herself was.

"Is there anything we can do to help him?" Tammy asked, and Helen felt a swell of pride for the girl.

"We can pray for him, dear," Helen answered the question. "We can ask God to take care of him."

"Best help he can have right now," Hiram nodded in agreement. "He's not bit," Hiram stressed again. "He's taking a large dose of precaution because he got a good bit of blood on him. No open wounds or scratches, so he should be okay. But he wants to make sure and I can't blame him," the older man admitted. "If it was me out there, and it has been more than a few times, I'd want to know before I came dragging back here bringing something that could kill everyone around. He's just playing it smart, which in this case means careful. We should hear from him in three days when he starts back for home. Until then, like Helen said, pray."

Tammy wanted to scream at Hiram to do more, but one look at the old man's wounded face told her that doing so would be a waste. He was obviously blaming himself for the fix that Ringo was in. There was nothing he could do, either. Realizing that she decided she'd try instead to make him feel better.

"Well, all that talking is probably dry, hungry work," she said lightly, trying to break the gloom and doom atmosphere in the kitchen. "I guess I could find a fresh slice of bread for an old goat who had the manners to ask nicely. In fact," she added with a grin, "if he were to ask nicely enough, I might could find some butter to go on that bread."

"Ah, child, you are a comfort to an old man on a hard day, you know that?" Hiram smiled. Tammy stuck her tongue out at him, then laughed and turned to get Hiram some fresh bread and something to drink.

The three of them sat together in the kitchen trying to cheer one another up. It was all they could do and it helped to alleviate their worry about Ringo being all alone in what was becoming an increasingly crazy and dangerous world.

-

Ringo saw the barn through the trees sooner than he'd expected. He was tired and knew that was affecting his sense of time and distance. He'd stopped already and filtered enough water to fill the one-gallon collapsible bag he had kept in his pack, as well as his canteens. He'd used a different creek to bathe in, using the disinfectant and bleach to cleanse himself and his equipment. The shirt, pants and web gear he'd been wearing had been discarded, buried in the ground fifty yards or so from the water to avoid contaminating the creek any worse than he already might have. Hopefully it would work.

He felt clean, at least. Water and soap, after his thorough disinfecting, had left him refreshed if still tired. Seeing the barn made him start to relax but he caught himself before he'd really started. He couldn't afford to relax until he was secure. He might be infected, he might not. He didn't know. But if he wasn't then there was no point in taking chances. If he was clean but got attacked and bitten, that would be a complete waste.

He made his way carefully around the small barn making sure it was still abandoned. He watched the house in the distance for fifteen minutes, seeing no signs of occupancy during that time. He saw no movement, no traffic on the road in the distance, nothing. Satisfied he was clear for the moment, Ringo made his way back into the loft. He quickly secured the entrance again and then set about making himself comfortable.

With his meager camp set up, Ringo removed another MRE and popped the fuel tab, heating the slightly palatable meal for a late lunch/early supper. He was not surprised at all to see the cat appear once the meal started to give off a fairly pleasant aroma.

"Well, well," Ringo chuckled aloud to the feline. "Look who's still here." The cat sat down just out of reach, ignoring him as she used a paw to clean her face. Shaking his head in amusement Ringo cut the bottom from the package the MRE had come in and used it to fashion a small bowl. He poured a small amount of water into the make shift container and set it toward the animal.

The cat looked at him suspiciously for several seconds, then leaned forward sniffing carefully. Finding nothing wrong with the small package, she stuck her head inside and drank slowly at first, then more greedily. When the water was gone she licked the package for any missed drops. Ringo smiled and used his canteen to add another drink, which the cat took after only a few seconds hesitation while Ringo moved away again.

"Thirsty weren't you girl?" Ringo asked. He had a sudden urge to pet the cat but resisted it. The cat was all but feral. While it might accept a pat to its head, it could just as easily bite him. No sense borrowing trouble.

The meal now heated, Ringo opened the package to let it cool and the smell of Beef Stroganoff brought him the cat's undivided attention. Chuckling, Ringo took a sizable portion out of the bag and set it on a makeshift plate made from the remainder of the packaging. He slid the 'plate' closer to the suspicious animal, who retreated a few steps, back arched. Ringo ignored the cat, setting the food out where the cat could reach it and then returning to his own meal, leaning against his bed roll.

The cat obviously remembered getting a meal from this human before, and that memory coupled with the inviting smell of another hot, meaty meal won her over quickly. She kept a wary eye on Ringo, but attacked the small meal with gusto.

"You're that hungry already, huh?" Ringo smiled. Talking to the cat seemed silly he supposed, but it was better than just sitting here in silence. He would be here for three days at least and these might be the last lucid days of his life. He really didn't think he had been infected but the only way to be sure was simply to wait and see. He expected that to be a long three days.

He had food, water enough for the three days, and he was dry and comfortable, considering. He had a book he could read and he had a tablet with other books on it, one of the few things he possessed that wasn't a blade or clothing. He had one small box with a few trinkets that had belonged to his parents, which he had left behind in his room at Hiram's. No sense in risking it, he had figured. The tablet could be replaced even now and the books were all copied to a flash drive along with the music he had downloaded over the year or so he'd had the tablet. If he lost it he could replace everything that was important.

So, he would stay put, stay quiet, and see what happened. If the cat was around to keep him company then so much the better. Ringo finished his meal and leaned back, allowing himself to relax for a while. The shotgun was close to hand and the pistol was lying across his chest, still in its holster. His sword was never out of reach by long habit. With the door blocked again, Ringo was about as safe as he could be in the situation he found himself in, so. . . .

He was asleep before the thought finished. Five minutes after that, her belly full again and warm, the cat was once more curled up on Ringo's belly, purring softly.

Neither noticed when it began to rain softly.

CHAPTER ELEVEN

-

Ringo woke sometime later to a gently falling rain. He checked his watch, seeing that it was around midnight. He moved slightly and grinned at the cat curled up on him. For her part the cat stirred slightly, glaring at Ringo for daring to disturb her sleep, then settled in again. Ringo sighed.

"Sorry, Grouchy, but some of us need to take care of some business," he said softly and gently moved the cat off him. The cat allowed that contact with a jaundiced eye, not biting or clawing. Ringo sat the animal down in a curl on the hay he was using to pad his bed and rose to his feet.

Across the loft was a five-gallon bucket that Ringo had appropriated as a latrine. Shredded hay from below mixed with sawdust taken from a pile under a side shed made a fairly convenient repository and should keep the odor down. Business done, Ringo added another handful of the hay and then crushed some pine needles he'd collected from the trees nearby, dropping the fragrant pins into the bucket.

Cleaning up with the wipes and hand sanitizer, Ringo eased to the open loft door and stood looking out at the area around him. The rain prevented him from seeing much but he could see the distant glimmer of security and street lights. Apparently, the power was still on.

For practice more than anything, Ringo took the night vision scope from his pack and used it to scan the surrounding area. Other than two deer munching at the uncut hay in the field to his east there was nothing moving he could see. He moved to the rear opening and repeated the process, studying the woods. Again, he could neither see nor hear anything out of the ordinary. Satisfied for the moment, he sat down and began to clean his weapons. He hadn't had time before and his impromptu nap had stopped him earlier.

They wouldn't be damaged by a little rain and time, but he

wanted them clean anyway. Sword and knife could rust if left uncleaned and firearms could ruin if allowed to rust. He cleaned them all, even those he hadn't used since they would have gotten wet, paying close attention to any damage he could see. All was well.

Once the guns were cleaned and reassembled he loaded them and laid them aside, close to hand but out of the way. He took a small stone and ran it over the blade of his katana and then his knives and the small throwing axe he carried. The spikes didn't require that sort of thing. Seeing the empty holder reminded him that one spike was still on the interstate, buried in the head of the infected woman who'd tried to kill him earlier in the day. He didn't really want it back and certainly not bad enough to go and get it. He could make a new one. He'd made that one, after all.

Once his chore was finished Ringo eased back onto his pack again, considering his position. There really wasn't much he could do until the time passed. He decided that any time he had to confront the infected again he'd be wearing a balaclava. Hopefully one that was resistant to water. Between that and the goggles he shouldn't have to go through this again.

He would also make some gauntlets, he decided. They would need to be light, yet strong enough to stop a biting attack. Perhaps some kind of aluminum shrouded with Kevlar? That might work. He used the writing function on his tablet to make a few notes, careful to keep the screen low and block the light it let off from escaping the barn.

Next Ringo considered the tactics needed to fight the infected. Noise was death, especially in a large group. They could also see fairly well. But could they tell the difference between one of their own and someone healthy? Close in he was pretty sure they could, since the three he'd taken had attacked him without pause or hesitation, but what about at a distance? Could an infected see a person walking in the distance and know whether it was one of them or not? And why didn't they attack each other? The only altercations he had observed had been individual infected fighting or struggling over something both seemed to want, whatever it was.

How was their sense of smell? He'd had no way to test that and hadn't thought of it even if he had. No one else had mentioned it either. He needed to find out if they could smell. That meant finding another infected and trying to get downwind of him/her with something they'd want. He didn't know what that might be, so that was something else he'd have to wing. But he was convinced it was good information to have.

He thought back to the three he had killed at the interstate. They were not drained of blood despite their wounds, which meant their blood was still congealing as it should, still clotting. Maybe the virus made their blood thicker? The blood that had spilled over on him had been very thick, almost like oil in both color and consistency. That could mean that the virus was changing the make-up of the blood in its victims, maybe? Or was that what blood from a head wound looked like when it hit the air? He made another note but was shaking his head. He could come up with all sorts of questions, but he didn't even know where to start on answers. Ringo wasn't dumb by any one's measuring system, but he lacked the training and education to figure out something like this. So, he made notes of things that occurred to him, figuring to pass them along to Baxter.

You know, if I don't become an aggressively violent hydrophobic maniac sometime in the next couple of days.

Tired of this line of thought for the present, he opened a book he had been reading before the start of all this. He hadn't had time to read any the last few days, but here all he had was time. Might as well read, he figured.

Taking a ration bar from his pack, he nibbled on it as a snack while he read, laying small pieces on the floor for the cat, who would sniff disdainfully but then gobble the pieces up when she thought Ringo wasn't looking.

The two passed the rest of the night like that with the sound of falling rain as a background noise.

By morning it would be raining much harder.

-

"Glad we got the rest of the early stuff in the ground," Hiram said as he sat on the front porch the next morning, coffee in hand. "Won't be working in the garden next few days looks like."

"No, I expect not," Helen agreed, sitting at his side. "Have you heard from Ringo?" she asked gently.

"Don't expect to," Hiram shook his head. "He'll call if he starts showing symptoms or when he starts home and not before, unless he's got something to report."

"I see," was Helen's reply. She took her husband's hand and squeezed gently.

"What set you off yesterday?" she asked, and Hiram stiffened, but didn't pull away.

"Just worried about the boy," Hiram answered, and while not the whole reason it was still the truth. "I know he could have said no, and hell, I even sort of prodded him to say no," he admitted, "but I still feel like it was my fault he was out there...is out there, right now."

"I can see how that would bother you," Helen nodded, "but, as you said, he could have said no. Your influence might have helped him say yes, but I get the feeling that he wanted to be away for a few days. Alone." Hiram looked at her, nodding slowly.

"I thought that too and it's probably accurate," he replied finally. "He's been through a lot for a kid his age and that's the truth. Talking to him is almost like talking to someone that's a ten or twelve-year vet. With combat time at that," he added, sighing. "He's had a rough time."

"Want to tell me about it?" Helen asked.

"It's his to tell," Hiram shook his head. "And I know just enough of his story to tell it completely wrong. I will tell you this," he turned to look at her. "Beneath that lamb exterior is a dragon, ready and waiting to breathe fire on anyone who wakes it. That, you can count on."

"I thought as much," Helen nodded once again. "He seems like a sweet boy and he is, I'm sure, but there's an edge hiding beneath. I probably wouldn't see it if not for living with you for so long," she added, partly teasing.

"Me?" Hiram looked at her with raised brows. "Why I'm as pure as the driven snow!"

"Oh, my dear Hiram," Helen laughed. "That's one of the things I love about you so much. You don't look or act dangerous and yet you are. Ringo hasn't your years of experience in hiding it though. The edge to him is much closer to the surface. Unlike you, Ringo doesn't seem to care if anyone sees it or not. I'd say he doesn't advertise it, but then I'm fairly sure he doesn't have to, either."

"I'd say you've got him pegged pretty fair," Hiram nodded, grinning slightly. "That boy is dangerous, there's no question or doubt about that. I just hope he comes through this okay," he said, looking back out at the falling rain.

"Lord willing, he will, husband," Helen's voice rang with a confidence Hiram wanted to share, but couldn't. "Lord willing, he will."

-

Ringo startled awake, unsure when he had gone back to sleep. His tablet was lying beside him so he must have just drifted off. He realized it was getting light outside when he looked toward his feet and saw the cat.

The cat was looking toward the opening to the front of the barn with her back arched and a quiet hiss showing on her face. Ringo tensed slightly. Whatever had woken him up had also upset the cat.

Getting quietly to his feet Ringo started to move over to the loft door then thought better of it. Some of the boards creaked, he knew from experience. Moving across the hay scattered on the floor would also cause some of that hay to fall between the cracks in the boards, giving away that someone was up here.

He took his seat again, careful not to disturb the hay beneath him or make any noise. He wondered who, or what, was around the barn. Was it someone who was infected? A thief maybe? Someone looking for a place to hide, like he was doing? There was no way to know.

It could just as easily have been the farmer who owned this barn, Ringo realized with a start. There was no equipment stored here but there was the hay he was sleeping on and there might be other things downstairs. He hadn't paid attention to most of the storage other than to ensure he was alone. He really wanted to look outside and see what he could see, but to do so might give him away.

The cat was still as well. Ringo thought that if it wasn't something to worry about, the cat would have gone to investigate or gone back to sleep, one or the other. Instead she was still on guard, watching the entrance to their loft.

Ringo lay back carefully and pulled the shotgun to him, making sure the safety was on. He wasn't proficient enough with firearms to go around with the safety off, not that he thought it was a good idea even for a professional. That done, all Ringo could do was wait; which would be more difficult because he needed to pee. Really bad.

-

Tammy looked outside from the window in her room, sighing at the rain and the generally gloomy day it was causing. Thankfully they had completed the garden work yesterday afternoon, so they weren't being held up by the rain. Hiram had even said it was a good time for a slow, gentle rain like this since it would help give the garden a jump start.

Still, it meant that she was pretty much stuck in the house unless she wanted to get soaking wet, which she didn't. So, she was resigned to a day inside. Fortunately, Helen and Hiram had a nice library and she'd picked herself a book, a mystery, and settled into the chair in her room to read.

She kept drifting away from the story, though, to look out the window and wonder where Ringo was and how he was doing. He wouldn't call unless he was headed in or had started showing signs of infection. If it was good news they wouldn't know until at least tomorrow and probably the day after. If he called before then it would probably be bad news.

She could tell that it was working on Hiram pretty hard. It was clear the older man blamed himself for Ringo's predicament. While Tammy would like to have someone to blame and be angry at, the fact was that Ringo had gone because he had wanted to. There was no blame, including for Ringo really. He had done something that needed doing, something that few others had been willing or able to do. Perhaps his work would give the doctors and scientists what they needed to combat the virus. She hoped so, for more reasons than one. Sure, it would be nice for things to start getting back to normal, if that were even possible, but also it would mean that whatever Ringo was going through would mean something. It wouldn't be wasted.

As much as she didn't want to think about it, Tammy had to admit that she was afraid for him. She would give almost anything reasonable and few things unreasonable to be able to help him in some way. But there was nothing she could do. She didn't even know where he was and Hiram had been remarkably reluctant to give any details about his location. And she couldn't do anything even if she knew where he was and went to him, except add to his burdens.

She exhaled heavily, her mood slipping. She returned to the novel in an attempt to put those concerns from her mind, but sooner rather than later she would find herself looking back out the window again. Thinking about what Ringo was doing and how he was feeling.

How he was making it.

-

At that moment Ringo was crawling to a small hole in the floor of the loft, trying to get a look at what was happening below. He'd heard a muffled cry a few minutes before and the cat had scampered away to whatever hiding place or secret entrance she used. Ringo had heard what he was positive was a low voice though he wasn't able to make out the words, then what had sounded like a blow and a thud. He was almost sure there were at least two people beneath him. Who they were or what they were doing he had yet to figure out.

He made it to the hole and very carefully moved the tiny pieces of hay from around it so he wouldn't knock them through and call attention to himself. Peering down into the barn, he tried to see what was happening.

Movement caught his eye and he stopped, trying to get a good look at what was happening. Suddenly the top of a man's head came into view. Long, dirty hair tied back in a ponytail. As the man moved a step or two further on, he could see it was a pretty good sized old boy with a tee shirt and overalls. A beard was visible from one side but Ringo couldn't get a look at his face.

Barn owner? Farmer? Traveler looking to get out of the rain and somewhere safe? Ringo had no way to know and elected to stay quiet for the moment.

"Get up, bitch," the man suddenly growled, his voice low but carrying now that Ringo was closer. Ringo heard a reply that he couldn't quite make out, though it sounded like a woman.

"I said get up!" the man ordered, louder this time, punctuating the order with movement. Ringo saw him lean into a stall, arm extended. When he pulled back he was dragging a woman by the arm. The part of her face Ringo could see was smudged with dirt, and her clothes were torn. Not yet to the point of exposure, but looking at the way the man treated her coupled with the fact that her hands appeared to be bound behind her, Ringo decided that point probably wasn't far off.

She wasn't a small woman, he noticed, which meant that the guy was stronger than he looked. The woman wasn't really fat, she was just. . .well, a big girl. She wasn't exactly attractive in her present state, though Ringo allowed she might be in another setting. Clearly this guy wasn't interested in what she looked like.

"Go ahead and yell," the man told her as she struggled. "No one around to hear you, no way. And if you bring one o' them down on us, I'll leave ya here for 'em and head out myself. We'll see if you like their company more's ya do mine, how 'bout that?"

Ringo had seen enough by now to know that he'd have to do something. He could never justify lying here and allowing this thug to hurt a woman. Of course, he wouldn't be able to do much else for her considering his own problems, but he could at least get her free of this hoodlum. Ringo eased the suppressed pistol Hiram had given him from its holster and checked the safety. He knew there was a round chambered. He eased the tip of the suppressor into the hole, and waited.

"You and me, we'll just hang out here a little while, get to know each other better," he heard the man say. The woman's reply was muffled and Ringo couldn't make it out. He was pretty sure it wasn't agreement, though. He waited for the man to move back his way, but after a minute or two, that hadn't happened. Reluctant to move, Ringo was about to do just that when suddenly the man moved almost directly beneath him.

"It ain't like you got a lotta choice, here, sweetums," the man was saying. Ringo aimed carefully and his finger tensed on the trigger.

"Fact is, you should be thankin' me, since I'm keepin' ya safe," the man told his captive. "I figure I got some kind o' pay comin' for that. Only right, wouldn't you sa--"

The shot surprised him, just as it should have. The bullet went into the top of the man's head and seemed to have gone through since Ringo could see blood shoot from the bottom of the man's chin, or so it appeared.

He could hear the woman scream, again muffled, and realized that she must be gagged. Not to mention scared out of her mind. Ringo watched for a minute longer, making sure the man had been alone. When no one else appeared, he moved to his hay block and moved them out of the way. He stuck his head through the hole then drew it back, taking a quick look around. Nothing. Satisfied that maybe no one was waiting to ambush him Ringo eased himself down the ladder.

Lying in a stall out of sight of his peep hole, the woman was struggling to get to her feet, eyes wild with fear, tears flowing, nose running and her mouth sealed with what looked like a bandanna held in place with duct tape. Ringo held his hand up slowly and stood still, trying not to look threatening. He realized he was still holding his pistol and quickly tucked it into his waistband after making sure it was on safe.

"Lady, easy now," he said gently. "You're okay. Just take it easy a minute please and let me untie you, all right?" The woman screamed into her gag and tried to move away from him but without the use of her hands she couldn't get very far.

Ringo slowly took a small knife from his pocket and pulled her arm toward him. She fought him the whole way and he tried not to hurt her. Finally, he got a look at her hands and realized they were tied with binder's twine, a cord used by farmers and craftsmen. He also saw that they were tied far too tightly and the circulation in her hands had to be cut off.

"Easy lady, and let me cut that line, all right?" he asked. The woman redoubled her efforts to free herself from his grasp.

"Lady, listen!" Ringo hissed. "He's tied you tight and the line is cutting into your skin. It's cut off the blood to your hands, understand? If I don't get this loose, it could hurt you a lot worse, okay? Let me cut it. I can't do that with you jerking around because I might cut you by accident. Now please, hold still, just for a minute. All I want to do is free you."

The woman suddenly went limp, sobbing into the hay she was lying on. Ringo felt sympathy for her, knowing she had to be terrified. He gently cut the twine holding her hands together and then stepped back from her, giving her room. She watched him for a second, then groaned into the gag as she pulled her hands from behind her back. Ringo guessed she must have been tied that way for a while. There was a small trickle of blood where the twine had cut into her skin, but her fingers appeared to be working so maybe the circulation hadn't been hurt after all.

It took her a moment working with her numb hands to remove the tape, but Ringo let her do it rather than get close to her again. She finally managed to get the tape off, and ripped the bandanna from her mouth, spitting the taste of the dirty rag out. She looked at Ringo. With the immediate danger passed, the woman's fear seemed to have been replaced with a haughty expression that was completely out of place given her circumstance.

"Who are you?" she almost demanded.

"Uh, I'm nobody special," Ringo replied. "I'm just trying to stay out of the rain. You and your friend woke me."

"He's not my friend!" the woman almost yelled and Ringo put a finger to his lips to try and quieten her.

"Let's not make too much noise, okay?" he said gently. "Noise draws them."

"Don't tell me to be quiet!" the woman snapped. "I asked who you were!"

"I'm the guy who just helped you," Ringo said evenly. He knew she was scared, or should be, but that was no reason to be ugly to him, was it?

His answer did seem to calm her, though, and she had the good manners to appear embarrassed. She mumbled an apology, getting shakily to her feet.

"Where's your car?" she asked. "I have to get to town and report this."

"I don't have a car, ma'am," he told her. "Don't know how to drive."

"What?" the woman looked stunned. "No car? How did you get here?"

"I walked, ma'am," Ringo replied evenly. "Like I said, I don't know how to drive."

"But I have to get to town!" the woman protested.

"I can't help you with that, ma'am," Ringo told her. "Sorry."

"What are you even doing here?" the woman demanded. Again.

"I'm hiding from crazy people and trying to stay dry," Ringo answered. Again.

"And you just happened to pick this barn?" the woman asked suspiciously.

"Well, it looked dry and no one was around," Ringo

shrugged. "Isolated seems a good thing right now."

"Well, I need you to take me to town, so get your car," she ordered. Ringo just looked at her for a moment. Was she in shock? Or maybe she just wasn't listening?

"Ma'am," he said finally, "I've already told you, I got no car. I've never owned a car and never drove one. I walk everywhere I go. I can't take you to town because I don't have a car. How did he get you here?" Ringo asked, nodding to the dead man.

"His truck, but it's out of gas," she answered. "That's why I need your car." Ringo fought the urge to shake his head in defeat. Hello, Earth to lady, come in lady.

"I. Don't. Have. One." Ringo said slowly. "I really don't."

"Everyone has a car for God's sake!" the woman snapped.

"Not me, lady," Ringo abandoned his polite address. "Can't drive. Never learned how. You might try that house up there," he pointed. "Don't think anyone is around, but there might be a car."

"I guess you've already been up there?" the woman almost sneered. "Take whatever you could carry?"

Ringo's face froze at that, a mask falling into place. Without a word, he turned away and grabbed the ladder.

"Where are you going?" the woman demanded.

"Back where I came from," Ringo said, climbing the ladder. "I was trying to sleep when you and your boyfriend woke me."

"I told you. . .he wasn't my boyfriend!" the woman screeched. Ringo stopped and looked around at her.

"If you keep screeching like that, you're going to draw infected down on you. When that happens, you'll be sorry. At least for as long as it takes them to kill you or infect you. Better get that mouth under control if you want to make it." With that he kept climbing.

"Come back here!" she ordered. "I need your help!"

"Should have thought of that before you accused me of being a thief," Ringo told her without turning around. "I helped you all I'm going to lady. Good luck to you and please get the hell away from here with that yelling, okay?"

The woman was about to reply when she heard a screech in the distance. Ringo hurried the rest of the way up the ladder and started closing the hole off.

"What was that?" he heard her call.

"The infected," Ringo told her as he finished shutting off the hole. "And thanks to you, they know where I am. If I was you I'd start running, lady. They'll be looking for you."

"Let me up there with you!" she shouted and Ringo could only shake his head as he heard another infected shriek.

"That's not going to happen, lady," he told her flatly. "You'll just get me and the cat killed with that mouth of yours. Now you better head out and do it quick because they usually run to noise and you're making plenty of it."

"I demand you let me up there!" she yelled. "I'm the Circuit Court Clerk!"

"Don't care if you are," Ringo said softly. "They'll get you just as quick. Now you better hurry. They'll be on their way. If you can't get into the house then I'd just start running. You might make it."

"I'll see you in jail for this!" she threatened.

"Not if you don't start moving, you won't," Ringo told her, then decided not to answer her anymore. No sense in attracting them to his own presence. Below the woman claiming to be the Circuit Court Clerk finally realized the danger she was in and took off running for the house, still cursing as she did so.

"You'll pay for this!" he heard her shout and heard at least two infected answer her.

"I doubt it," Ringo muttered. He made sure he was secure and then went belly down at the loft door to see what he could see.

The last view he had of the erstwhile Court Clerk was her running down the driveway after failing to get into the house. She was still shouting.

Two infected followed her.

Ringo waited thirty minutes, watching all the time. He saw no more infected and heard nothing. Finding himself in the clear, he packed his gear and cleaned his mess. He needed to find another place to hide. This one had just become untenable.

Five minutes later the barn lay behind him as Ringo made his way through the woods in search of new shelter. His last thought as he headed out was that he would miss the cat.

CHAPTER TWELVE

-

Ringo made pretty good time, wanting to put some distance between himself and the barn. Mentally he cursed the woman and her loud mouth along with the man who'd brought her there. The last thing Ringo had done before leaving was drag the dead thug outside and away from the barn. There was no sense in letting him ruin the little building.

He had covered most of a mile when he stopped to get a breath and listen. He couldn't hear any screeching or yelling. In fact, he couldn't hear anything at the moment. The rain was keeping animal life under cover. It was eerily quiet and Ringo felt a shiver through his spine. He wrote it off to being damp, but deep down he knew better. This whole thing was creepy.

He found a dryish place under a fir tree and pulled out his map, trying to shield it with his body to keep it mostly dry. He wished for a moment that he could just head for Hiram's place. If he pushed it and didn't have any trouble, he could probably be there just after dark. Sighing, he shook the idea away. He couldn't do that and time spent thinking on it was just wasted.

He put the map away, satisfied that he knew roughly where he was. He knew there were other houses in the area but he'd already decided houses were off limits. They might be empty now, but the owners could be on their way home even as he went inside. Not a good situation. No, he'd find another barn, or failing that a shed. If he had to, he'd find a sheltered place to go head down and huddle under his poncho, but that was a last resort. It would likely be cool tonight and he needed a place he could dry off and maybe use his small stove. Outside wasn't that place.

Shrugging his pack straps higher on his shoulders, Ringo set out again, eyes open for anything that looked like it might provide him shelter and safety for the next two days.

-

Doctor Baxter met the helicopter on the pad above the

complex. An assistant took the samples and hurried below with them while Baxter waited for the men from the retrieval team. The team leader, a large man with crew cut white hair, stepped to her upon seeing her waiting. He would have been handsome, she thought, if not for the scar that marred the right side of his face. It ran from his forehead down the length of his face, disappearing beneath his shirt. Whatever had made that scar had taken his right eye along the way, a patch now covering the empty socket.

"Doctor?" Williams asked. "Something you need?"

"I don't suppose you were able to find the boy," she asked. Williams shook his head.

"Long gone. No sign of him at all."

"I was hoping to get him into quarantine," she sighed. "It would be nice to have a live specimen to study."

"You don't know for sure he's infected," Williams shrugged. "No sense going to that trouble without knowing, is there?"

"We could always infect him ourselves if he failed to show symptoms," Baxter's voice was detached, clinical.

"That's not really something I'd want to be part of, Doctor," Williams told her. "Our mission is to find a cure, if there is one. Not to make things worse by infecting healthy people."

"Many distasteful things are done in the name of science," Baxter waved the complaint away. "And it would serve that Colonel right, having the nerve to threaten me."

"What Colonel?" Williams asked.

"The man who set this up," Baxter told him. "Apparently, he knows you," she added, remembering that part of their conversation. "Calls himself the Goblin, and said to tell you he sends his-- what?" Baxter cut herself off seeing the look on Williams' face. "You recognize that name?"

"I'll give you one thing, Doctor," Williams said evenly, shaking his head slowly. "When you make enemies, you don't mess about. You just go out and make the worst one possible right off the bat."

"What's that mean?" she asked, concern showing on her face.

"What did he tell you?" Williams asked instead of answering.

"He said that if anything happened to that boy he'd make

me beg for death, or something like that," she tried to wave it off.

"Listen, lady," Williams voice was suddenly harsh. "That man is dangerous. If he met the devil on the sidewalk, the devil would step aside and let him pass, understand? If he said he'd kill you, that is exactly what he meant. I've never known him to make threats, just promises. And he's kept every promise he's ever made."

"I don't appreciate you trying to put me in his sights either, while we're just talking. He'd kill me as quick as he would you and yes, I know him. Knew him, anyway, a long time ago. Best thing you can do is forget him and that boy, understand? And if you put me in a position opposite him again, I'll kill you myself. I'd rather face an army of your creations than face that man alone and I'm in no way exaggerating. Put me in that place again and you'll be riding this out alone because my men and I are history."

With that the large merc grabbed his gear, shouted orders to his men, and disappeared down the stairs. Baxter watched him depart, wondering what kind of man could have that impact on Williams, a man she would have sworn was afraid of nothing.

Perhaps it was better that Just Ringo was still free after all.

-

Tammy and Helen fixed supper in silence, each occupied with her own thoughts. Even the meal itself was subdued with little more than simple pleasantries passed between the three. Tammy cleared the table afterward and cleaned the kitchen while Helen washed and dried the dishes. Chores finished, the women were somewhat at loose ends and took seats at the table again, talking quietly.

"He's listening to the radio," Helen sighed, looking through the door toward the small room that Hiram used for his radio room. "Marking that map and making notes. He just can't let go of who he was."

"Who he still is," Tammy observed just as softly. "You can't stop being a soldier, Helen. Not after that long. My father's been a soldier since he was old enough to serve and he doesn't know anything else. I doubt he could do anything else, in all honesty. Him or his friends." Helen was pleased to hear Tammy speak of her father in the present tense, but didn't mention it.

"Oh, I know that, dear," she replied instead. "Don't misunderstand me. I'm not fussing so much as simply worrying.

Hiram looks at this as some kind of personal challenge and he's just not as young as he once was. We're not old as such, mind you," she added primly. "But we certainly aren't children, either. And don't let his grumbling fool you, either. Hiram is in excellent condition, especially for a man his age. But this is too big for him to get involved in and he knows it."

"If he were still active, he would be in the middle of this, I'm sure," Helen continued after a pause. "I don't know exactly what he did when he was away but I do know that for most of his later years in the service he wasn't part of an active field unit. He doesn't think I know that, of course, but you can't hide much from Army wives. You would think soldiers would realize that at some point, but they never do," she sighed theatrically.

"Lucinda used to say the same thing," Tammy nodded, smiling at the memory. "Lucinda was the woman who looked after me when my father was deployed," she explained at Helen's look. "My mother died when I was still a baby, not quite four, and Lucinda Steele, the wife of one of my father's friends, looked after me when he was away. She was sort of a surrogate mother," she smiled.

"Bless her heart," Helen smiled. "When we lived on-base I would do that kind of thing for younger officers, especially those who had young wives that worked or where going to school. I know that not everyone is like that, but most of the people I knew when Hiram was in the Army pulled together like that in times of need. It was almost like having a very large extended family."

"Sounds like me," Tammy nodded. "I don't know how many 'aunts' and 'uncles' I had," she laughed. "Someone was always dropping by to see if we needed anything or how we were doing. I miss it," Tammy admitted. "It was one of the hardest things I've ever done, leaving home to go to school. If I hadn't, I'd still be there," she added softly.

"Dear, if you hadn't then you might be in dire straits right now, too," Helen reminded her. "Remember what your father said about losing contact with Bragg. That's not something that happens, Tammy, regardless of what novels say. Base communications are very secure."

"I know," Tammy nodded absently. "And truth is I couldn't have landed anywhere better than right here," she looked up, smiling at Helen. "I can't thank you enough for how you've taken me in, Helen."

"It's been my pleasure, dear."

-

Ringo was crouched low in the fading light, watching for signs of life. He had traveled maybe two miles from the Cat Barn as he'd taken to calling it and he was soaked to the bone. While it wasn't full dark, it was close and the light was fading fast. The last thing he wanted to do was use a light.

Sitting maybe fifty yards ahead of him was a small house that looked deserted. From this distance, it didn't look like it was in the best state of repair, but he couldn't tell for sure and even the binoculars weren't much help in the low light. He considered his options for a moment, slim though they were. He took a few seconds, more to curse the dead thug and loud-mouthed woman who had cost him the Cat Barn with its warm hay bed, then shook the thought away.

He could either move in toward the house, hoping it was empty and could serve as a place to dry out and warm up, or he could spend a miserable night in the woods huddled under a poncho. When he thought about spending the night like that even a possible confrontation with infected looked better.

He wiped a hand down his face to clear away the water, knowing that it wouldn't really help. He was cold, wet and thoroughly miserable. If he didn't get out of this weather soon, he'd have a fever whether he was infected or not.

And wouldn't that be some shit? he thought to himself. Die of the flu or pneumonia before I get a chance to die of rabies or whatever? He shook his head at the irony of it.

And then he started for the house.

He moved carefully, aware that he couldn't see very well. It was still too light out to use the night gear Hiram had given him, but dark enough that he had a hard time seeing clearly. All he needed was to trip on something or step on a nail.

And then die of tetanus instead of pneumonia or super rabies, he thought sourly. This day has really sucked.

He reached the house without any disaster befalling him and breathed a shallow sigh of relief. He edged his way to the corner to peer around into the front. No car or other vehicle of any kind. The grass in the yard hadn't been cut either. Returning to the back of the house, he tried the door, surprised to find it open. He was instantly on guard. There was just no way that this was a good sign. He wasn't having that kind of day.

Drawing his pistol, Ringo cautiously made his way inside, careful to allow his eyes to adjust as much as possible to the darkness. Very little light was able to penetrate the curtains, however, and Ringo finally resorted to a small but powerful flashlight, its beam cutting through the house like a laser.

The house was neat and uncluttered. It had very little furniture and only a few decorations of any kind. He noticed a collection of fishing gear filling one wall along with an empty gun rack. He finally put two and two together; this was a weekend place for someone. That's why it looked deserted.

He continued his search of the house making sure he was well and truly alone. Satisfied that he was the only occupant, Ringo secured the rear door. He checked the front, finding it locked, then checked the windows. All were intact and locked from the inside.

He allowed himself to relax just the tiniest bit. He walked into the single bedroom and hit the light switch. The light came on just like it was supposed to. Off to the left was a bathroom. Ringo considered his situation for about ten seconds before he started stripping out of his wet clothes. He returned to the kitchen long enough to secure a chair from the table, then returned to the bedroom, closing the door. The door had a lock, he was glad to see and he threw the bolt before shoving the back of the chair under the knob to secure it further.

Two minutes later he was in the shower, allowing warm water to run over him. He leaned over against the wall as the water warmed him, resting for a moment. He knew he was taking a chance doing this, but he needed to be warm. Being clean and dry would just be a bonus. He scrubbed himself vigorously, remembering his hurried creek bath only this morning after the incident. He stayed in the shower until the water began to run cold then shut it off and toweled dry.

He had one remaining suit of clothes in his pack which he donned with his hair still wet. He took his wet clothes and rung them out in the tub, then hung them on the shower rod to hopefully drip dry. That done, Ringo unblocked the door and eased into the living area once more. There was no television but there was a stereo. He turned the radio on but found nothing but static and a religious station that was warning everyone this was the End Times. Apparently, the people who owned this place used the CD player and not the radio.

He went into the kitchen and looked around. As he'd expected, he found no food other than a few canned goods. Leaving food in a place that wasn't always occupied was a good way to attract vermin. He examined the cans but decided to stick with his own food instead. He was not really hungry, but knowing he should eat a bite, Ringo took one of the ration bars and slowly munched on it as he consulted his map and GPS unit. Slowly he worked out where he was and nodded to himself. Despite the urgency of his departure from the Cat Barn he had moved more or less in the right direction. He was still several miles from Hiram's place but that was fine.

He put the map and unit away and leaned back on the bed. It was fairly comfortable and he was grateful for it. As he started to drift off to sleep he thought of something. Rising, he closed and locked the door once more, replacing the chair beneath the knob. He placed the Remington beside him on the bed, the pistol beneath his pillow.

Tired to the point of exhaustion, Ringo fell into a fitful sleep hoping that he woke up still in his right mind.

-

Baxter reviewed the video that Ringo had taken, fascinated that the young man had thought to provoke the infected in order to record their reactions. The video from the bridge area was especially interesting as she noted the same behaviors that Ringo had. He really had done remarkable job gathering information.

The specimens were also collected and labeled properly; something that two of their volunteers had not been successful with, resulting in the loss of their hard-earned collections. All of Ringo's were excellent and were sent immediately to the lower labs in the secure area where others were waiting for them to begin testing.

The head was secured in a cryo chamber and she had to wonder where the 'Goblin' Colonel had gotten it. It wasn't as if these things were standard issue. Still she was glad he had it, since it practically guaranteed that the head would still be workable in their research. Once she was in an isolation lab with the temps set to just above freezing, she broke the seal on the canister and removed the head for examination. It would have been much better to have a live specimen to work with, of course, but Williams was not willing to risk his men to retrieve one for her. This would have to do. She set the head on the table before her, preparing to take samples of the brain tissue.

"Well Mister Doe, let's see what kind of brain you had," she murmured. She estimated that the John Doe had likely been in his late thirties to early forties, but an exact age was impossible to tell. She hadn't thought to ask for any identification that the body might have had and regretted it. If she had been able to pull the man's medical records, it might have assisted her in her research.

But then, none of this was supposed to have happened. She sighed in regret at the loss of life and of years of research in the African lab. One little mistake by an over-eager research assistant had brought almost a decade of work crashing down and now threatened to end the world as it was known. Baxter knew from experience how deadly this disease was since she was one of the team that had weaponized it. She had no qualms about that, knowing that the virus had been intended as a last resort against the spreading threat of radical terror groups that were slowly taking control of the Middle East and Northern Africa.

It had never occurred to her that all the careful planning and safety precautions would be completely undone by stupidity on the part of a staff member and the outright incompetence on the part of security forces charged with preventing what had happened.

There had always been plans for a vaccine, of course. You didn't manufacture a weapon like this without one, for a number of reasons, self-preservation chief among them. But the virus had still been in the developmental stage at the time of contamination. And all of the work they had done had been lost when the lab was contaminated. There had been back-ups of course, but those servers had been in Africa and they were lost now, probably for all time.

Legal issues had prevented them from bringing any of that material into the States, though she had argued unsuccessfully that USAMRIID should have had received copies of everything as a back stop to her program. But the Army was not aware of this program so her argument had been shot down.

And now she was starting from scratch trying to find a vaccine for the Pandora's Box she had opened. To make matters worse, all of her team had been killed in the original contamination and she alone remained of the science unit that had developed the virus.

That was part of the reason that Williams and his men were here, she knew. Despite the White House's immediate treatment of her, the people who really wielded the power had secured her release in mere minutes. She was the only one alive that had first-hand knowledge of the virus and how it had been created. She was literally the most important person in the world at the moment.

The world's most important person had allowed her mind to wander over all these things as she worked, and that turned out to be a mistake. John Doe had a metal crown on his very front tooth. Years of neglect and days of harsh treatment since his infection had left that crown with a sharp edge to it.

As Baxter prepared to take a sample from Doe's head, her left-hand glove caught on the razor-sharp metal, slicing her glove and her finger. As soon as she felt it Baxter froze, eyes wide in horror.

With her heartbeat slamming in her ears, she slowly lowered her gaze to her hand, hoping she would not see blood.

But she did. Her finger was bleeding. From a cut caused by a crown in the mouth of a dead infected.

She carefully placed her tools back on the table and moved to decontamination. She stripped the gloves off inside the chem shower that cleaned her suit, daring to hope that the combination of liquid nitrogen the head had been frozen in and the chemical bath would prevent her sickness. She grabbed a bandage from the first aid kit and quickly wrapped it around her finger, grasping the bandage in her hand and placing the hand in her lab coat pocket and out of sight.

Moving hurriedly, but trying to appear calm, Baxter kept her hand in her pocket as she walked briskly down the hallway to her suite. Once inside, she locked the door and leaned her forehead against the cold steel, trying to stop shaking.

She was violating protocol by leaving the lab and she knew it. Had there been a full staff on duty she would never have been allowed to leave the lab. The current crisis had robbed them of most of their staff, however, and working alone had become the norm rather than the exception. No one knew she had been exposed.

She managed to make it to her desk on shaky legs and sat down, her entire body trembling in fear. It had seemed so clinical just a short time ago to speak of casually infecting someone so that she could study the virus and try to find a treatment. She had never imagined that it would be her that was infected.

Of course, she might not be infected her mind reasoned. She had been handling a dead specimen, one that had been completely frozen for several hours. There was every reason to believe that she was safe. And she was due for a rest period.

Justifying her behavior with the knowledge that she was the only hope of finding a vaccine, let alone an actual treatment, Baxter decided she would not report her possible exposure. She was sure that if the virus began to manifest itself she would have ample time to isolate herself and prevent any damage.

In the meantime, she was very tired and a short rest would be good for her. She stood carefully and made her way to her bed, removing her lab coat and loosening her clothes. She would just lie down and rest for a short time. If she were infected, she would know it soon enough.

If needed, she would take immediate measures at that point, she promised herself. She would isolate herself and make sure that she didn't contaminate the lab. There was absolutely no point in exposing herself to the tender mercies of the infection protocol that she herself had written. One that required immediate isolation and containment of anyone who might have contacted contaminated blood or body fluids.

She was a special case, she assured herself. Not at all like the masses that were even now suffering from the hell she had allowed to be unleashed on the populace. She was different.

Having justified her behavior to herself, she allowed her eyes to close and sleep to claim her. Her last thought was that she would awaken later, all would be well, and this little mishap would simply be an unwritten footnote in the travesty that was the unnamed virus that was turning the world on its side.

CHAPTER THIRTEEN

-

Tammy was awake early the next morning, something she was getting more accustomed to. The first two days she had been here she had been on the verge of exhaustion. That, coupled with hard work and intense worry, had made her sleep later than normal while conversely not actually letting her get much rest.

Today seemed to be different. Not that she didn't have plenty to worry over with the world going to hell on a skateboard, her father missing, her home 'off the grid', at least for now, and with no way to know if her friends were still alive and safe. On top of that was the fact that she was essentially homeless except for Hiram and Helen who had literally taken her in as an act of kindness and that her friend was out there somewhere in all this craziness waiting to see if he turned up infected.

So, all in all, there was plenty for her to be worried over, yet not a single thing she could do about any of it. That realization had been rammed home by the news that Ringo might be infected. She was powerless to help him, but there were things she could do and should do. There were chores to be done here at what she had started calling Birdsong House, preparations to make in case this situation spiraled out of control even worse than it already was. She meant to survive, if it was possible. She owed her father that and her mother. She owed it to Ringo, too. He had helped her get this far, after all. She would like to believe that she would have made it anyway, but there was no way to know.

So, she owed it to him to live, to survive in this crazy world even if he couldn't. Even if her father and everyone she had known before was gone now. To just lie down and quit was a foreign thought to her to start with. She certainly wasn't going to quit now.

With that in mind she walked into the kitchen to start breakfast. She intended to start taking over most of the household chores from Helen, at least as far as the older woman would allow. Not to take over the house, but simply to be useful. To be productive. She might not be able to accomplish anything else, but she could at least take some of the burden off of her hosts.

It would also give her something to do besides wait for a call from her father or from Ringo, calls that might never come.

-

Hiram was sitting on his riverside bench looking at the water flow by him. His satellite phone was next to him and he would look down at it every now and then, wanting it to ring but dreading to hear it at the same time.

He shook his head again at the memory of how he had handled all of this. Mishandled might be a better word. He should never have mentioned any of this to Ringo. He had known the boy would be willing to try and do the mission. Why hadn't he just ignored it?

Maybe Helen was right. Maybe he just couldn't let go of the life he'd once led. He had thought he could when they had bought this place and settled here. He had retired after thirty years in the Army and its various incarnations of service. He had left without looking back, or at least he'd thought he had.

Over the years since his retirement he had consulted on certain issues a time or two but had balked at ever returning to the field. He wasn't exactly an old man but he knew that field work was properly a young man's province. He had been there and done that as the saying went, and his time had passed.

Yet here he sat, ten years down the road, watching his nation, hell, the whole world, fall apart right in front of him. A nation he had given far too many years of his life protecting from one threat or another. Years where he had missed birthdays, anniversaries, years that had cost Helen the chance to adopt a child because he was never around. He stood suddenly, his self-loathing reaching the point that he had to move and burn off some adrenaline. He wandered down the path he had laid for his visitors, hands stuffed in his pockets, head down. In his despair and self-condemnation, he left the satellite phone on the bench behind him.

So engrossed was he in retrospection that he didn't notice the lone figure moving out of the trees.

-

Helen descended the stairs of her home to the sound and smell of breakfast being prepared in her kitchen. She smiled softly to herself as she realized that Tammy was cooking this morning. Rather than jog her elbow, Helen turned to the left instead of the right and walked into the library where she went about dusting and straightening.

The presence of Tammy Gleason was a comfort to Helen. Not because she needed help, because she didn't. As she had told the younger woman, Helen and Hiram were in no stretch of the imagination old. They were older, yes, as both were in their fifties, but they were both fit and able. But their home had always lacked children and while Tammy was not in any way a child, she was young enough to be Helen's daughter had she had one.

She had taken to the younger woman at once, something she wasn't wont to do, if she was honest. Over the years she had become accustomed to people coming and going but rarely getting to know them very well. She and Hiram had few close friends and none of them were really nearby. They both had made acquaintances in the area since settling here ten years before, but neither of them were the kind of people who made real friends easily. They had moved about too many times and too often to allow them to make those kinds of friendships except in the rarest of cases. She sighed sadly at the thought of those few friends, people she would likely never see again, if this situation was a bad as Hiram believed it to be.

There was the chance, of course. At least one couple had made plans to come to Birdsong should an event like the current situation occur. That was assuming they could make it here, of course, and that they themselves were not infected. There was no way to know at this point.

Hiram had tried in vain to reach Charles and Amanda Reilly since this madness had started. Every contingency the two men had made to keep in contact had failed thus far. Perhaps the two of them would simply show up one day, but Helen admitted, if only to herself, that she doubted it. Charles was certainly capable of taking care of them and Amanda was in no way helpless, but it was a long way from their place in Huntsville, Alabama. It was perhaps a three to four-hour drive in normal times. But her current houseguest was here because she could not find a way across the river to get home. Charles and Amanda would certainly face similar challenges on their trek to Birdsong.

"Helen?" She heard Tammy call and shook away the

feelings that had begun to settle on her. Ever the hostess, Helen was smiling when she turned to face the younger woman.

"Breakfast is ready," Tammy smiled and Helen nodded.

"Thank you, dear," she smiled again. "I'll call Hiram." She started for the door but before she could get there both women heard a gunshot.

-

Ringo stormed into Birdsong house covered in blood and gore, eyes wild with rage. Moving through the vaguely familiar home he searched for a target. He found one.

"Ringo?" Tammy looked stunned at the sight of him. "Ringo, what's wrong?"

Rather than answer, Ringo fairly growled as he lunged toward her. The woman evaded him at the last second which only served to enrage him further. Screaming, the woman ran for the stairs, Ringo hot on her trail. She had made perhaps three steps before he grabbed her ankle, pulling her down.

Tammy flipped onto her back and used her free leg to kick Ringo in the face. He recoiled but did not let go, so she kicked him again, then a third time. Finally, she managed to hit him hard enough that he stumbled back slightly, nose broken and bleeding. Tammy was on her feet in an instant, taking the steps two at a time. Despite the pain of his injury Ringo was only steps behind.

He followed her down the hallway that looked strangely familiar to him and slammed into the door that she just managed to close in his face. Screaming in rage, he pounded on the door, then began kicking it. He kicked again and again until the wood began to splinter and he could see into the room.

The gun in her hand didn't register in his rage and fever-damaged mind as she backed away from the door, pleading.

"Ringo, please! You know me! You aren't like this! Stop!"

Ignoring her, he concentrated only on getting into the room. There was enough of the door damaged now that he could crawl through the hole and he did, ignoring the skin on his arm tearing as a shard of the broken door dug a deep channel through his skin. Blood dripping from this new wound, he was a terrifying sight as he straightened to his full height.

He charged across the room and suddenly felt a hammer hit his chest. . . . .

Ringo sat straight up in the bed still yelling. He yelled for several seconds until he realized that it had been a dream. He was bathed in sweat, hair matted to his head, the sheet beneath him and the pillow he had been using soaking wet.

"A nightmare," he breathed to himself, shaking his head slowly. He got to his feet shakily, evaluating himself. Was he infected? Did he have a fever? Was that what had caused his nightmare? Nightmare. He had woken up screaming. Had anyone heard? Galvanized by that thought, Ringo grabbed the pistol from beneath the sweat-soaked pillow and eased the curtain back, peering outside.

The rain had stopped, he noted, but he saw no one in view and no movement. He crossed to the door and removed the chair, unbolting the lock. He moved through the house from window to window, repeating his inspection. Nothing was visible around the house anywhere that he could see. Sighing in relief, Ringo allowed himself to relax, returning to the bedroom and securing the door once more. Stripping off his sweat-soaked clothes he entered the bathroom and checked the clothing he'd hung there the night before. Mostly dry. He took them down and crawled into the shower, turning the water on and allowing it to cascade over him.

The nightmare had seemed so real that he hadn't realized it wasn't even when he'd woke up. It had taken several seconds for it to register.

"I was tired," he told himself aloud, the sound of his own voice comforting in the silence. "That's all. I was tired and I'm probably half sick from being out in the rain. Just because that nightmare made me sweat is no sign I've actually got a fever. And even if I do, it doesn't mean I'm infected. I might be running a fever from being cold and wet for so long yesterday."

Once more he allowed the shower to warm him, standing beneath the water long after he had washed, waiting until the hot water began to taper off before shutting the shower off and stepping out. He toweled himself off and dressed in the nearly dry clothes from the day before. He used hand soap to wash the clothes he had slept in in the tub, wringing them out by hand and then hanging them in the shower to drip dry.

That done, he moved into the bedroom and stripped the damp sheets from the bed, tossing them into a corner. He looked through the drawers of the small chest in the bedroom and found another set of sheets. He quickly re-dressed the bed then took the damp sheets into the kitchen where he spread them across the chairs to dry. It was then that he noticed a small closet at the back of the kitchen. He hadn't seen it the day before, or at least if he had, he'd ignored it.

He opened the door to find a small washer and dryer. He stared for a minute before laughing out loud at the find.

"Always the hard way," he shook his head. He had just spent twenty minutes scrubbing his clothes by hand when there was a modern washing machine sitting right here. He went to get his clothes. Ten minutes later he was sitting in the kitchen naked as both of his remaining suits of clothes ran through the wash cycle. He was taking a chance he supposed, but it wasn't like he could just leave. He had to wait out the incubation period and see if he was infected or not.

He had found a thermometer in the bathroom and had it under his tongue as he sat at the table. When it beeped he removed it, looking at the readout with a combination of dread and hope.

99.9°

"Well, that's not too bad," he told himself, not sure if he should be worried or relieved. It was too soon to tell for sure.

Hunger began to make its presence known so he took an MRE from his pack and let it start heating. He really didn't feel like eating but his body needed food. As he waited for the heat tab to work, he thought again about the nightmare.

It had to be psychological. His worse fear had been to go back to Tammy and the others carrying the infection with him. Hiram and Helen had been too good to him in the short time he'd known them for him to risk them that way. He just couldn't take the chance. And he would never put Tammy at risk either.

He snorted to himself slightly at that admission. What was Tammy Gleason to him? He had elected on a whim to accept her offer because she had helped him out. He acknowledged he hadn't needed it, but she had still done it. That meant something to him, perhaps more so because it wasn't something that happened to him. It just didn't. People didn't help him. Didn't care whether he lived or died, usually. Yet she had. That made her special as far as he was concerned. People that were willing to help someone they didn't know were rare.

So, he had decided on a whim that he would make sure she got somewhere safe. When he had found out she was heading for her home that became his focus. To makes sure she got home. All he owned was in his duffle bag or his backpack so there was nothing keeping him in Memphis. He was free to go where he pleased at that point and helping her gave him something to focus on.

He had to admit that she had done very well. She might not have fared well with the three men he had killed defending her, but otherwise she had held it together in the face of ever-increasing danger and difficulty and Ringo admired her for that. He suddenly found himself hoping to meet her father one day. A man that could raise a daughter like that had to be okay. The thought made him think of his own parents. He had only a few shards of memory of them. Nothing he could really cling to just flashes here and there. He wondered what they had been like. Had they been like Hiram and Helen? Had his father been like Tammy's?

The smell of his meal getting warm drew him away from those thoughts as his stomach growled. He discovered he had an appetite now and dug into the meal with gusto.

-

Helen and Tammy ran outside at that sound of the gunshot, Tammy's hand going to her hip where her small pistol was riding in its concealed holster.

Both saw Hiram standing at the far side of the yard proper, near the tree line. His pistol was in his hand and there was a figure sprawled at his feet. Without thinking, Tammy scanned the area for any other intruders, but she saw nothing. Hiram looked up at Helen's call and waved to her that he was okay. Tammy and Helen walked slowly to him and Hiram met them several feet from the body.

"Mack Bodine," he told Helen softly. "Came at me out of the woods."

"Oh, no," Helen almost whispered back. Mack Bodine owned a boat repair and servicing business just two miles away from them down river. He and Hiram had spent many hours fishing the river together and solving the world's problems, at least to their satisfaction. They weren't exactly friends in the way Hiram figured such things, but he had liked Mack and enjoyed his company.

"I guess I need to go and check on Celia," Hiram almost sighed. Celia was Mack's wife.

"Was he infected?" Tammy asked, eyeing the body closely.

"I didn't ask," Hiram replied dryly. "Why?"

"I'm assuming he attacked you with that crowbar?" Tammy asked, pointing to the crowbar in question lying near Mack Bodine's body.

"Yes, using it like a club," Hiram nodded. "Why?"

"I haven't noticed any infected using tools before," Tammy shrugged. "just curious." Hiram stared at her for a moment as the gears in his mind shifted.

"Huh," he grunted at last, eyes showing thoughtfulness. "Hadn't considered that."

"Me either until right this minute," Tammy admitted. "But I've seen several infected up close and personal and none of them were using anything as a weapon." She looked at him steadily. "If they're starting to do that then we might have a bigger problem than we thought."

"How did he get in?" Helen asked, frowning suddenly. "He's inside the perimeter."

"I don't know," Hiram admitted. "I suppose he could have crawled over it. The fence is only four feet high in most places."

"I think we need to try and find out how he got in," Helen insisted. "If he opened a gate then that implies that he could think clearly enough to open the gate, not to mention that the gate is probably still open. It also may imply that the infected can remember things from their lives before they were infected."

"Good point," Hiram sighed. "I'll walk the fence and check it out."

"Not until you've had breakfast," Tammy almost ordered and Helen nodded, suppressing a smile. "And not alone, either," Tammy added. "This is a game changer, Hiram. We're going to have to be extra cautious from now on."

Hiram glared at the girl for even suggesting that he couldn't take care of himself, but Tammy had endured 'the Glare' before and stood her ground firmly. Hiram realized that she wasn't going to back down and finally conceded the point, much to Helen's silent delight.

"Fine, just don't start getting the idea you can tell me what to do," he said firmly. "I'm doing it because it's a good idea, that's all."

"Of course it's a good idea," Tammy replied smugly. "Now, breakfast is ready. After we eat I'll help you get rid of your friend and check the fence.

"He wasn't my friend," Hiram said without thinking. "I just knew him, that's all." Tammy almost stumbled at the words but managed to keep walking. Her father had used those same words more than once about people he would hear of being killed in action. "Guy I knew," would be all he'd say.

It seemed like some things were universal. Including how men who couldn't afford to be ruled by emotion dealt with the loss of 'people they knew'.

CHAPTER FOURTEEN

-

Ringo sat in the small living room of his refuge, reading. He had his ear buds draped across his ears listening to music but where he could still hear sounds around him as well. It was a poor way to relax, but it was all he had. He found himself wishing he could sleep since it would be a good way to pass the time.

Of course, if he was infected and the virus hit him while he was asleep then he wouldn't have the chance to call Hiram and let him know. He wondered if he should call before he went to sleep later, assuming he could sleep later, and tell Hiram he was going to sleep, just in case.

But then he'd have to call when he woke up too, wouldn't he? And if he started calling it would raise their hopes back at the house and he wasn't sure there was anything to be hopeful about. His temperature was 100.9 the last time he'd checked it, which had been about a half-hour before. He had found a half-bottle of Ibuprofen in the bathroom's medicine cabinet and taken three of the tablets. They were meant to be a fever reducer, after all, and he might have a fever because he'd been in the weather, right? A simple fever didn't mean anything.

He laid the book he was reading aside and rubbed his face with both hands. No matter what he did, he couldn't escape the simple fact that he was sitting here waiting to see if he was going to become like the three people he had killed the day before. Or was it the day before that? He frowned, trying to think back. How many days had it been? He had to wait three days, right? Had it already been two? If it had, then if he was still good tomorrow he could head home.

No, he was certain it had been yesterday morning early. He had gotten back to the Cat Barn before noon, and had napped until late afternoon when he had been. . .no, no that was wrong. He'd slept through the night, hadn't he? It had been raining when the thug had brought the woman into the barn for. . .well. So, this was Day

Two then.

But did the first day really count as Day One? Seventy-two hours didn't necessarily mean three sunrises, now did it? It meant seventy-two hours. It had been roughly nine in the morning when he might or might not have been exposed. So that meant he had to wait for three full days, seventy-two hours from then.

Okay so it was three sunrises, wasn't it? He had to wait three full days. So, about nine o'clock on the day afterward would be one day down on his countdown. That meant that when he woke up in the morning, it would be two full days. One day to go and he could head back.

Unless he woke up infected. But then if he woke up infected he wouldn't know it, would he? Or would he? Some of the behavior he had witnessed the day. . .no, two days ago, had been a little disturbing. He might end up being a raging lunatic that could remember everything but still couldn't control himself. Be aware of everything he was doing and still be powerless to stop it.

He stood suddenly, his thinking filling him with the desire to move and burn off some of the stress he was feeling. He walked around the small living room several times as he tried to focus himself. On a whim, he dropped to the floor and began doing push-ups. He did so many that he lost count. It no longer mattered how many he'd done, he just kept going, pushing himself until his arms refused to lift him from the floor again.

He turned to his back and hooked his feet beneath the couch and started doing sit-ups. He didn't take a break, just launched right into the sit-ups. He worked until he couldn't and then still did crunches until his abs flatly refused to continue. He lay back, looking at the ceiling and waiting for his breathing to settle. When it did, he rose from the floor and went to take a shower. He was obsessed lately with being clean, it seemed. He hoped that wasn't some kind of sign, at least not a bad one. He could do with a good sign right now.

He was in the shower when he felt a tickle in his nose. Raising a hand to wipe it away, he was shocked to see the hand come down bloody. The shower washed it away almost immediately but he had seen it. He turned immediately and got out, looking at himself in the partially steamed over mirror.

His nose was bleeding. The left nostril.

Panic seized him for just a second, but he managed to get it under control. He pinched his nose together, tilting his head forward. Why was his nose bleeding? Was that one of the signs? He couldn't remember. Oh, God, I can't remember!

He forced himself to stay still for a slow count to one hundred. Once he reached the end he released his nose and looked up at the mirror.

Nothing. No more blood. It had stopped. Would it have stopped if he were infected? Why hadn't he asked that? Maybe Hiram didn't know anyway. He started to call and ask, but then thought better of it. He would have to tell Hiram why he was asking. Admit that he was bleeding.

He thought about the three Ibuprofen. Would that make his nose bleed? Did it work like Aspirin and thin the blood? He didn't know that, either. Why hadn't he bothered to learn things like that? Why didn't he know the things he needed to know?

How the hell was I supposed to know I'd need that? he asked himself silently. How does one train himself for the end of the world?

He took three deep, calming breaths, and then stepped back into the shower. He hadn't cut the water off and it was lukewarm at best now, the small hot water heater exhausted for the moment. He washed off in the rapidly cooling water and shut it off, getting out again.

Once he was dry and dressed with his freshly clean clothes he sat down to consider his options. His spontaneous burst of exercise had left him tired enough he could sleep he thought. Maybe he should call Hiram anyway, just in case. What if he didn't wake up? Or what if he did, but wasn't himself anymore. Would Hiram come looking for him? No, Hiram was smarter than that. He wouldn't leave Helen and Tammy alone to try and find someone who might be infected.

Or would he, if he blamed himself? Ringo was surprised his head hadn't exploded it was going so fast. He dug into his bag and withdrew the satellite phone. He stared at it for a long time before suddenly punching the number into it.

Hiram deserved to know.

The phone rang…and rang…and rang some more. But Hiram didn't answer. Ringo allowed the phone to ring until it simply stopped ringing. He lowered the phone slowly, wondering why Hiram wasn't answering. Was something wrong? Had something happened at the house? Was he just away from the phone?

He had told Hiram he wouldn't call unless he knew he was infected or when he knew he wasn't and was headed in. Maybe Hiram wasn't expecting a call this soon. Maybe he was asleep. Maybe, maybe, maybe.

He shut the phone off and lay back on the bed, mind swirling with what might be. He closed his eyes, both hoping for and dreading sleep.

No more nightmares, he pleaded silently. Just let me sleep. He slept.

-

Hiram led the way as he and Tammy walked the fence around Birdsong Bed and Breakfast. Helen was on the porch with a two-way radio, the mate to it in Tammy's hand. Hiram was carrying a rifle in his hands now, one Tammy recognized as an M-4. She had a sneaking suspicion that this rifle was not the civilian model, but she didn't ask.

Hiram was quiet as they made their way toward the gate in question. Tammy kept her head on a swivel, reasoning that if one infected, or not, could get inside the fence and attack then so could two or ten for that matter.

Hiram stopped in front of her, hand raised, and Tammy froze. His hand slowly came to a point and she followed it to see the gate.

It was standing open.

"Dammit," Hiram cursed softly. "Did he manage to open that gate infected? Or was he still sane and attacked me anyway?" Tammy had no answer for that and didn't think Hiram was really expecting one. She watched as he reached into a pocket and pulled out a padlock. She followed as he continued to the gate and stood guard as he pulled it closed and locked it.

"That might keep it from happening again," he told her and she nodded. The two of them walked the rest of the way in silence, Hiram stopping at each gate to secure it with a padlock. They made the entire circuit, ending up once more at the front porch.

"Well?" Helen asked.

"Gate was open," Hiram pointed toward the offending gate. "He had to have opened it. If he was infected and managed to open that gate, and was using the crowbar as a weapon, then you're right," he looked at Tammy. "We may have a bigger problem than we thought."

"Let's don't borrow trouble," Helen advised. "We still need to get rid of Mack's body," she reminded him.

"I know," Hiram nodded. "I'll take care of it."

"I'll help," Tammy said at once, but Hiram was shaking his head.

"No. I'll get it. He might have been infected. If he was, then we want the least exposure possible."

"What are you going to do?" Helen asked.

"I'm going to use the forks on the tractor to carry him down the road to the dumpster, drop him inside and then burn him. The dumpster will make sure the fire doesn't get out and the fire should make sure that any trace of the virus, if he had it, is gone."

"Hiram, that's almost two miles," Helen pointed out, and he nodded.

"I wish it were ten," he replied. "But it is what it is." With that he went inside to gather what he needed before starting out. Helen looked at Tammy, her face stony.

"I need to go with him," she said evenly.

"I can go," Tammy told her. "I'll follow in my car. If anything happens he can abandon the tractor and we can come running back here."

Helen considered that for a moment before nodding her reluctant agreement.

"Take the radio," she ordered. "Call me when you're almost back and I can have the gate open. The less time we're exposed, the better."

"Amen to that," Tammy breathed. The statement made her wonder how exposed Ringo was at the moment.

"Leave that for later," Helen ordered her, knowing the look. "Worry about him when you're safe again. That's what he would want. What he would expect." Tammy nodded, knowing the truth when she heard it. She made sure she had her pistol and knife secured on her belt and thought about getting her bat but decided against it. If she were attacked, she'd be shooting. Her father had made sure she knew how to handle most any kind of firearms she might come into contact with, including some that she probably shouldn't be able to come into contact with. Reese Gleason was a careful man.

Hiram came around the side of the house on his small tractor a few minutes later, a set of forks that were probably originally meant for hay attached to the front. He slowed at the steps, idling the tractor down to be heard.

"I'll be back as soon as I can," he told them. There was a small gas can beside the seat.

"I'll be following you," Tammy told him. "If something happens we'll use the car and run back here. We can try to get the tractor later if we can."

He looked as if he was about to object but the two women had what he called 'the Look', which meant they had already made up their minds and that meant he had too. He was accustomed to seeing that look from Helen now and then, but he hadn't realized that Tammy had it too.

No wonder they get along so well, he snorted mentally. He nodded his acquiescence and started the tractor moving again. Tammy got her car and prepared to follow while Helen stood on the porch with the remote for the driveway gate.

Hiram lifted the body of his former neighbor off the ground, managing to center the weight in one try. With a gentle wave to his wife, he started down the drive. At the road, he turned left and increased his speed, wanting to get this over with. Tammy followed a few spaces back, eyes constantly scanning for threats.

Behind them Helen secured the gate, worry in her eyes as she watched them depart. She glanced at the shotgun leaning against the porch post near her side. Out of sight of casual onlookers or passersby, it was still ready for instant use and Helen knew how to use it. They had thought they were safe here from the madness. Ringo had pointed out that might not be the case, saying that 'as the crow flies' they weren't all that far from the bridge. But Helen hadn't given that statement much thought and she didn't think Hiram or Tammy had either. Ringo had the kind of mind that was needed in a crisis like this.

If he still has his mind she thought wryly, a pang of sadness hitting her at the thought of Ringo being infected. He was a genuinely good young man or she was badly fooled. And fooling her was hard to do. He had helped Tammy when most men, especially at his age, would have, at the very least, made some kind of unsavory demand on her for that assistance. He had defended her against an attack by men who were even worse than that and Helen was thankful that Ringo had been there. Helen had taken an instant liking to the younger woman, seeing in Tammy something of herself at that age. The idea of her suffering like that was heart-wrenching.

She offered a silent prayer for Ringo as she stood on the porch waiting for her husband and houseguest to return. It was a prayer for his well-being, his safety, and his safe return. It was all she could do at the moment.

-

Hiram pushed his tractor throttle to the stops, moving down the road as quickly as the small tractor would go. It seemed faster than it was. Tammy was looking at her speedometer as she trailed him and it was resting at 20 mph. She sighed in frustration at how long it was taking.

In reality, it hadn't been that long. In less than fifteen minutes from when Hiram had used the forks to lift Mack Bodine's body from the ground, he was tilting the forks to drop his neighbor's body into a dumpster as Tammy stood lookout for him. Backing away as the body fell inside, Hiram positioned the tractor where he could see into the dumpster and upended the gas can inside it, saturating the body of his one-time fishing buddy. The guy he knew.

Just a guy I knew. That's all.

Once he was done Hiram moved away from the dumpster and dismounted the tractor, leaving it idling. He motioned for Tammy to retreat and she obeyed. Hiram took a road flare from the tractor and lit it, allowing it to spark fully into life before tossing it toward the dumpster.

He hadn't used much gas, less than a quart by his estimation. The fumes had already formed an invisible cloud around the dumpster and they ignited before the tossed flare even reached the trash bin. A loud whump that seemed to shake the ground was followed by a flash of fire. By the time Tammy had looked back toward the dumpster flames were licking at the sky from within. She looked at Hiram but the man was stoic as he watched.

They stood there for perhaps two full minutes watching the flames before Hiram turned back to the tractor.

"It ain't goin' nowhere," he told her, climbing back into the seat. "Let's get home. We're too exposed out here like this. Even if it gets out, rain soaked everything. It's fine." Tammy nodded and got back into her car, turning around in the road as Hiram moved away toward home. She caught up easily and resumed her post behind him. As they neared the house she called Helen to tell her they were almost to the gate. There was no reply, but Tammy could see the gate opening as Hiram approached it. Soon they were both back through the gate and it was closing behind them.

As she parked her car, she noted Helen on the porch with the shotgun, a grim look on her normally cheerful and pleasant face. Tammy was sure the look on her own face matched it. She had allowed herself to believe she was safe here. And she might be.

Then again, Mack Bodine had opened that gate. As she got out of her car she looked southeast, the direction Ringo had gone. She wished he were here. She trusted Hiram but Ringo was a known quantity. She knew for a fact that he was more than capable of making a difference.

If he wasn't infected himself, that is. That thought brought her crashing back to reality. There was a lot to do today, considering what they had learned. Might have learned, she corrected herself. She could think about Ringo later once she had helped make sure that Birdsong Bed and Breakfast was really secure.

-

Hiram was reclining on the front porch when he realized something was wrong. Something was missing...

"Where the hell is my phone?" he asked aloud, looking around the porch as he patted down his pockets. Nothing. He walked inside, checking the vestibule and then the counter in the kitchen. Still nothing.

"What is it, dear?" Helen asked from the table where she was cutting potatoes for supper.

"I can't find my satellite phone," he replied, still absently patting his pockets even though he'd already checked them.

"Where did you last have it?" Helen asked.

"You can use mine," Tammy offered at almost the same instant.

"Ringo won't have the number for yours," Hiram shook his head. "And I've had it with me all the time since he left. I must have dropped it when we carried the body off," he all but groaned. There was no telling where the phone was or if it was undamaged.

"I don't think so," Tammy shook her head. "I was watching pretty close, Hiram, and I didn't see anything going or coming. Are you sure you had it with you when we left?"

"Of course I. . ." he stopped.

"The bench," he almost breathed the words. "I left it on the bench where I was sitting this morning. I forgot it after Mac. . .after this morning," he corrected himself. He walked away headed for the bench. Tammy and Helen followed after to help look in case the phone wasn't there.

It was there. Blinking.

"Shit," Hiram muttered, his step increasing slightly. "Shit, shit, SHIT!"

"Hiram," Helen chided gently.

"I left the son-of-a-bitch and Ringo tried to call!" Hiram almost yelled but caught himself. He held the phone up so the other two could see the screen. "Dammit!" He punched a series of numbers, calling the teen back. Ringo might be in trouble and he had forgotten the damn phone!

He listened as the phone rang and rang some more. It kept ringing until the service interrupted to tell him that the number he was attempting to call was not available at the moment and then disconnected.

"Not available?" Hiram looked at the phone incredulously. "What the hell do you mean not available! It's a damn sat phone! The whole point is that you're always available!"

"Hiram!" Helen's voice was stronger this time. "Control yourself. You aren't on a parade field." Hiram glared at her and for just an instant Tammy saw a glimpse of what Hiram must have been like when he was in the field. Just as quickly it was gone.

"Sorry," he muttered to both, looking back to the phone. "Dammit, he tried to call me and I left the damn phone sitting here!"

"You were attacked this morning," Tammy pointed out. "And we had to check the fence and dump the body. It's not like you were just ignoring him."

"You don't get it," Hiram managed not to snarl. "When

someone's in Indian country you do not leave them hanging. There is always someone for them to contact, even if there's nothing that can be done to help them. I left Ringo hanging." He spat the last four words out as if they were a foul taste in his mouth.

"He could have been calling to say he was in trouble, to warn us of trouble coming our way, or to tell us. . . ." He trailed off.

"Tell us he's infected," Tammy finished for him evenly. "We get it, Hiram. It's not your fault."

"It's all my fault!" Hiram shot back and again made a visible effort to get control of himself. "I'm the one who sent him out there! He wouldn't even be in this predicament if it wasn't for me and now I've just left him hanging when he may have really needed to talk to me!" He almost threw the now hated phone into the river but caught himself just in time. Replacing it now would be a cast iron bitch.

"Hiram, calm down," Helen ordered briskly. "He will call again and this time you'll have the phone with you. Until then that is enough of this nonsense." Tammy watched how Helen handled the situation, wondering if she would someday have to do the same thing for Ringo. As soon as the thought hit her, it jarred her to the core.

Why would she have to 'handle' Ringo? She wasn't his wife, or even his girlfriend. She didn't need to know how to deal with this. Did she?

"Now, I have work to do," Helen was saying. "And so do you two. I suggest you be about it." With that she turned and started back to the house, her back straight.

"Well, she told you," Tammy said smugly, trying to get Hiram to think about something else. She needed to think about something else too.

"I think that should be she told 'us', young lady," Hiram snorted, eyebrows raised. "She's right. We do have work to do." He pocketed the phone, determined not to let it out of arm's reach again. Not until Ringo was back.

"He'll be okay, Hiram," Tammy said softly, wondering all the time if she was reassuring him or herself.

"I'm sure he will," Hiram nodded, wondering the same thing. The two of them followed Helen back to the house in silence after that. There really wasn't anything else to say, anyway.

CHAPTER FIFTEEN

-

Supper was a subdued affair at Birdsong House. Tammy and Helen had set a good table and the three of them had eaten hardy, but had done so in silence. Afterward Tammy washed up as Helen cleared the table and put away the leftovers. Just as they were finishing up the lights began to flicker. Helen stopped for a moment, almost as if considering something. Suddenly she walked straight to the back door and opened a utility door in the wall that Tammy hadn't even realized was there. Without a word of warning she flipped a series of breakers in the box and the house went dark.

"The power is going," she told Tammy calmly. "We have solar power to back up the meter but it won't pull everything in the house. We'll have to prioritize from now on." She opened a drawer near the sink and removed a flashlight. The beam cut across the darkened kitchen.

"Hold this for me," Helen told the younger woman, and Tammy took the light. Helen returned to the drawer and removed three candles and a lighter. She set one on the bar, one on the counter and the third on the table, lighting each one as she went. She reached out to take the light then.

"I'll go and make sure Hiram is okay," she smiled. "He's afraid of the dark, you know," she added and Tammy had to laugh in spite of herself. Chuckling softly Helen went in search of her husband, leaving Tammy in the candlelit kitchen.

She had never imagined the power going out and now that it had she couldn't understand why it hadn't occurred to her. Power had to be generated somewhere and that meant people had to be on the job to make that happen. If too many were sick then there would be no power generated.

Hence no electricity. She shook her head at her naiveté. She was smarter than this. She'd been taught better, too. Military bases were targets in peacetime as well as wartime and her father had taught her how things could happen and what to expect.

She blamed her absentmindedness on the loss of her home, the traumatic experience of her trip after leaving Memphis, including her near victimization at the hands of three thugs, the brief call from her father that had sounded like the last time she would ever hear his voice, the list went on and on.

Added to all of that was the fact that Ringo, someone she was really starting to care for, was out in the mess the world had become sweating out whether or not he was infected. He was probably no more than ten miles away but he might as well be on the moon for all the help she could offer him.

Tammy Gleason was not accustomed to being helpless. She was strong, intelligent, and, as Hiram had pointed out, she was the daughter of a warrior. She was not a silly 'Deb', as Ringo had said, prone to flights of hysteria and panic.

"So, it's time to start acting like it, Tammy," she murmured to herself. She stood suddenly and took the small, but powerful, flashlight from a pouch on her belt. It was a small kit of things she might need in an emergency including a multi-tool, lock blade knife and this tiny AAA flashlight. No bigger than a pen, it produced a wonderfully bright light in the now darkened house. Using the light, she made her way to the library.

It was time to start studying up on what she needed to know if she was going to keep on surviving in this new world and Hiram was bound to have some books she could use to prepare herself better. She ignored the sound of voices from the porch where Helen had found Hiram. The latter had apparently lit a lantern as one was burning on the table. She could hear them talking but not enough to make out what was being said. And it wasn't her business. She had work to do, anyway.

-

"I can crank the genny if you want," Hiram said softly, looking out into the dark. While they were isolated here there were always lights visible in the distance, more so in the fall and winter when the leaves were off. There were no lights at the moment. He had observed the same flickering from them that Helen had noted in the kitchen before they had gone out and not come back on.

"We don't need it and we may need the fuel worse later," Helen replied, laying a hand gently on her husband's arm. "Hiram, I know you're worried, but remember this. If he is infected, there's no help for him and so there's no point in worrying about it. If he isn't then he is wonderfully capable, as you yourself have noted. He can take care of himself. I seem to recall that when you were his age you were sneaking into North Korea to play. . .'tag' I think you called it." Hiram's head snapped around at that.

"Who told you that?!" he demanded. "That's Top Secret!"

"Nothing is over the clearance level of an Army wife, Colonel Hiram Tompkins. You should know that by now." Helen managed to keep any trace of smugness from her face as she spoke. Hiram stared at her for almost a full minute during which Helen calmly met his gaze. Finally, he turned and looked back out at the river. Or toward it since it was stone black dark.

"Whoever told you that should be tried for treason," he muttered, and Helen actually laughed at that which only seemed to make Hiram more determined.

"They should!" he insisted. "That's the kind of thing that can start a war, right there!" Even as he said it, she saw the light dawn in his eyes. He shook his head finally, laughing at himself. The world was burning up with fever and he was still worried that something he had done nearly three decades ago was going to start an incident. He really needed to reassess.

"That's more like it," Helen encouraged. She knew that her husband felt responsible for Ringo and his current predicament, but there really wasn't anything he could do and it was time for him to accept that. There was too much happening for him to be distracted.

"You may want to move any keepsakes and mementos, pictures and the like, to the bunker tomorrow," his voice broke into her thoughts. "just in case."

"You think it will come to that?"

"No idea," he admitted with a shrug. "But if it does then you may not have time to gather them up. It's just a precaution. That's all."

"All right," Helen nodded, sobered by the thought. They had made similar moves in the past, but very rarely. Each had been a false alarm, but sometimes it had been close.

"Don't fret too much," Hiram told her, leaning back. "We're isolated, we're well-provisioned and we're well-armed. There's not much reason for anyone to be out this way unless it's fishing and if they're fishing they shouldn't be a problem for us. Shouldn't be," he stressed. "If they are, we'll deal with it. The bunker is just in case, like it always has been."

Helen nodded again but remained silent. She heard something behind her and turned to see a light in the library. She excused herself and got up from the table, going inside to check on Tammy. She found the younger woman looking through the titles on the shelves.

"Are you looking for anything in particular?" Helen asked, moving to Tammy's side.

"No, ma'am," Tammy shook her head. "I just realized that I've been living with my head somewhere dark and smelly the last three or four days and it's time to take it out," she grinned, and Helen laughed.

"I think that's the nicest way I've ever heard that phrased," she admitted.

"Learned if from Lucinda," Tammy smiled at the memory. "Anyway, I just thought I'd see what there was in here for me to read up on. This looks like it could be long term if not permanent and I'm not sure I know enough to keep up or be useful. So, it's time to change that." Helen heard the steel in Tammy's voice and almost smiled. This young woman was made of stern stuff. She would do.

"Well, let's start with these," Helen led here to a collection of books on the lower shelves behind her desk. "These are rather old I admit, but the information in there is priceless if you need it and don't have it. They aren't exactly a How To series, but rather stories and anthologies of people who lived through what we call 'old times' nowadays. Many of them tell how they lived without electricity or modern conveniences, how they cured this or that, and how they made things they needed. There aren't always detailed instructions but it's still a good place to start." She paused, looking at Tammy closely.

"If this is as bad as it looks, Tammy, then we may be looking at a return to that kind of living. Knowing how things were done way back when is a good place to start in preparing yourself for that eventuality."

"Where would you start?" Tammy asked.

"Why, at the beginning dear. That's always the best place." She took the first volume and handed it over.

"Enjoy."

Ringo stirred slowly, fighting his way out of a deep sleep as his bladder insisted that he get up. He rose slowly since he was stiff and sore from his impromptu exercise session earlier. He stumbled into the bathroom to relieve his bladder, hitting the light switch as he went.

Nothing.

He flicked the switch again and then once more for good measure, though he wasn't sure what that would accomplish exactly. Shaking his head, he used his flashlight to take care of his business and then went to check the rest of the house. No power anywhere.

"Well, it was too good to last," he muttered, glad that he had washed his clothes earlier. No more hot showers either. He sighed mightily at that one having really enjoyed having that option. It was amazing how just two days in the 'wild' could sharpen your appreciation of modern appliances.

He made his way around the small house checking out the windows. It was dark outside, not a light in sight anywhere. So, the power's out all over, then, he thought to himself, figures.

Ringo had expected the power to go out, but had assumed it would be in another few days. So much for optimism. He made his way back to the bedroom and checked his temperature. 100.5°. He frowned.

That was lower than before. Wasn't it? He closed his eyes in resignation.

"Why in the hell didn't I think to write that down?" he asked the wall. Wall had no answer for him, of course. He quickly scratched out his temperature on the inside cover of his notebook. It had been. . . what? 100.9° before? Yeah, he was pretty sure that was right. So, his temperature was falling. That was definitely a good sign. At least he fervently hoped it was.

He shook two more Ibuprofen out of the bottle and swallowed them with a healthy drink of water. With nothing else to do and no way to do much in the dark, Ringo lay back on the bed and tried to get comfortable. His temperature was falling. He couldn't tell if he was sore or not from infection since he was sore from his calisthenics earlier. Still, he felt better than he had this time the day before. At least as far as he could remember he did, anyway.

His head didn't seem as off as before and he hadn't bled anymore, either.

Maybe I'm going to be okay, was his last thought before sleep claimed him again. He never once thought to check the sat phone.

CHAPTER SIXTEEN

-

Tammy woke early the next morning. She went through her new morning routine of workout then shower, (cold this morning thanks to the power being off) and then went to fix breakfast. Of course, there was no power. She looked around the kitchen for another means of cooking but found none. On a whim, she ventured to the garage where she found a Coleman stove, complete with a small oven rig for it. She carried her finds to the back porch then set about preparing for the morning meal.

She decided against eggs this morning since she didn't know where they could get more. She decided to keep things simple and fixed pancakes and bacon, using one-half of the griddle top for each. Before she was half finished Hiram and Helen were in the kitchen. Helen used a small propane 'eye' and an old-fashioned percolator to prepare coffee, Tammy watching her every move.

"Never used one of these before?" Helen asked with a smile.

"Never even seen one," Tammy admitted. "Whenever we camped we just used instant and boiled the water for it."

"Well, this is old-fashioned to say the least, but it's effective," the older woman assured her. "And Hiram isn't much use without coffee," she added, raising her voice just a bit so that he would hear.

"I heard that!" he called back. "I can function just fine without coffee, but it does help me deal with you, woman!" Helen chuckled at that and Tammy marveled silently once more at their obvious love and devotion for one another. It warmed her heart to see it and she again felt the spark of hope within her that one day, even in this new, ever so messed up world, she might have that.

She shook those thoughts away as the smell of an almost overdone pancake made its way to her nose. She quickly pulled the cake from the griddle and poured another, then did the same on the bacon side.

"You two should go ahead and eat while it's still hot," she told Helen. "I'm almost finished and when I am I'll join you."

"We'll eat out here, I think," Helen nodded and went inside, returning with plates and utensils. She set the table, then went back inside for glasses, water and juice.

"Might as well drink it as not," she said with a smile when Tammy looked at the orange juice. "It won't last forever. We do have some concentrated powder. Not as good as this," she nodded at the bottle, "but better than nothing." Tammy nodded her understanding. Things were changing. She had to learn to change with them.

Hiram walked out onto the porch, satellite phone firmly in hand. He sat down but waited for Helen before fixing his plate. Once the blessing was said Tammy quickly finished, shutting off the stove and joining the older couple at the table.

"We'll go through the house today and prioritize what we use power for," Helen told Tammy as they ate. "We can run various appliances during the day but not all at once. There are three inverters in the house attached to the battery bank. There is one in the kitchen, one in Hiram's radio room, and one upstairs. We can use them to keep various appliances charged and to run a few items that will make our new circumstances more bearable."

"There is a separate system for the garage if we need power there, but the two are isolated systems so we can't use that power here in the house without a good deal of trouble. Frankly it's not worth it." She didn't mention the bunker. Tammy wasn't aware of it as yet and the two hadn't discussed whether or when to tell her. Helen knew that Hiram had told Ringo but that had been a have-to case.

"What do you need me to do?" Tammy asked after washing down a bite of pancake with her OJ. She savored the taste, knowing she might not get anymore.

"For now, we need to just be thinking about what we need the most, long term," Helen said after a moment's thought. "There's always the possibility of resupply at some point, but we have to accept that what we have now might be all we ever have. We need to start thinking about conservation in everything. We can't afford to be wasteful."

"I didn't fix eggs this morning because I wasn't sure there

would be any way to get more," Tammy admitted.

"We can get eggs," Hiram told her. "There are several people around here that raised chickens and sold eggs. We usually bought from them rather than the store. There are also several orchards within reasonable walking distance; apple, pear, and peach trees for the most part, along with a few cherry trees and the like. The main thing we won't be able to get is citrus," he pointed to the orange juice glass. "That's always been a weakness for this area, but it is what it is."

"You could always use a greenhouse," Tammy mentioned. "That would allow you to grow oranges and lemons. It would be limited of course, but it should work."

"Something to think about," Hiram nodded. "I considered it once before, but it was more cost and trouble than it was worth with produce always available from the farmer's markets. Still, maybe using Plexiglas sheeting. . ." he trailed off, obviously considering what could be done.

"Anyway," Helen turned the discussion back to the present, "we can start today by listing the items that we need to be aware off. For instance, we have a good supply of rechargeable batteries. We need to make sure we don't overcharge them or allow them to develop 'memory' so that they won't acquire a full charge. There's also the handhelds, which are very important now since cell phones are probably a thing of the past."

"Power tools?" Tammy asked.

"That's in the garage," Hiram re-entered the conversation. "Batteries for those are already marked and were all charged when this started. They should be good for now."

"What about appliances?" Tammy asked. "Refrigerator, freezer, things like that?"

"We can run them a few hours a day," Helen said cautiously. "The freezer will be fine for several days so long as we don't fan the door. There are several blocks of ice in there to keep things cold without power for a few days. Eventually they'll melt without the freezer running. We'll have to work out a schedule for that. We'll probably eventually use the refrigerator as a chiller more than anything, to preserve left overs and things like that."

"Okay," Tammy nodded, trying to keep everything straight. "What about fuel?" she asked. "My car has almost three-quarters of a tank of gas. That's about. . .twelve gallons, I guess, give or take. Say ten to be safe. You can have that of course."

"Thank you," Helen smiled. "We have some reserves, but every little bit will help. I was about to say that we have a generator that can help with the freezer and refrigerator. It runs on propane and has its own tank, I think five hundred gallons. Or is it pounds?" Helen mused to herself. "Anyway, we can use it sparingly since we can't be sure that we can get more fuel so, again, think conservative."

"Cool," Tammy nodded.

"And that's another thing," Hiram sighed. "Conditioned air is a thing of the past I'm afraid. In the next few days we'll need to get the awnings up over the windows since they'll need to be raised most of the time other than winter."

"Awnings?" Tammy asked.

"Think of them as an umbrella for the windows," Helen told her. "Like the coverings at store entrances? They allow us to keep the windows up even when it's raining by preventing the rain from blowing into the house. A storm blowing through will air the house out quite efficiently," she grinned.

"I'd guess so," Tammy smiled at that. "Okay, it looks like today and tomorrow have a full schedule."

"Oh, we'll have a full schedule from now on, I'd say," Hiram snorted. "All those wonderful time-saving and work-saving gadgets we're so dependent on are pretty much history. Although," he mused, "I have a plan for a water wheel around here, somewhere. I'll see about that as soon as we're set everywhere else. That might provide a good bit of help to the solar panels. Use a car alternator or generator to charge some deep cycle batteries. The river current will move a good-sized wheel pretty good." He frowned.

"What is it?" Helen asked.

"It just occurred to me that we have no idea what TVA has done with the dams," Hiram admitted. "If they at least opened some of the flood gates then the water will keep flowing, at least some, but it won't be regulated. The lake level here may drop. That might prevent us from using the wheel, or even getting a boat into the water. Our boathouse may end up on dry lake bottom eventually," he told her.

"Well, that's nothing we can control and we have plenty to worry over as it is," Helen declared. "though I'd forgotten that we do have a lake full of fish to depend on to stretch our food stocks. We've already planted the garden and we can use the outdoor kitchen to prep and can the food."

"Outdoor kitchen?" Tammy asked.

"You haven't seen that, have you dear?" Helen almost murmured. "If we can talk Hiram into clearing the table I'll take you there now. Hiram?" It might sound like a question but Hiram obviously knew better.

"Of course, Mrs. Tompkins," Hiram nodded, rising from his chair. "Right away, Mrs. Tompkins."

"Whatever." Helen snorted in amusement and looked at Tammy. "Come along, dear."

"Of course, Mrs. Tompkins," Tammy grinned, getting to her feet. "Right away, Mrs. Tompkins."

"You are a horrible influence on young people, Hiram Tompkins," Helen gave her husband a mock glare.

-

"Wow," Tammy said softly as Helen opened the door to what Tammy had thought was a picnic pavilion. "This is pretty neat."

The interior had a concrete floor with a wooden half-wall. Screen material covered the rest of the wall with Plexiglas coverings on the outside to protect the screens and interior. There was a long bench down one side complete with a sink. Across from there sat a magnificent wood cook stove, its flue piped through the ceiling. Cast iron cookware hung from racks along the ceiling and down the one solid wall. Shelves with canning equipment, stock pots and boxes of jars, rings and lids for canning lined that wall as well.

"You could live in here!" Tammy exclaimed, laughing.

"Well, I wouldn't want to live here but it would make a decent emergency shelter," Helen chuckled. "Anyway, I use this for my canning. That," she pointed to the older model electric range, "probably won't be any good anymore but the Monarch," she pointed to the wood burning stove, "will still work just fine. So, when the garden starts coming in you and I will be in here putting up food for the winter."

"What about Ringo and Hiram?" Tammy asked, ignoring the fact that Ringo's future was still uncertain.

"We'll need them to do the heavy lifting and bring in the veggies from the garden," Helen smirked. "It's a fair division of labor, though," she added more seriously. "This is a hard, hot job to say the least. But at least in here we have plenty of room to prepare everything. And we should be able to spare enough power to run a fan plus we'll have the glass off to catch any breeze that happens through."

"Sounds like we'll be busy," Tammy was smiling. "But I have to warn you, I know nothing at all about canning."

"That's fine, dear," Helen assured her. "I have books that will prepare you and then I'll be able to give you plenty of hands-on experience. By the time we're done this fall you'll be an old hand at it."

"I'll be glad to learn," Tammy nodded. She looked at Helen then, growing serious.

"You know, there's no way I can thank you enough for all this, Helen. I mean, taking us in, teaching me how to survive like this. My dad taught me a great deal. I know how to shoot and to hunt. I can even skin game, though I don't like it. But I never had anyone to teach me things like this," she waved her hand to encompass the outdoor kitchen. "If not for you, I'd be. . .well, I'd be homeless," she finished, the idea settling on her truly for the first time. "All I still own is whatever is in my room or in my car," she said softly. "I don't have anywhere else to call home, now."

"My dear girl," Helen hugged the younger woman to her gently. "It's not all one way, you know. Without you and Ringo, we would be here all alone. We would be able to survive just fine on our own, but without anyone else it would be lonely, to say the least. It was our amazing good fortune to have two such fine young people come knocking on our door during the end of the world as we know it. You know that Hiram and I are only children, and our parents were only children as well. We've no close family left. Poor Ringo has no family any more either, as I understand it. Your father may still be alive and I hope and pray that he is, and maybe can even make his way here since he knows where you are, but do you have any other family outside the woman who cared for you when he was deployed?"

"No ma'am," Tammy shook her head. "I don't. It was just us."

"Well then, the four of us will be family to each other from now on," Helen said firmly. "And we'll take care of each other. How's that sound to you?" Tammy pulled out of Helen's hug to look at her.

"That sounds wonderful."

-

Ringo woke once more due to the pressure from his bladder. He could see light coming in around the curtains and guessed from that that it was daylight, at least. He made it to the restroom and relieved himself. He moved through the house as usual, checking outside all the windows. There was no sign of anyone being around, or having been for that matter. He checked his temperature. 99.0. He checked the time. Nine o'clock. Day Two, and no fever now.

No. Day Three. If he woke up tomorrow still himself then he was probably in the clear. That would be his seventy-two hours. He went to his pack and removed an MRE, activating the heating tab. Another roast beef meal he noted absently. Good. They weren't too bad. Made him think of the cat, oddly enough. He wondered how the cat was doing, then snorted mentally at himself.

"Cat's doing at least as well as I am," he said aloud. While he waited for the MRE to warm he got his tablet and thumbed it to a novel he had been reading. His reading material might have surprised some people, but this was simply a time passer. Something to do while he waited.

He fixed his meal and set down at the table, reading while he slowly ate. He found he couldn't really concentrate on the novel so much as his mind kept wandering. Wondering, really. Wondering what was going on in the world, wondering what was happening at Birdsong. . . .

Abruptly, Ringo set his spork down and went to retrieve the sat phone from his pack. He had tried to call yesterday and gotten no answer. He had slept soundly last night, no nightmares, no waking up drenched in sweat. He didn't have a headache today and was no longer lightheaded at times. He was starting to be more sure that his earlier problems had been related more to his being out in the weather than because he was infected.

He took the phone and went back to the table, dialing the

number for Hiram's phone. He heard it ring.

Please, pick up this time, he thought to himself. It wasn't that he still needed to talk to Hiram since things were looking better. But the fact that Hiram hadn't answered yesterday worried him. Had something happened to the others while he was away? Were they--?

"Ringo?" the voice caught him by surprise. "Ringo, is that you?" Hiram sounded anxious.

"Yeah, it's me, Hiram. I'm okay. How about you guys? Everything okay there?" Ringo asked.

"Yeah, kid, we're good," Hiram sounded relieved. "Had a little excitement yesterday but turned out to be nothin'. Sorry you called and I wasn't here to answer. I had set this damn thing down on a bench and then walked off and left it. I tried to call back but got the unavailable message. I was afraid something had happened to you."

"I turned it off to save the battery," Ringo explained, breathing a sigh of relief. "What kind of excitement?"

"Neighbor came calling," Hiram replied. "Reckon he got the fever from somewhere. Either that or he decided he didn't like me after all. Tell you the truth I couldn't tell for sure before I shot him. He was comin' at me with a crowbar."

"Damn," Ringo murmured. "I haven't seen. . .well, that's not true, exactly," he stopped himself.

"What?"

"Well, I saw some of the infected trying to do different things. Open car doors, things like that. I mean with keys... and one trying to open a trunk. One even trying to get a leg over, if you know what I mean," he laughed.

"Kid, that's a scene I really didn't need in my head," Hiram said after a minute, and Ringo could tell the older man was trying not to laugh.

"Hey, you should have to see it live and in person," Ringo snorted back. "Anyway, you can look at the vid if you want when I get back. I used that card for the CDC pickup and kept the camera. It's on the internal memory."

"Good deal," he could almost hear Hiram's nod. "Might be interesting to see at that. Tammy said she hadn't seen any of them using tools. This one also opened a gate on the far side of our property."

"I hadn't seen any of them doing that either until I got back to the bridge," Ringo told him. "I don't know if they're remembering or if they're re-learning. But I haven't seen any of them worrying about eating or drinking or anything else. I don't think they'll last long at that rate."

"That might be the best news we've had since this started," Hiram replied. "We lost power yesterday, by the way. Well, last night would be more accurate. No way to know but it's probably permanent."

"Yeah, I noticed," Ringo said. "None here either. I think I'm about eight miles from you at this point. Give or take a mile depending on the route."

"How are you doing, Ringo?" Hiram asked. "How are you feeling?"

"Well, I was a little worried yesterday, but I'm better today." Ringo explained about being out in the rain and how he was pretty sure that his problems had been caused by that rather than infection.

"I'm good this morning, to be honest," he told Hiram. "No more fever and I feel fine. No soreness other than normal from a pretty good workout. I. . .I think I'm okay, Hiram." It felt good to be able to say that.

"Thank God," Hiram breathed out. "That's the best news I've had so far. Kid I'm really sorry you had to call and get no answer. That wasn't right."

"Sounds like you had your hands full, man," Ringo told him. "It wasn't a big deal. I. . .honestly, I was calling to tell you about the nose bleed, just in case. . .well, in case I was losing it. I had told you I would and I was about to go to sleep so it just seemed like a good idea to call in case I couldn't later. I didn't really need anything. It's not a problem, Hiram. Don't worry about it."

"I appreciate that kid. All of it. What are you going to do?"

"Well, I guess I'm going to ride out one more day here to make sure and then start home. That's the plan, anyway."

"Sounds like you could come on in now if you wanted to," Hiram said evenly. "I'd say if you don't have a fever by now, you ain't gonna get one. But that's just me, now," he added.

"Nah, I've stuck it out this long, I'll wait the last day," Ringo told him. "No sense in taking chances. And I'm in a pretty good spot right now. I, uh, might have a little bit of a problem, though," he added.

"What kind of problem?" Hiram asked at once.

"Well. . . ." Ringo briefed Hiram in on the events at the Cat Barn.

"Tall woman? Beefy lookin', mouthy?" Hiram asked.

"Uh, yeah," Ringo replied.

"Yeah, she's the Court Clerk all right," Hiram almost chuckled. "Maybe we got lucky and she got. . .no, I'm not goin' there. Anyway, don't worry about it. There ain't much she can do and anyway it's her word against all of us, since you've been here the whole time waitin' to see what happens. Right?"

"Oh, yeah," Ringo stammered finally, taking a second or two to catch on. "Good thing I decided not to be out in this mess, huh?"

"Right," Hiram said firmly. "Since you didn't mention nothin' she can use don't let it bother ya. If anyone does come callin' about it, we'll just talk 'em out of it." Ringo noticed, not for the first time, that Hiram tended to pick up an accent when he was talking about things of this nature.

"Well, now that I know you guys are good, I'm going to get off here and save the battery. I'll call in the morning before I head in," he promised.

"Good deal, kid. Keep your powder dry, hear?"

"Will do." Ringo shut the phone off and then killed the power. He felt better now knowing that all was well with the others. He returned to his meal, now growing cool, and picked up his tablet again.

He was able to concentrate on it now.

-

Hiram set the phone down on the counter and almost whooped for joy but contented himself with just a firm 'Yes!' before heading outside to tell Helen and Tammy that he had some good news for a change.

News that was received joyously and tearfully by both women. It was a very good way to start the day.

CHAPTER SEVENTEEN

-

Chores seemed a bit easier after the good news that Ringo was okay and might in fact be completely okay and on his way home by the next day. Once Hiram was finished he decided to take advantage of a lull in activity to run an errand he'd been wanting to get done but had kept putting off. He found Tammy sitting on the front porch reading. She was almost half-way through the first Foxfire book.

"Wanna take a little trip?" he asked. She looked up at him, startled.

"Uh, sure. Where to?" she asked, rising.

"I want to go to where you and Ringo were attacked and get that truck if it's still there," Hiram admitted. Tammy frowned.

"You don't have to go if you don't want to," Hiram told her. "I know you might not want to be around there."

"Oh, I don't mind going," Tammy waved off his concern. "I was just wondering if it would still be there and if we can. . . ." She trailed off as Hiram held up the keys Ringo had given him.

"May be gone or vandalized by now," he admitted, "but Ringo locked it up and brought the keys. He said it was a nice club cab rig, four by four. Might be nice to have it if we need to go somewhere."

"It looked nearly new," Tammy nodded. "Let me get my bag." She went to get the carry bag she was using while Hiram went to tell Helen what they were doing.

"What do you want it for?" Helen asked.

"Just an asset," Hiram shrugged. "Might come in handy, especially if we need to make a run somewhere. Nice roomy rig with four-wheel drive and what not. No sense letting it go to waste. Or in using our own when we can use this one," he added. "If we ditch this one, or lose it or whatever, it's not like we lost ours, right?"

"Make sense," Helen agreed. "Tammy taking you?"

"Yeah. Figured she can drive me right to it. Be watchful. Shouldn't take us long. Twenty minutes or so at most, I figure."

"Be careful and don't let anything happen to her," Helen warned. Hiram nodded and met Tammy in the hallway.

"Ready," she nodded. The two got into her car and were soon on their way out. Tammy took them straight to it, surprising Hiram slightly that she could remember the twists and turns with so little effort considering what her mental state was when she arrived at his house that night.

The truck was still there, sitting on the side of the road right where it had been left. There was no sign that it had been tampered with or that anyone had even bothered to check on it. Not unusual considering, Hiram supposed. He got out and checked the truck over while Tammy stood watch. Climbing inside, Hiram put the key into the ignition and gave it a twist, the truck firing right up. Three quarters of a tank of gas he noted. Nice.

In less than a minute he was headed back to his house, Tammy right behind him. Twenty-two minutes after they had left the two were in the driveway at Birdsong B&B once more.

"Nice," Helen nodded, giving the truck the once over. Hiram rummaged around the glove box until he found the registration, but didn't recognize the name. He held the paper out to Helen who shook her head. She didn't know the name either.

"Well, I'd guess it's stolen," Hiram sighed, replacing the paperwork. "Happens the world manages to right itself, we'll see to it that it's reported." He still had a bag full of recovered valuables that Ringo had given him. Hopefully they would get the chance to return at least some of them to their rightful owners. In the meantime, the truck might come in handy.

"How likely do you think that is?" Tammy asked, and Hiram, lost in his thoughts, looked at her questioningly.

"That the world will right itself," Tammy clarified. Hiram nodded then, understanding.

"I really don't know, Tammy," he admitted, closing the truck door and stepping up on the porch. He took a seat and accepted a glass of water from Helen who had a pitcher and glasses on the table. Tammy accepted one as she took a seat.

"Things look a little bleak at the moment," Hiram went on. "Things like the power going off seem to indicate that this might be a long-term problem. It's possible it's just a line down or blown transformer, of course, and that it will be repaired, just slower than normal. That's best case."

"Worst case is that the NRC, Nuclear Regulatory Commission," he added for clarification, "has idled the nation's nuke plants. It's a sensible precaution, but also a pain in the ass. It cuts a lot of available power, especially after Dumbo the Clown has all but eliminated coal-fired steam plants. Now just the hydro-electric dams and whatever green systems are still working and that's probably not enough to keep power everywhere, so they'll prioritize. Rural areas like ours will be out of luck. Power will be shunted to wherever the most people still are and especially to critical infrastructure. Military bases, hospitals, refugee centers, shelters, that kind of thing."

"That doesn't seem fair," Tammy frowned.

"It's not about fair," Hiram shrugged. "It's about doing the most for the most people. Decisions have to be made about where to send what resources are available." He paused, taking a drink and weighing his words.

"This country is accustomed to plenty," he told her finally. "We're not used to need. Sure, we have people we consider 'needy', but compared to some places in the world, the poorest person in America is still better off. Hard to imagine I know, but I've seen it for myself. We really do live in the land of plenty. I won't say 'milk and honey' because I'm not sacrilegious, but we're in a good place. Or at least we were," he sighed again.

"Thing is, living in all that prosperity has made us soft. Each generation has had it easier than the last and that's led to a softness in this country that just fifty years ago was still only a crisis on the horizon. We've grown dependent on just a few hard men and women standing between us and the wolves at the door. There's nothing wrong with that except in times like these when people really need to be strong to survive and they aren't. If this is as bad as it seems to be, then a lot of people who survive the initial crisis will still perish in the crisis to come."

"What crisis to come?" Tammy asked. "I mean, if they find a way to beat this thing, that's it, right?"

"Is it?" Hiram asked. "I doubt it. How many people will die before this burns itself out? How many people will be left defenseless because they live in an area that restricts gun ownership for protection? How many will die for lack of clean water in cities where the utilities aren't working? For lack of medical treatment because the hospitals will have suffered the effects of this, this, whatever it is, first and without any warning or preparation?"

"Many of the people and services that we depend on in this nation will be gone, at least for some time. They may return as things get sorted out, assuming they do, but how many will suffer in the meantime? And that's not even considering people like the three goons who tried to attack you and Ringo," he nodded to the truck. "Don't think for a minute that those three were an aberration. There are predators all over the world held in check only by the threat of reprisal. With that threat gone or at least diminished, you can bet they'll be roaming the streets, or roads in our case, taking whatever they can get their hands on. Literally."

Tammy had paled slightly at the mention of the three hoods Ringo had killed protecting her. That won't happen again, she promised herself and her hand fell to her side where her pistol rested, as if to reassure her of that. Hiram noted the movement and nodded.

"That's right," he told her. "Keep that gun handy, and don't hesitate to use it when it's necessary. It may be what saves your life. I assume your father taught you to use it?"

"Yes," she nodded emphatically. "This and many others, in fact," she added. Hiram's eyebrows rose at that.

"Really? Like what, for instance?"

"Like that M4 you were carrying when we checked the fence, for one," she told him. "I've been hunting, using a bolt action Browning rifle which I wish I had with me, to be honest. A .270 with a Zeiss scope. I learned to use a shotgun as well. Come to think of it, I think I'd rather have it than the rifle," she mused. "A Mossberg 590 with extended tube, collapsible stock and ghost ring sights. I don't have an M4 but I had an AR platform from Bushmaster called a Carbon 15. Light, optics ready and very dependable."

"Yes, it is," Hiram nodded. "Not on the same level as some but still an excellent package if maintained properly. You know what the hardest part of using an AR platform is?"

"Finding reliable ammunition," Tammy replied. "AR rifles

tend to have a much closer tolerance than say a Mini-14 Ruger. They'll feed just about anything without much difficulty. My father has two. Had two, I guess," she frowned. "Whatever we owned may be completely gone, now." She looked a bit sad at that.

"Possible but not certain," Hiram noted. "I think we can outfit you just fine ourselves, though. How hard is the twelve gauge on you?"

"Not too bad," Tammy grinned slightly. "I'm a good-sized girl," she laughed.

"Well, what say we see what we can come up with then. After lunch, we'll run through a few things and see what you're comfortable with. I've put off setting out some backups too long anyway. We need a weapon in every room from now on, and spare ammunition too. We'll see to that after we eat."

"Sounds like a plan for the day."

"Well, that's two references to lunch in as many minutes," Helen chuckled. "I'm assuming that you're hungry, dear?"

"I could eat," Hiram admitted. "Wasn't a hint, really, but since you're offering. . . ."

"Yes, yes, I know," Helen got to her feet. "I think it's time you showed Tammy around," she gave him a pointed look. "I'll fix some lunch and ring you when it's ready."

"Are you sure?" Hiram asked and Tammy got the impression that there was more to that question than seeing if Helen needed help with the lunch.

"Oh, yes," Helen's voice was firm. "We're in this together. You may as well. . .'brief her in' I think is how you would say it."

"Okay," Hiram nodded, getting to his feet. "Tammy, come with me. The woman of the house has determined that you need to be brought up to speed."

"Uh, okay," Tammy rose as well, not sure what was going on.

"Come with me."

-

"Holy cow," Tammy breathed out, looking around her in amazement. "This is cool."

"Glad you like it," Hiram smirked as he watched Tammy take in the Bunker.

"I take it Ringo has already seen this?" Tammy asked.

"Yes, I brought him down here to get him outfitted. Had to place a lot of trust in him, and we're doing the same with you. But Helen's right. We're in this together, so it's time to let you in on what's available. I wasn't kidding about those three idiots not being the only people like that. We need to be prepared. One of the most common held misconceptions of city dwellers is that the countryside is full of food waiting for the taking. We can expect survivors to be out scouring the area for anything they can eat sooner or later."

"I'm not against helping those in need, but not at the risk of ourselves. Just not going to do it. And if you help someone today, they'll be back tomorrow and bring others with 'em. And they will have convinced themselves that because you have something they need, it's only 'right' that you let them have their 'fair share'."

"Fair share?" Tammy frowned. "But it's not theirs to start with. How do they rate a share?"

"Exactly," Hiram nodded. "They don't. I worked hard on all this, for everything I have. I won't see it taken from us or ruined by people who can't be bothered to plan for their own survival. I'm not talking about something like this," he waved his hand to encompass the bunker around them. "This was something I did partly because of who I am. Was," he corrected. "And partly because I know what the world is really like and how quickly things can go to hell in a bucket."

"My dad was like that," Tammy nodded. "Is like that," she corrected firmly. "Our house had food hid everywhere. Like that," she pointed to where cans of freeze-dried foods sat on a shelf. "He had MREs, of course, and others things like medical supplies, ammunition, things like that. If the house is still standing and hasn't been ransacked, it should still be there."

"I figured you'd seen something similar since you weren't bowled over by all this," Hiram grinned.

"Well, we don't have anything like this," Tammy shook her head. "hard to build something like this on an Army base. But yes, I've seen places like this. My dad believes in being prepared. He's like you in that he's seen bad things in other places. He never bought into the idea that 'it can't happen here'. He mentioned Sarajevo once as an example."

"And a good one," Hiram nodded. "Hosted the Olympic

Games once and now it's a war-torn piece of hell. And there's plenty more just like it. We may be on the way to becoming like that ourselves," he added. "The only consolation is that most everywhere else is going to be just as bad, looks like. If it were just us, then we could expect an invasion at some point. May still can in the future," he admitted. "But our first concern is to survive. To do that we have to protect what we have, and keep ourselves alive and from becoming victims." He led her to the 'armory' room.

"Oh, wow," Tammy repeated getting a look inside. "My father would have a field day in here," she laughed.

"Sounds like my kind of soldier," Hiram nodded.

"You two would get along famously I'm sure," Tammy agreed. Hiram picked up a rifle and tossed it to her, testing her reflexes. She caught the M4 deftly and worked the slide checking it for a load before putting the weapon on safety. She did it by reflex rather than conscious thought and Hiram nodded in satisfaction.

"Nice," he told her. "Let's take a look at what we need upstairs."

-

The three of them ate lunch and then spent the rest of the day making defensive preparations and plans. Weapons and ammunition were placed in each room and in the garage, out of sight but always within reach. Once that was finished Helen and Hiram sat down with Tammy and began explaining their contingency plans to her, altering them now to allow for her presence and that of Ringo when he returned.

Tammy was impressed by the depth of preparation the older couple had made. Far from just a general list, they had made as complete a plan as possible. While they had no plan for any specific problems other than natural or man-made disasters and attacks from without or within the nation, there were some very specific plans with reference to defending their home and themselves.

If that happened, this was the response. If it was this, there was a different response. If attackers reacted this way, they would respond that way. The list wasn't complicated but it was thorough. Tammy wasn't surprised by that considering Hiram's background.

They spent the rest of the day planning, with Tammy being quizzed on and off at times about what she'd learned so far. She took it just as seriously as they did, knowing what was at stake. As supper neared, it was Helen who put an end to it.

"I think that's enough for today," she declared, getting to her feet. "Tammy all of this is written out so that you can study it on your own. Learn it all, dear. Commit it to memory and always be alert, inside or outside. It might make the difference if we have a difficulty." With that she left to start their evening meal before the natural light was gone. It still took some getting used to not having electricity.

"I know it seems like a lot," Hiram told her. "But a failure to plan--"

"Is a plan to fail," Tammy finished, and Hiram started before laughing.

"I guess your dad taught you that," he said through his laughter.

"Among others," she nodded. "I get it. And I'll make sure I know it all as best I can, too. You can rely on me, Hiram. I promise."

"I already do, Tammy," he told her. "I already do. We'll make it. I don't know what shape the rest of the country will be in, or even our own little county, comes to that, but we'll make it so long as we work together and keep our heads."

Tammy went to sleep that night still thinking about all she had learned that day and about how glad she would be when Ringo showed up again.

-

Ringo lay down that evening almost too excited to sleep. He had made sure he was packed and ready other than just what he would need to get started in the morning. He had gone through another workout, exhausting himself so that he might be able to sleep despite his excitement. He really wanted to go home.

Home. He rolled that word around his head a few times. He didn't know exactly when he'd started to think of Birdsong as home. He hadn't really spent that much time at the place but there was just something about it that made him feel at home. He didn't understand it, but it wasn't a bad feeling and he rather liked it.

Tomorrow, assuming he woke up still him, he would start for Birdsong Bed and Breakfast as soon as there was sufficient light for him to do so. He had already mapped out a route and a contingency in his head, reluctant to put anything on paper or into the GPS in case he should lose it. No one had to teach him to be careful. He'd been that way all his life.

He went to sleep thinking about something other than an MRE or an energy bar for a meal. He'd be glad to get 'home' and have a good home-cooked meal.

CHAPTER EIGHTEEN

-

Ringo was up and awake long before daylight. He took a very quick, very cold shower and got dressed. He fixed an MRE for breakfast, hoping it was the last one he had to eat ever. It wasn't bad if you were hungry but it left a lot to be desired in the taste department.

He made sure the small house was clean and that the only dirty linen was the towel he had used and the sheet currently on the bed. At the last minute, he decided to leave a note explaining what he had been doing and that he had taken pains to leave the house as well as he had found it. He didn't bother with his name. It wouldn't mean anything to whoever found it, anyway.

By the time it was light out he was on the move, crossing the open areas carefully but wanting to be into the woods and the cover they afforded before the day was any brighter. Consulting his compass, Ringo struck out on the heading he needed, following a path he'd memorized over the last three days.

He was going home.

-

Hiram was awake early, as well, for an entirely different reason. He awoke suddenly, lying completely still as he listened. The house was quiet which was normal enough without electricity. The alarms were still working since the PV system was able to keep them running and it seemed a reasonable precaution considering the situation.

He got up, careful not to disturb Helen, and made his way to the bathroom. He dressed quickly and ventured downstairs, careful to avoid making any noise. Making rounds through the house he was satisfied that nothing was wrong, at least inside. That done he eased outside, standing on the back porch and just listening. Nothing seemed out of place, so he left the porch and began making his rounds, rifle in hand.

It usually took him twenty minutes to make a round of the

fence around their property. Ten acres wasn't that much land really, but there was a fence all the way around it and he walked that fence every morning. After his altercation with Bodine he made sure to check each and every gate as he went.

He took his time, stopping every so often to just listen. He finished his rounds only a little slower than normal, satisfied that the perimeter was secure. He eased onto the front porch and took a seat, rifle on the table in front of him. The fact that he hadn't found anything out of place didn't mean that everything was okay. Something was bothering him and that kind of feeling was something that he'd learned not to ignore.

The sat phone ringing startled him. He was glad Helen or Tammy wasn't there to see it. He answered it on the second ring.

"Ringo?"

"It's me," Ringo confirmed. "I'm on my way in. I'm already in the woods and making good time. I'm clean, looks like."

"Thank God," Hiram said reverently. "All the gates are locked around the property so give me a call when you get close and I'll come open one for you."

"Will do," Ringo's voice was confident. "I don't suppose you've heard from Baxter, have you?" he asked suddenly. "I'd like to know if this has been worth it."

"Haven't heard a word, but then I haven't made any attempt to contact them, either," Hiram admitted. "When you get in, we'll see what we can find out. That work?"

"Only after I've eaten something besides foil-wrapped cardboard," the teen said wryly and Hiram had to laugh at that.

"I did warn you," he reminded Ringo.

"So, you did, but tasting is definitely believing. I think I can be there before lunch, assuming that I can keep this pace and don't run into any trouble."

"We'll be waiting on you, kid," Hiram promised.

"See ya then," said Ringo and then hung up. Hiram placed the phone back onto the table, smiling despite his unease. There was something wrong, but he just couldn't put his finger on it. Not yet. At least it didn't seem like anything was wrong around the place.

He eased back in his chair, watching and waiting. Both required patience and Hiram had learned patience in spades over the years.

-

Tammy woke slower than normal for some reason, but soon she was up and moving. A brisk cold shower left her facing the day with wide eyes indeed. She heard Helen stirring as well and decided to head downstairs to get a head start on breakfast. As she came down the stairs into the foyer she could see Hiram sitting outside, just putting the satellite phone back on the table.

"Good news?" she asked, stepping outside. She wanted to know but was afraid of the answer.

"Ringo is on his way home," Hiram told her simply. "He's clear. Might be here by lunch if he's lucky."

"Yes!" Tammy shouted and then instantly covered her mouth. "Sorry," she said sheepishly.

"Completely understandable," Hiram smiled again. "We do need to keep noise down some but this is definitely a special occasion. He did mention he'd love to have something to eat besides an MRE," he added.

"I'll see to it," Tammy promised, still smiling. She made her way inside and started breakfast, whistling as she went. Helen found her a few minutes later and added her smile to the good news and her help to breakfast.

-

Ringo fought the urge to hurry. He wanted to be back as soon as he could. At least there he could have a bit of down time. The weight of thinking he might be infected was gone and he felt as if he could breathe again for the first time in he didn't know how long. He knew it had only been three days, four if you counted how long he'd been out, but the waiting had made it seem like a month or more. If felt good to be moving and it felt natural to want to move quickly but he couldn't rush.

He was still in what he considered enemy territory and it would be the height of irony to have waited out three days to see if he were infected only to fall victim to an attack on the way home. Odds were, he wouldn't encounter any infected in the woods, but who knew? And not all the danger was from infected. He'd learned that the hard way over the last several days.

He did make good time, though. Crossing fences and avoiding gullies cost him time, but he was taking as direct a route as possible to Birdsong. Thanks to the map and the GPS he could eliminate the need for most landmarks and he didn't need to follow the highway again since he wasn't looking for infected. In fact, he was actively trying to avoid them.

Even though he stayed alert, his mind was working as he moved. Had his efforts helped? Had Baxter made any progress at all? Perhaps they were already well on their way to finding a way to stop this virus. He knew things had gone too far for the world to go back to 'normal', but perhaps they could have some kind of new normal, at least. One where the terror of the last few days was just a bitter memory. He hoped they could salvage something, anyway. For him it didn't really matter since his life before all this started hadn't really been anything to celebrate. Not that his Uncle had mistreated him because he hadn't. But his mother's brother had never been a very emotional individual. He hadn't hesitated to take Ringo in and had never made the boy feel unwelcome, but the man hadn't been a nurturing soul. He simply hadn't known how to be.

Coupling that with the problems any small child would have after seeing his parents murdered in front of him didn't leave a lot of room for 'sunshine and puppies' as the saying went. Ringo had dealt with his problems internally, often suppressing his emotions in order to keep them at bay. His uncle had tried to get Ringo to take interest in a number of activities but to no avail. Until one day when he had taken Ringo with him to his dojo.

His uncle had been a martial arts instructor for most of his adult life. A competitor in several disciplines, he also had studied the sword. He had spent a year in Japan training with the katana and becoming efficient enough at it to earn the right to teach certain styles as an officially accredited instructor. Ringo had watched the classes that day that his normal babysitter had been ill and been mesmerized by the flashing steel and graceful movements of his uncle and the students alike.

His uncle had noted Ringo's interest and encouraged it, using the study to draw the boy out of his shell and into the open for the first time since the death of his parents. Ringo had been an apt pupil, devoted to being the absolute best no matter how hard he had to work.

His uncle had urged Ringo to compete in competitions, but that had never been his aim. His aim had been to become so dangerous that he would never again feel alone and afraid. That he would never again be a helpless victim, unable to defend himself or others he cared about. At nineteen, Ringo had been using a sword for almost fourteen years. He held belts in three separate disciplines and was proficient in two others.

He had been preparing to become an instructor at his uncle's academy when things had turned upside down. It hadn't been a dream or a goal, but it was a way to earn a living while continuing to hone skills that he had to admit had no real-world value.

Until now.

He had used his sword many times in the last week. He had never really expected that to be the case. He had begun his journey with a child's hope of one day turning his blade on the men who had killed his parents, but as he'd grown older he had come to realize the folly of that dream. He would never likely find the men responsible if the law had not. He was separated by time and distance from that night and that place, neither of which he could overcome. It was very difficult to hitchhike from Memphis to rural west Texas with a sword. That was asking a bit too much of the average traveler.

Ringo slowed as he came to a road ahead. He would have to cross it to continue on his way. He looked at his watch and was surprised to see that he had burned almost two hours thinking about his past. He shook his head, a bit startled that he had allowed his thinking to drift so far away from the present, again. That was a good way to become a victim.

He checked the GPS and was surprised to see that he was now less than two miles away from his destination. He could continue through the woods and be on Hiram and Helen's front porch in an hour, perhaps two at the most.

Excited, he put his map and the GPS away and slid down the slight rise to the side of the road, intent on crossing the narrow back road and returning to the cover of the woods as soon as possible. He never saw the infected man until the, now all too familiar, screech of rage startled him. Turning to his right he saw an older man in bib overalls stagger toward him.

Before Ringo could react the man suddenly stopped short, arm raised to attack though he was still several feet away. Ringo had drawn the pistol by now and had it ready, but for some reason he hesitated, watching the strange behavior.

The man looked confused, Ringo thought, a look he hadn't really noticed on the infected he had seen at the bridge or on the highway. He'd seen frustration, anger, and what passed for boredom, but not confusion. This was new.

The man took another step, this one halting. It was as if he was suddenly having trouble making his limbs obey. Ringo noticed the man's face was flushed and growing more red by the second. He watched in macabre amazement as the man gasped for air and then fell to his knees, one hand clawing at his chest with a partially closed fist.

Is he having a heart attack? Ringo wondered to himself. Stroke? Or maybe it's a progression of the virus? He finally thought to check around him for more danger but could see nothing anywhere around. Turning his attention back to the kneeling man, Ringo watched as the man's eyes bulged slightly. His mouth moved silently, reminding Ringo of a fish removed from water. And then he just fell flat, face first, onto the road and was still.

What the hell? Fascinated, Ringo waited for two full minutes for the man to get back up, but he lay still upon the road. No breathing, no movement of any kind.

This guy's dead! he thought to himself. He just died with me looking at him! Ringo eased forward, his fascination overriding his sense of danger. He prodded the body with a foot, pistol aimed right at the man's head. Nothing. He repeated the measure harder. Still nothing.

Ringo knelt beside the body and reached into the back pocket of the man's overalls where the bulge of a wallet could be seen. Removing the leather billfold, he pocketed it quickly. There would be ID inside. Hiram might know him and might know if he had a history of heart problems or something.

Still shaking his head at the scene he'd just watched play out in front of him, Ringo hit the woods again, taking a great deal more care than he had been before. There would be no more reminiscing as he made the rest of his trek home.

-

Hiram jumped slightly as the phone rang. He'd been expecting it but it still startled him.

"Ringo?"

"I'm at the gate I left through," Ringo's voice rang across the phone. "And I'd really like to come inside," he added, chuckling a bit.

"Be right there!" Hiram promised. He was already on his feet and moving. Rifle in hand he was off the porch before he thought to call out to Helen and Tammy.

"Ringo's here!" he tossed over his shoulder as he headed for the gate. He made record time crossing his property to where Ringo stood waiting.

"Damn it, boy, you're a sight for sore eyes, I tell you!" Hiram exclaimed, quickly opening the lock and allowing Ringo into the yard. He replaced the lock and then enveloped the younger man in a hug.

"It's damn good to see you, son," the older man told him, drawing back to take a good look at him. "You look fit."

"I'm good," Ringo smiled slightly. "I got something I want to show you," he said, holding out the wallet. Hiram took it, looking inside.

"Ben Wallace," Hiram said, a note of sadness in his voice. "Where did you get this?"

"Off his body," Ringo said flatly. "He was about to attack me when he just. . .stopped, Hiram. I think maybe he had a heart attack or something. I mean, I don't know just what that looks like, but he looked like he couldn't breathe and then he sorta grabbed at his chest like, and then he fell over. I mean that was it. Gone." Ringo snapped his fingers.

"He had a heart problem," Hiram nodded. "Maybe three, four years ago he had to have surgery for it. Poor old Ben. You say he was infected?"

"Yeah," Ringo nodded. "Sorry about him, Hiram."

"Is what it is," Hiram shrugged. "We knew him from church and from around the way. Not really friends but we knew him." Hiram sighed and put the wallet in his pocket. "Well, come on. I'd say Helen and Tammy have a feed waiting on you by now."

"That's the best news I've had in a while other than I'm not infected," a grin broke Ringo's face at that. "Lead on!"

Tammy and Helen were on the porch and Tammy ran to meet him, throwing her arms around him in a bone-crunching hug.

"Oh, I am so glad to see you," she told him. "Welcome

back!"

"Thanks," Ringo smiled, though he looked uncomfortable. Tammy noted that and stepped back a bit, but then leaned forward and kissed his cheek, surprising them both.

"C'mon!" she told him taking his hand. "We fixed you a good meal and it's waiting on the table. Hiram said you'd been eating those horrid MREs for all this time. That's too much for anyone to endure for long."

"You've had one then?" Ringo laughed.

"Soldier's daughter, remember?" Tammy said impishly. "I've had one. More than one since my dad always brought them along on camping trips. 'Saves time', he said." Ringo was happy to see that Tammy could mention her father without turning morose. That was a good sign. And Reese might be all right, after all.

"Do please lead me to this food," he settled for saying and allowed Tammy to pull him toward the house. Hiram watched closely at how Ringo fidgeted over the contact but smiled to himself at how well Ringo dealt with. He really was a good young man.

Helen embraced him as well once he was on the porch but more reservedly than Tammy had.

"We're so glad to see you home, Ringo," she said gently. The word 'home' hit Ringo by surprise, but he found himself liking it. He had felt comfortable here from the first and reminded himself that one of his initial thoughts was that had it not been for Tammy he would have jumped at the idea of staying with them.

"It's good to be home," he said, meaning every word and was rewarded with a warm smile from Helen. She was pleased to hear him say that.

"Come on then and get washed up," she told him. She, Tammy, and Hiram each helped him shed gear and equipment which was deposited in the hallway for later.

Five minutes later Ringo was eating heartily and telling the three of them what he'd seen and experienced while they shared their own story of the last few days. There was a lot to catch up on.

-

"So anyway, to say it's weird out is an understatement," Ringo finished. "It's really odd in places. There's almost no traffic right now and with the power off its creepy quiet. Which is kinda helpful, actually, because you can hear better."

"It is more peaceful," Hiram agreed with a nod. "Course once summer hits full on and we're missing the conditioned air we'll be singing a different tune, I imagine."

"Maybe the power will come back on by then," Tammy shrugged. "I mean if things aren't terribly bad anyway. Once things straighten out we might get at least some services restored."

"Might at that," Hiram said, more to keep from dashing Tammy's hopes than because he agreed. And she might be right.

"I think no matter what things are gonna be a lot different from now on," Ringo shrugged. "I wonder what Memphis is like right now," he mused.

"Radio is full of reports of one kind or another, but when you sift through them way too many are just 'I heard' stories," Hiram told them. "Not many operators in any major cities seem to be on the air at the moment. That might be because of the power," he shrugged. "Generators are loud and hard to use in smaller places and solar isn't always an option either for people in apartments and what not. Most commercial radio is off the air and there's been nothing on television since the power went off. The last reports were bleak to say the least," he admitted.

"What about Baxter?" Ringo asked. "Did you ever hear anything from her?"

"No, but like I said, since you're back we'll try and give her a call," Hiram said, getting to his feet. "No time like the present if you want to give it a try."

"I'd really like to know if she's managed to get anywhere," Ringo replied, getting up as well. Hiram looked at Tammy and Helen.

"You two want to come along? You can hear what she has to say. Just stay out of the camera. No sense in her seeing more than she already has." The two women exchanged glances and then nodded.

"If you talk to her, you might ask if she has any news about my dad's unit," Tammy said hopefully. "He said they were in Atlanta. Maybe they were nearby, I don't know."

"Won't hurt to ask," Hiram nodded. "She might well know at least some news. If she doesn't, maybe we can find someone who does."

The four of them made their way to Hiram's radio room in silence. There was hope for good news mingled with dread of bad news and no one wanted to speak about either. It was the work of just a few minutes for Hiram to get his gear connected and powered up. He placed the call over a video link, expressing surprise that line was still up.

"It's a dedicated line, but still it's a wonder it's working," he explained. Tammy nodded in understanding. Ringo didn't know the difference and didn't react. Hiram made a shooing motion to Helen and Tammy and both moved away from the camera, out of sight. The call ended without an answer and Hiram frowned at that.

"Might not be working as well as I thought," he murmured, placing the call again. This time someone responded and Hiram was shocked to see Williams looking at him out of his one good eye.

"And speak of the devil," the other man smiled grimly. "I sure wish you were here right now you old bastard," he said though there was no heat in the words.

"What's happening Willie?" Hiram asked, frowning. No way should he be answering this call.

"Hell done come to breakfast, Gob," Williams told him. "That stupid bitch Baxter got herself infected and went through half the staff before anyone realized it. Whole place is in an uproar. We're trying to save who and what we can but we're gonna have to abandon this place. Whatever you want, make it quick."

"I was just wanting to see if those samples did any good," Hiram managed to get out. "I can see that they likely didn't."

"Sorry, Colonel," Williams shook his head. "Most everything of that nature was lost when we lost the lower lab levels. Some data was saved but nothing hard. I'd have been reluctant to release anything out of here anyway. You know the protocol for something like this."

"I do. You got a back-up?" Hiram asked.

"An off-site just out of chopper range," Williams grimaced. "We're gonna get as close as we can and try to hump the rest of the way. It's almost to the Florida line. We may have some ground transport waiting but I can't count on it."

"You had any word from the Eighty-Second?" Hiram asked. "Friend of mine's father was with 'em. Haven't heard any news."

"I know they were here," Williams nodded. "Last I heard some of them were holed up in several buildings downtown but low on supplies. If we have the time we're gonna try and drop some stuff to 'em, but our priority has to be the squints. If we can hold out long enough to load a couple choppers with goods for 'em it might help. All we can do," he shrugged.

"If you can, outlast them, they're dying from medical problems," Ringo offered. Hiram looked a little annoyed but Williams perked up at that.

"You must be the kid she thought might be infected," he said and Ringo nodded. "Glad to see you made it, kid. If it wasn't for her being about the last person alive that might have stopped this thing I might o' killed her for suggesting we bring you in. Turns out I didn't have to. I'd say it serves her right, but like I said she was about the last brain we had that might have figured something out."

"Thanks for the info, Willie," Hiram said. "Watch your six," he added.

"Always do, Gob. Wherever you are, stay there. Ain't no place for old men like us to be." With that the signal was gone and the four of them were left looking at an empty monitor.

"Oh my God," Tammy spoke first. "There's nothing left?"

"Didn't sound like it," Hiram's voice was grim. He turned to Ringo.

"Nothing," the teenager said bitterly. "It was all for nothing."

"I'm sorry, kid," Hiram said gently. "More than once it was me."

"What are we going to do now?" Helen asked, ever the pragmatist. "I'm assuming that this back-up plan of theirs doesn't come with more doctors and researchers."

"No, it won't," Hiram sighed. "It'll be a fallback to store and preserve the data they have in case someone turns up who can use it. From what he said," he nodded to the screen, "they don't really have many left to do the work. And probably no one who can replace that bitch Baxter."

"Hiram," Helen scolded gently.

"She was," was all the defense Hiram offered. "Well, we are definitely in for it now."

"What are we going to do?" Tammy asked, still thinking

about the news of what was left of her father's unit. Maybe he was alive still, but if so, then he was trapped in a building in the middle of Atlanta.

"All that we can do," Hiram said turning to look at all three of them. "We survive."

The words sounded hollow even to him. But it was all he had to offer at the moment.

-

Even as Hiram spoke the world burned, sometimes literally with both fire and fever. The virus had been engineered to be spread quickly and the engineering had worked to perfection. Throughout the day the situation deteriorated, growing steadily worse until finally there simply wasn't anything left of society. In just a matter of days, less than two weeks total, the virus had swept around the world, taken by commercial airliners into the industrialized world where it spread quickly. Individual infected became groups of infected traveling with a herd-like mentality focused only on attacking anything within reach. In larger cities groups became crowds. In some areas crowds then became hordes.

The problem was that once you were bitten, that was it. There was no treatment and no cure of any kind. Again, the engineering used to construct the virus held, fighting off any and every attempt to counter it. There was simply nothing to be done with someone who was infected.

As realization of that spread, people began to take drastic measures. Anyone who exhibited any signs at all were shot out of hand. Anyone bitten wasn't even given a chance to say goodbye to loved ones before being shot in the head. These types of measures initially made matters worse as body fluids, brain matter and blood from those 'sanitized' were not treated as level four hazards. Believing that only a bite could infect them, it took an entire day for people to realize that they were exposing themselves to the virus even as they tried to prevent it from spreading.

To prevent more of that, those suspected of being infected were rounded up and trucked to isolated areas where pits had been scooped into the earth with bulldozers. The 'suspects' were unceremoniously forced into the holes and shot, the bodies then burned to ensure the virus was eliminated.

Once the trucks made that run once and returned empty, as

those 'suspected' of being infected decided they had nothing to lose and started fighting back. Until that moment many had believed the lie that they were simply being isolated as a precaution. Others were firmly convinced that a cure was imminent, awaiting only an effective method of distribution. All they had to do was 'hold on'.

As the truth began to sink in the last vestiges of order simply collapsed. Those who were trying to cooperate with the authorities ceased to do so, in many cases joining roving gangs of criminals who were taking advantage of the sudden absence of order and authority.

The last official estimate provided to the world governments were that fully eighty percent of the world's population was either infected or exposed. The last straw for those in positions of power was a frantic call from the CDC informing the White House that the virus had escaped quarantine inside the medical lab and that the majority of the staff were now infected or exposed. There would be no help from that quarter ever.

There was no last resort. No golden bullet or magic formula. There was no last-minute cure or vaccine, no heroic doctor working for days at a time to provide the answer at just the last second.

And so, the world as it was known ended not with a bang or a whimper or even a whisper, but in the blood curdling scream of those infected with a bio-engineered virus that induced a debilitating rage in anyone who came in contact with it.

Those in power always had a fallback position, and as the dark clouds of disaster rolled over them they scurried away like rats deserting a sinking ship. Unfortunately for many of them, several of their number had been exposed to the virus and hid that fact, carrying that sickness into the bunkers and retreats and hideaways of the world's most powerful rulers.

Some would survive, but many more would not. Those who did survive would find their power base eroded, their authority and the ability to enforce it gone. Anarchy in its truest form would rule the world for a long time to come.

The only good news was that the virus was as deadly as it was virulent. Ringo's observations had been right on the money. Those driven mad by it would ignore water and food; ignore injuries and illnesses, medicines and treatments. It would take some time, in many cases a long time, but eventually the infected began to die of dehydration, heart attack, stroke, high or low blood sugar, bleeding wounds that refused to clot, the list was as long as one's imagination. The infected may have conquered the earth, but they would not live to rule over it.

That would rest in the hands of those few who remained.

THE END

A MESSAGE FROM AUTHOR
N.C. REED

I hope you've enjoyed Tammy and Ringo. It was a challenge to write but it was also fun. It's always exciting to see something you've spent so long working on come to fruition

I wanted to say "Thank You" to my readers and express to you my appreciation for your patronage and your support, and most certainly for your kind words about my work. There has been many a late night when that encouragement was what kept me writing when I was ready to throw in the towel and give up.

If you enjoyed Tammy and Ringo or any of my other works, please let me know with a review on your book seller's website, or Goodreads, or you can visit my blog at badkarma00.wordpress.com. There are links there to my Facebook page as well.

You'll find a lot of odd and end stuff there that I work on to piddle when I can't get anything else done. Feel free to leave a comment. I know that it doesn't get updated often enough but I do try to post important notices there, and ANY books released by me will always be posted there and on my Facebook page. Of course, I would also encourage you to visit my publisher's page at www.creativetexts.com. They have links to purchase all of my books, as well as special giveaways and promotions from time to time.

Again, thank you.

N.C. Reed

THANK YOU
FOR READING!

If you enjoyed this book, we would appreciate your customer
review on your book seller's website or on Goodreads.

Also, we would like for you to know that you can
find more great books like this one at
www.CreativeTexts.com